Among These Savage Thoughts

Astro Teller

ISBN 978-0-6151-8003-8

Printed in the United States of America
Designed by Astro Teller

A hunter's moon shone down on the gates of Karabas. The only road connecting the city with the outside world wound up through the foothills, past a patchwork of terraced farming, and in between two giant stone monoliths, roughly carved but so worn by the centuries that they were more like gnarled fingers. Stern warnings pointing skyward. On the threshold between these fingers the stout visitor paused, a tall shadow stretching out behind him.

The man stood for a moment staring up at one of the snow capped ancient markers to the edge of Karabas. Then dropping his eyes to the road ahead, he moved through the gates and his shadow followed him. Adjusting the courier's bag slung across his back, he kicked his feet in the white powder, disrupting the fleeting purity of the road and wetting his fancy leather boots.

Beyond the gate, hovels, shanties, and the most meager houses of wood and tarp began to sprout. Slowly at first, then faster and faster, one on top of the next in a dense and squalid profusion, like hairs bursting out on the hide of some great animal asleep in the snow. A few weak lights winked at the stranger as he continued up the road, but there were no sounds, for all the evidence of population on either side of the road.

Continuing its rhythmic curves up through the hills, the road left the slums of Karabas behind in favor of what was referred to as the Lower Bank. The narrow passages that branched off from the main road were walled on both sides with wood and clay brick buildings two and three stories tall. With the laundry and carpets that hung outside even on such a mid-winter evening, it was clear that a noontime sun on a clear day in summer would produce nothing more than a dim dusk down in the alleyways.

These branches off the only road into Karabas turned from alleys to streets to avenues so that by the time the traveler reached the river, the structures had become solid works of stone, massive and imposing, drab and unornamented. His round face turned left and right with a friendly, awkward smile, looking up and down the river at these buildings. From the perspective of the long shadow behind him, he looked almost embarrassed in those two brief profiles. Karabas did present its underbelly first, and relief that it improved on the road to its center was a common reaction.

In front of him stretched the principal bridge connecting the Lower Bank of the city to the River Island. This island sat in the middle of a wide river of white rapids, fed by never-ending snow runoff from the towering mountains in the distance. Though the island was half a mile long and a quarter mile wide, only two bridges on either side arched over the torrent to the heart of Karabas. If he had bothered to look downstream, he would have just been able to make out the smaller bridge connecting to the tip of the island.

At the far end of the bridge before him, a father and mother were sheepherding their three children off the bridge and into the edge of the now audible island festivities. He hailed them, but they either did not hear or were too eager to stop and wait. He set off across the bridge in a clumsy half run but stopped near the middle under a huge pitch torch, panting, and brought his bag around over the hilt of his sword to rest on his round stomach. His hand fishing through the bag, he grunted under his breath. Porcine snuffling turned to a satisfied cluck as he pulled an oversized folded parchment out of his bag, fumbling it over a few times in his hands, and began to rummage in reverse, putting the letter back where it apparently belonged.

Quietly, patiently, gracefully, his shadow rose up behind him. As it loomed, the dark figure resolved into a tall, wiry youth with a blond mane full of snowflakes. The traveler pushed his bag back around his side and the youth nestled in behind him, embracing the plump little man with one arm across the chest and the other under the pink chin and up, covering the traveler's rosy cold ear. The taller figure moved slowly but the start of surprise shook the shorter man's frame only just as his head was lifted up and back of his shoulders. In the cold air, the sharp snap inside the fleshy neck echoed a little off the far walls on both sides of the river.

Lane supported the small man as he sagged and, slipping the bag to the ground, caught him up like a cradled infant. Playfully, Lane spun on one toe, surveying both ends of the bridge through the snow that had begun to fall again. Then he stepped to the rail and gently lowered the body into the midnight rapids.

Lane, kneeling by the pouch on the ground, explored its contents and withdrew the letter. It had the seal he was looking for and he grinned as his thumb caressed the red wax chop. Looking around quickly, he broke the seal and glanced inside the folder parchment. After turning it twice, he wrinkled his nose, shrugged, and refolded it. Standing up on his toes he passed the corner of the letter through the torch above his head and waved it slowly to and fro, watching it burn and light up the nearest falling snowflakes like tiny feather jewels.

When the letter was nearly gone, Lane dropped the smoldering remnant into the bag. The bridge was relatively free of debris, so it took him a minute to gather together a pile of rocks and pebbles next to the sack. A group of dirty children, bundled in multi-colored rags, waved to him as they ran past, heading to the island to be there before midnight. Lane waved back as he loaded the stones into the bag. When he had finished, he buckled the sack closed and dropped it over the bridge rail to follow its owner.

The bridge was empty again and Lane allowed himself the luxury of throwing back his head, thrusting open his mouth to the falling snow and stretching out his arms as he spun slowly around in the center of the bridge. A few wet strands of his shoulder length hair stuck to his temples and his open mouth further accentuated his long face and handsome features. Slowly his large hands moved towards his hips and his spinning stopped. No sound escaped his open mouth but his body pulsed and his fog gray eyes sparkled and shown like brilliant smoky lamps. Then he closed his eyes, inhaled a deep, penetrating breath and started an ululation that began as a soft howl but turned gradually into a sound of both pleasure and pain - an elemental rushing out of raw emotion. With his eyes closed, there could have been a fountain of fire erupting from his lungs – a wild blazing spire that lit the world like a hundred suns and consumed him as it burned. Snuffed out as his eyes reopened.

His outburst echoed off the high walls of the River Island and the shoreline buildings on both sides. The reverberating sound mixed with the noise of rushing water below and the clatter of approaching cartwheels on the Lower Bank end of the bridge. Lane pulled a strand of hair from the corner of his mouth and set off at a trot for the River Island, the New Year festival already at its peak. His long loping strides were easy and unhurried, but a moment later two men at the front of a coach peered across the bridge through the snow and could see no source for the sound still lingering in the air.

‡ ‡ ‡

Lane rolled over onto his back and experimentally opened one sleepy eye, studying the temple's attic ceiling and noting with satisfaction that he was still alive. The gossamer films of light drifting in through the roof were already strong enough to illuminate the crawl space between the temple's nearly flat inner ceiling and the pyramidal roof just above it. Lane knew he should be gone already, but he took his time rolling off the dusty mat and over to the ceiling panel. He slid the wood slat away, exposing the scene below, and it was as he knew it would be.

There were more people than usual milling in the temple and attending the two titanic wooden statues on either side of the main floor. Which was normal for the first day of the New Year. Directly below Lane sat the twenty-eight foot image of the incarnation of Addiction. Oren was depicted kneeling on one knee. In his open hand he held three rectangular gambling dice he was about to cast, and in his other hand, a bottle of spirits. Though it was not directly shown, most of Karabas could recognize from Oren's bare feet this moment in his life when he stakes his daughter in an effort to win back the rest of his possessions.

Across the hall stood a similarly sized statue of Ardo, the incarnation of Madness. This carving showed Ardo as a middle-aged man in filthy rags, tied to a tree to prevent him from eating himself. His head was thrust to one side as his jagged teeth tried bite into his shoulder. As the story went, Ardo believed consuming oneself was the only path to immortality.

Lane watched as the few visitors came and went, lingering dazed in front of Ardo or leaving and occasionally taking offerings from in front of Oren. Lane had chosen to make a nest in this temple exactly because these were two of the least popular avatars in the Karabas pantheon. In addition, this particular temple was poorly placed, as it was in the middle of the Upper Bank. For the most part, the sorts of citizens who would attend to the statues of avatars such as Oren and Ardo were farmers, the poor, and the criminal elements of Karabas. And they tended to live on the side of the river that led down out of the foothills, the Lower Bank. Still, it being New Year's day there were bound to be a few visitors, which necessarily delayed the moment when Lane could drop the few feet onto Oren's head, climb down his back, and slip out the front door.

Looking down at an old woman standing quietly in front of Ardo, it was hard to believe that people came to the temple at all. Attending to Anna, the avatar of Beauty, to recognize the share one had and the fortune involved with having it, or attending to Dama, the avatar of Wisdom to remind oneself of its value or to try to have more by association, these made some sense. But to spend the time to dwell on negative aspects of oneself was weak and self-indulgent. Still it was an excellent place to roost. A drunkard patted Oren's big toe affectionately and wandered back out into the daylight, leaving the temple empty.

Lane slipped a thick, cream-colored linen tunic over his faded gray pants and laced up dark boots. Then lowering himself through the ceiling hole made by the missing plank, he dropped a few feet to land on all fours in the gambler's sculpted hair. Lane slid to the ground in a simian flash, swinging from invisible holds so that in a moment he was on the ground behind the statue and then striding out into the cold bright morning.

Lane's illuminated hair made a sandy nimbus that swished as he moved through the city. The narrow cobbled streets were already full of the Upper Bank's people. Vendors and children and merchants and artisans and beggars and craftsmen and sweepers. Everywhere the sweepers went silently about their business, pulling the city's dust, dirt, and garbage out of the cracks and crevices of the streets and doorways and pushing it in growing mounds downhill towards the river. By twilight the mountains of refuse had all been sent over the bank by scores of long-handled straw brooms. The river whisked away these unwanted bits of the city, and the sweepers, like somnambulists in an endless sleep, drifted back uphill to start again at the high edge of the city.

The sun was bright but not strong enough to cut the cold, and the previous evening's snow was still sprawled out in the shadows. Many of the beggars selling nuts and buns and sweets from their impromptu stoves were fair-weather types

Lane could access only with the return of spring. Still, there were a hardy few, and Lane depended on these for most of his winter food. Turning into a deep alley, Lane moved along a shelf cut into a wall until he came to the wrinkled old woman who was always there, her feet tucked up under her, a blanket on her lap, and a little fire going in a square of bricks directly beside her.

Lane had purchased food from this bent woman on many occasions, yet she never showed any flicker of recognition when he appeared.

"Hey there tiny bundled bit. What are you cooking?"

"Sweet grass and morfa leaves," she croaked.

Lane reached into his shirt pocket, pulled out a coin, and tossed it onto her blanket. The wizened vendor took the coin, slipped it under her blanket and brought back out a small lump of dough and a handful of greens, all of which she spread out over the grill that lay across the bricks.

While he waited, Lane reached down into a long pocket that ran along the outside of his right thigh, extracting an instrument of dull gray metal. It was a thin stake about the length of his forearm and slightly thicker than his thumb. It had a complex pattern of undulations along its surface, rubbed smooth from heavy use and punctuated by abrupt nicks. At one end the metal converged into a fine point before which were a series of gentle ridges, just pronounced enough to make the tool barbed. He ran his hands across it a few times to warm it up and then began to play it through his fingers until it danced around his hand and forearm. Lane smiled absently, watching the tempered metal flit about like a hummingbird dancing around his wrists.

The stake snapped to attention in his hand, and he brought it down with a thud on the side and heel of his boot. Snow and mud dropped away and the other boot immediately received a similar blow. Lane tapped the grill with the tip of his wand.

"Am ready, so it's ready. Come on little bit."

She glanced up at him and then shrugged and darted a blackened hand over the coals and scooped up the leaves and the dough that had risen into a sticky bun. Digging out a little pocket with her thumb, she stuffed the leaves into the bun and flicked the doughy covering back over the hole. Lane dropped the metal stake back into its place and took the morfa bun. He turned to leave and then, feeling bad for having been brusque with the old woman who fed him often on winter mornings, he turned back and gave her another coin. It disappeared under her blanket where the first had gone, but she otherwise had no reaction nor expressed any appreciation for being paid twice. Annoyed with himself for having wasted the gesture, Lane wheeled back toward the street again.

Stepping over and around the children and animals that littered the sunny spots of the street, Lane made his way through a crowd of people, most headed for the riverbank. The buildings became older, larger, and more ornate as the bank and its desirable access to the river and the River Island drew nearer. These choice buildings near the heart of Karabas housed the more successful merchants and the primary craftsmen's guilds for the city. And the very best of these guilds held places directly along this main artery of the Upper Bank. A burly man he quite liked was setting a wheel in front of the cartwright guild's main entrance, and Lane waved to him as he strode past.

"Greetings, Milo. Good new year!"

"Lane! Greetings! It's an excellent year so far. Nothing to complain of yet." Then, as Lane raised his hand over his shoulder in recognition, "Stay clean!"

This was the sort of teasing jibe that the smiths and their apprentices could expect, particularly from the other guild members of Karabas. These friendly insults were protests against the location of the city's forge. At the end of the avenue, right on the edge of the foaming rapids of the right fork of the river sat the ancient and enormous blacksmith's cathedral. The building had one of the most coveted positions in the city, directly on the water, on the immediate terminus of the main Upper Bank bridge from the River Island. And because its unusually large footprint had been set early in Karabas's history, the building now seemed to hog the bank by the standards of contemporary Karabas. Eight enlarged chimneys protruded from the building's curved roof sixty feet from the ground, and it still managed to seem squat because of its unnatural length and width. Of course Milo had no way of knowing how very far from smithing Lane's apprenticeship had become.

There were no doors on the gigantic building, just a gaping lipless mouth that, when it exhaled, let out billowing smoke and the regular beat of hammers inside. Because it was the only forge in the city, its lungs were never still. In fact, the apprentices were told that at least one of the eight furnaces had been burning without fail since the day the building had been finished.

The great mouth sucked Lane in as he drew near, and he was immediately transported from a bright winter cityscape into a fiery pit. All eight furnaces were running, and even along the walkway down the spine of the building, the heat and smoke were ghastly. Warped figures shifted and twisted, shrank and enlarged to Lane's left and right as the waves of heat and clouds of smoke washed over them. A man turned toward him through the haze. It was an older vision of Lane himself, ravaged by years of the grinding slavery of the trade. Another wave of heat crumpled and uncrumpled the figure. Lane shuddered in disgust, turning away before the face could be reconstructed and wincing at the thought of the four years he had spent damned to feed those infernos after he had been sold to the guild.

Lane pushed past the stacks of raw ore and finished wares, wood and tools towards the very rear of the building. Taking a left at the far wall, he approached a closed wooden door in the corner where, blocking the way, Slate sat whittling a log. Lane had never seen this door without Slate in front of it, digging his knife into some piece of wood. Lane had seen these pieces near completion before, and they were often beautiful. A desperate hand reaching up out of the white rapids, the face of a sleeping child, or a diving hawk with its head thrust forward and its wings tucked to its breast. What Lane had never seen was any of Slate's finished work, and Lane suspected that in some slow moment Slate would rise from his chair, toss his latest creation into the nearest furnace and pick up a new log on his way back to his post.

"Greetings, Slate. Glad to see me around for another year?"

Slate freed his knife from the log he was gouging and motioned to the door behind him. "As glad as would be if you weren't." Slate's extreme slouch on his chair accentuated the sense that his body was literally foreshortened - huge feet, long legs, large hands, small torso, and tiny head.

"Ha! Proper, Slate. Well nice to know you'd miss me, but you won't see me in roses in your lifetime."

Slate flicked his knife towards the door again. "Do know several dead apprentices who've said the same."

At the ridiculousness of the idea Lane grinned, shook his head, and gave Slate a cheerful clap on the shoulder as he stepped around him and through the door.

Lane pulled the wooden door closed behind him and took a deep breath of the cooler, cleaner air. The room was no more than four paces on a side. The walls were full of odds and ends - aprons, tongs, more aprons, hammers, bellows, molds, and still more aprons. In the center of the room was a circular hole in the floor. The only light in the room came through the cracks in the door, but without waiting for his eyes to adjust, Lane stepped into the hole and began to descend the spiral stone staircase.

Down, step-by-step through the darkness Lane jogged. The spiral screwed down to the right, built to be defended by people fighting up rather than down the stairs. Lane's right hand brushed the rough rock surface of the central column as he took the stairs now two at a time. Even so the descent was monotonous and dark as death. A dull golden glow began to grow below him until finally Lane came out into a wide corridor. Along both sides of this hallway, shoulder-high sconces of oil sprouted forked tongues of dancing flame. These lamps were not attached to the wall but had actually been carved from them, the wall chipped away to expose each built-in oil reservoir. In fact, the waving firelight was strong enough to reveal that the entire hall was without seams. Lane was passing through an antechamber dug right out of the rock over many generations, which showed particularly in the corners that had not been perfectly squared.

Lane turned with the underground foyer as it exploded into a great hall. Pillars of stone grew out of the floor, rising over a hundred feet into the air and then melding back into the vaulted ceiling. Two rows of these gigantic ribs of rock filed down to and then curved together behind a circular, raised platform some thirty feet wide at the far end of the hall. Lane noticed as he passed each pair of stone pillars that the four rock sconces protruding from each column burned the violet flame of a special oil in honor of the New Year. These two hundred lights illuminated most of the ceiling, revealing that it was covered, for the length and width of the enormous hall, with intricate carvings depicting death, murder and execution in all their guises.

The stone platform rose eight feet out of the floor, and four sets of wide steps had been left after the carving so the stage could be mounted from the four compass points. Lane stopped at the edge of the first step and drew from each of his thigh pockets the twenty inch stakes. These twin devices he laid beside a pile of weapons and unusual equipment, carefully orienting the needle sharp points away from the stage. Having done this, he dropped his left ear to his left shoulder, then his right ear to his right shoulder, cracking a joint in his neck with each motion. Straightening up, Lane climbed the stairs to the stage.

The surface of the stage was packed dirt, swept level and raked. To Lane's left knelt nine well-scrubbed young and frightened new apprentices. Lane smiled and nodded, not to them but in nostalgia. No amount of scrubbing would keep those nine youngsters, who all had been smithing apprentices only a few days ago, from being referred to as "grubbies" for the next twelve months. He scanned the two new women, but neither face created that lovely ache in his chest, and Lane never changed his mind after his first impression.

Directly in front of him sat the seven apprentices who had survived into their second year. Who had made it to "the hump." Lane knew no other apprentice would dare to arrive as late as he was now. That meant someone had been dropped out before the hump. Lane checked off those kneeling in front of him, and found it was Miles who hadn't made it. The rest sat silently, visibly relieved that they had.

Lane's eyes swept to the right side of the stage and what remained of his fellow final-year apprentices. Four of them knelt, still, watching Lane like living statues. Only four. Wren and Wren sat side by side, watching Lane with blank faces, taking turns blinking. Wren was uncomfortably tall with a long down-hooked nose, and a handsome profile that in no way made up for the fact that their heads were so narrow that looking at either Wren straight on still seemed an incomplete view of his face. Lane could easily tell Wren and Wren apart from subtle differences in their wear and tear, but that distinction was useless since it was a distinction the Wren's themselves did not make. Wren and Wren were apparently not aware, or not interested, that there were two of them.

Next to Wren sat Cye. Though his face and body were young, someone ancient looked out of Cye's deep brown eyes. Lane locked gazes with those unnerving eyes and though they were friends, Lane made a point to show Cye no loss of composure in his own unblinking eyes. Cye's eyes were framed by aristocratic features, fine light skin, black eyebrows, and thin brown hair. Beside Cye sat Sona. Sona's large frame was still a little slight for his heaviness. Sona slouched into his kneel, long straight black hair falling forward over his dark skin and jet black eyes. Sona's eyes were watching Lane too. Watching with undisguised animosity and disappointment. Surprisingly, from their group the previous year, it was Victoria who was no longer with them. She had been, admittedly, less than fanatical about training during the prior year, but she had shown real promise and occasional sparks of brilliance that ought to have been enough to move her into the final year. She had also acted as a buffer between Sona and the other four and her absence was more palpable than her presence had ever been.

Facing the far side of the stage, Lane placed his hand on his thighs, fingers spread, and inclined his body from the waist toward the solitary figure on the far side of the earthen circle. Master Horn knelt too, dressed in a thick simple gray tunic and a black skirt that spread out along the ground like dark orchid petals. His face was hard and square, his skin the color of driftwood, wrinkles lined his face and neck, but those creases lay over a body tough and strong beyond its age.

Lane had heard it said in jest that Master Horn had met Time coming down the stairs from the forges above. So the story went, Master Horn had won from Time the right to choose the moment of his own death, after vanquishing Time in a grizzly struggle lasting a day and a night. Looking at him just now, the story almost seemed possible. The many tiny, faded scars around Master Horn's eyes framed two points of patience and anger. Lane closed his eyes and inclined his head in the required show of subservience to Cian's doyen. After a moment passed, Lane opened his eyes and without fully straightening, stepped to his right and knelt down beside Sona.

"Good new year," he whispered as he knelt, and then, still looking ahead towards Master Horn and without moving his lips, "Am glad to see they didna drop you this past week." Sona flicked his eyes towards Lane, then back again to Master

Horn without a word. Lane smiled and brushed a lock of hair away from his face.

The ageless gray and black figure had risen, and Horn's dress swirled around him slowly like eddies of ebony water lapping around a gray stone. As he flowed in complex patterns over the dirt platform, he began to speak, now to one group or another, then back out into the indoor twilight of the oil lamps in the great hall.

"Welcome," as he passed in front of the first year apprentices, "and welcome back" as he passed the second year apprentices, "to Cian. I will remind you, as I remind apprentices every year, that your job here is not to learn your trade. That trade is the purpose for the guild and for Cian, this place that each of you will help to enlarge, physically and metaphorically. Our trade is our purpose, but that is secondary. Your first concern must always be tokada - solidarity, honor, and right action. Your trade will come from tokada. Without it, you will not graduate this place. Those of you that do complete your apprenticeship here will leave Karabas to pursue your trade. And no matter how far you are from Karabas, no matter how you live, you will send your gabel each year back to Cian. Why? Tokada. It is your first and last allegiance. That is why it is your first and last lesson here in Cian."

Master Horn's voice had stopped, but his silent movement continued, tracing faint patterns in the dirt and occasionally brushing an apprentice as he passed. After a minute or two his voice returned, less stern than its previous incarnation.

"You," he said as he began a circle of the new apprentices, "will live here in Cian for the next year. Your body will learn combat and I will be your primary instructor. You," he said sliding off his circle onto a new curve around the second year apprentices, "will spend today with them so that they understand how they will live and work in Cian. After today you will return to Cian every day to work here from dawn until dusk, but you will no longer live in Cian. After today, you will concentrate on the construction and use of weapons. You will continue to see both Master Weaver and myself, but as of tomorrow, Master Maya will be your primary instructor for the year. After today," he moved gracefully to the final group of five apprentices, "you will be here from noon until your lessons are finished. In your final year here in Cian you will concentrate on the fine points of tokada and your trade. Wait here for Master Weaver."

So saying, he wheeled once more around the third years and then gestured with a swish of his dress so that, as he descended the stairs, the first and second year apprentices were drawn off their knees and after him as though in the pull of an invisible undertow back down the length of Cian's great hall. Master Horn swept down the great hall and disappeared through the double doors on the right hand that lead to the Cian dormitory. Trailing after him, first the new apprentices, then the second years disappeared from view. The dormitory doors swung closed with a faint thud and the hall was quiet.

The third year apprentices shifted in place slightly but remained kneeling.

"Is that a professional memory?" asked Lane of Sona, drawing his finger from his collarbone to his ear, mirroring a deep recent cut in that location on Sona.

"Na. Not. It's a personal memory and nothing too. My Spirit went cold with na fuss nor bother nor like trouble t'all. This," pointing at his neck "was just a bit of fun while curing. Your Spirit..."

"...will na get roses," Lane finished for Sona, waving his hand dismissively.

Sona twisted his head away from Lane. "Cye? Wren? Hear Wren's Spirit was tricky, gave you both the slip and altogether eluded you? Surprised to see you two back and here. The lead too much for clumsy paws?"

"He did," said Wren.

"not," finished Wren.

Wren's limbs were long, even for his height, and with his too large hands and feet, Wren looked just then like a giant greyhound back on it haunches.

"Sona, this apprenticeship is not winner take all." Cye was looking straight ahead, not at Sona. "If Wren is still a Jack, it's because they ought to be."

Sona grunted. "And you, for Judge, went well? You're so mercury and light that your Spirit doesn't even go like missing or in state?"

Cye whipped his head around to stare down Sona. "The lead was recalled in time and Spirit wasn't Spirit. Na my fault is it?"

Sona smiled, turned forward again, and said under his breath, but loud enough for them all to hear, "Donkey."

Cye, up on one knee instantly and on his way to his feet, froze there as Weaver's forehead appeared on the far side of the stage. Lane thought briefly of shooting out a hand to cuff Sona for insulting Cye and then retracting his hand all before the instructor's eyes appeared. He could. Smiling and shaking his head slightly at the amusing mind's eye scene, he let the moment pass. As Weaver mounted the steps, Cye inhaled deeply and lowered himself back into a full kneel. Weaver wore the traditional black floor length skirt and an immaculately clean white tunic. A body in its prime, young enough not to have faded and old enough to be precise, and relaxed. He put first one, then a second foot onto the dirt surface. As soon as his second foot landed on the stage, all five apprentices had their hands on their thighs, fingers spread, heads inclined and eyes closed. After a moment four pairs of eyes opened and rose to meet Weaver walking towards them. He knelt only a pace from them, and only once he had settled himself did Lane go through the motions of raising his eyes and his head.

"Thank you all. I'm glad to see each of you again." Weaver's eye's ran from one to the next, leaving each with the feeling that Weaver had meant that last particularly for him.

After a long pause, Weaver swept his eye across the five students again. "What do you imagine you have left to learn here at Cian?"

"How ta work the Spirits better and better how ta serve each Judge." said Sona when no one else spoke up.

"Just so, Sona. But what about taking, researching, and completing a job do you think you need to focus on improving this year?" Weaver sat silent to let them think.

"Form, not function." said Cye finally.

Weaver smiled. "That is the answer. But since you already know it, what else do you need to learn?"

Cye was quicker this time, "We must internalize the process."

Without agreeing or disagreeing, Weaver drew an arc in the dirt in front of him with his index finger. "For the past two years, you have been taught to draw as part of your training. Can anyone define for me precisely what makes a curve strong or weak?" Half a minute passed in silence. "Do you know a strong line when you see one?" Five nods came, but no sound.

"In every part of your life, you can perform with what we call 'character'. Each line you draw, each word you speak, and each job you complete, you leave your mark when you do these things. Your main task this year is to learn to act without simultaneous reflection so that the lines you draw are each just as they should be. You will learn that ultimately this artistry will improve your performance. You will also find, if you make it to the next New Year's day, that the internalization of tokada, the principles of the Guild, obedience to Cian, and right action in accordance with your nature, will go hand-in-hand with a strong, even sublime performance."

Weaver drew his palm across the same arc, and the arc faded back into the packed earth. "It is the nature of a task for Cian that, once done, it is forever what it is. You can prepare as much as you like, but the target will only die once and in one way. Drawing does not entirely share that characteristic. But sculpting does." And here he pointed to the ceiling. In the shifting light of two hundred lit oil sconces, the carved figures raised out of the walls and ceiling seethed across the surface. All forms of monsters and men crawled, marched, and leapt past each other to escape from or grapple with their nemeses. Serpents, lions, huge armed men, deadly beautiful women, and mythical creatures acted out in relief the stories of conflict and death from the Karabas pantheon. Lane had often lost himself looking up at a particular scene of the crafty child warrior, Hann. Dressed as a peasant girl, Hann passes unnoticed over the bridge to the underworld guarded by Dyna, the father of all ogres. Just the gigantic foot and ankle of Dyna could be seen towering over Hann's crouched figure, but Lane had seen the rest of that magnificent stone giant in his dreams.

Weaver continued. "This year each of you will pick a theme, select an uncarved patch of this room, and add your mark to Cian. Just like working for a patron, careful planning on this project can save you from mishaps both small and large. You will not have the opportunity to change your theme, begin again, or finish late, so be careful without being cautious."

The five seniors were quiet, and Cye, Sona, and the Wrens were probably listening closely and respectfully. Weaver had a way of meeting the eyes of each as he spoke so that they knew he was addressing each as an individual and not just as a group. And more, he liked them all and it showed in his eyes and in his knowing smile as he spoke. Weaver gave Lane the slightest wink as he continued.

"Each of you will be given at least two tasks this year, in some cases three when possible and appropriate. As Master Horn told you last year, neither the number of tasks you are given, nor the target's station in society, nor direct or indirect ability to protect themselves should be taken as other than what it is. You have always and will during your final year here, be evaluated on how well you perform, not merely on whether or not your target dies. Remember, no assignment is beneath you. I have been tasked to target mighty kings and lowly corzens and each offered unique opportunities for learning and improvement."

Weaver was quiet again and his students knelt in silence with him. A breeze passed down the length of the enormous underground hall, stirring Lane's hair and sounding the deep chimes that hung in the huge empty alcove at the back of the hall. Lane looked over Weaver's shoulder at the empty space, reserved since the hall was built for a replica statue of the member of their guild who might someday be recognized as an avatar and added to the Karabas pantheon. It was, in fact, because this person had yet to be added to the exalted list of avatars that Cian tradition forbade physical conflict in the Karabas temples. Not that Lane slept a few feet over Oren's head for protection. It just felt comfortable being in the temple. Most students preferred to keep their sleeping quarters more secret. A few students probably kept one eye open no matter where they slept. Students were not allowed to have fatal run-ins of any sort no matter the location, and when one student was killed by another, Cian usually didn't allow the surviving student to survive for long. Still, that assumed that the Cian Dons knew who to discipline. A smart person could control what the Dons believed they knew. The Cian Dons were, of course, allowed to discipline apprentices as they saw fit, and Lane's sleeping quarters would not protect him. What did that matter though? He had no cause to fear discipline, did he? The temple suited him and that was fine.

Weaver shifted his gaze to Wren and Wren and said, "What do you imagine you will do if you graduate?"

"I will leave Karabas," began Wren

"to take up work in a Guild chapter," continued the other Wren.

"in some other city," finished Wren.

"Have you ever been out of Karabas, Wren?"

"No."

"Have you any idea what city you might go to once you leave Karabas?"

"No."

"The Guild requires that you leave the city where you were trained in order to continue working, registering with the local guild chapter in your new city. But that doesn't mean you can't talk to me about what's out there. You should all think during this year about what you desire, and I can help you with introductions and guidance." Everyone but Sona nodded in assent. "Good. Now intone tokada and return tomorrow at noon for your first day of classes."

Slowly, in unison, the five seniors recited the transparent pledge in a toneless chant.

Cian is inviolate. Our first allegiance is to Cian.

Cian is inviolate and no place for taking life.

Cian and our Guild are inviolate.

Our lives are a small price to pay for the secrecy of Cian and our Guild.

Our trade is inviolate. No value can be put on the purity of our craft.

We are servants of Cian and the Guild and know no other master.

We owe our craft to Cian and can never finish repaying Cian for this honor.

We will practice our trade only at the direction of our masters, Cian and the Guild.

Cian is inviolate. Our trade is our honor.

Lane had intoned these words hundreds of times before and had built up a strong resistance to them. It was clear that the purpose of the words was to keep order in Cian, ensure the secrecy of Cian, and provide the fuel to keep the tithes to Cian coming in from students long since graduated. Once the rules had been laid bare, they could be bent to suit the need as long as the variations were discreet. Lane smiled to himself as the chant ended.

The students spread their fingers across their thighs, inclined their heads, then rose to go. Lane could hear Cye drop off the side of the platform as if the eight foot drop was a single step, sweep up a thin long dagger, slide it in one smooth motion into a sheath that ran up his spine beneath his shirt, and recede down the long hall at a trot before the rest were even on their feet. Down the stairs Wren and Wren collected two pairs of gloves spiked with tiny studs and followed Cye, legs no doubt swinging in unison. Off the platform, Sona picked up a small two headed hatchet with an unusually long handle. Slinging it over his shoulder, he paused for a moment, probably looking back up the platform steps at Lane, and then turned and strode after the Wrens.

Lane still knelt with spread fingers on his thighs and bowed head. At few feet in front of him, Weaver remained as he was, watching Lane make the submissive position look almost commanding through the relaxation of his body. It wasn't insulting exactly, but Lane's posture did not convey the fear and respect that the position was intended to. "What can I do for you, Lane?" Weaver finally asked.

Lane raised his head, looking again at the oblong face, its shape accentuated by a receding hair line. "Don Weaver, do hear you, all assignments are good assignments, but it's stone to learn on the Spirits you assign. Did keep the last one company, a little clumsy hog, all the way from Karabas gates to the main Lower Bank bridge at arms length and he knew na'thing. And did put him cold in public, with na but these hands, and hog didna even squeak. Na person saw." Lane paused, watching Weaver's face, then finished, "Test me. There's na work am not the equal of."

Weaver smiled enigmatically. "Despite what I said to the class, Lane, I will grant your request to the extent I'm able. You have a gift that I enjoy nurturing. Remember though that as the assignment becomes more interesting, its successful and correct execution becomes more," he paused delicately, "critical."

"Grats, Don Weaver!" and Lane rose to go, neglecting the proper bow that should have concluded the audience.

"You're welcome, Lane. I'll see you tomorrow after Combat and Weapons." Weaver rose too, but stood quietly and watched Lane drop off the edge of the stage, scoop up his thin stakes and stroll down the length of the hall, twirling the spikes around the fronts and backs of his hands.

‡ ‡ ‡

The mouth of the forge exhaled such quantities of smoke and hot breath turned to steam that in between the stifling interior of the building and the bright, cold, cloudless Karabas noon, Lane passed through a temperate white blindness. As Lane emerged from this mist, his features slowly resolving from silhouette to specifics, both hands caught up the whirling rods and dropped them into their respective pockets. Lane stopped at the edge of the main road, tilting his head up to smile back at the midday sun, and stood with his eyes closed for a long moment, drinking in the light. Then turning to his right, he set out across the Upper Bank main bridge.

This bridge spanned three hundred feet of pounding rapids that would have worn through any bridge supports in a single generation. Instead, the bridge was suspended from two massive towers, one on the riverbank and one on the island bank. The steel cables, thick as tree trunks, were braids upon braids of metal so long ago fused by the elements that Karabas now lacked the skills to either bring the bridge down or to rebuild it.

The noise on the petrified bridge planks of the traffic flowing into and away from the River Island was as loud as the water. The total effect of the rushing rapids below, the streaming people, horses, and carts, and the constant hum of the Island Fountain, visible ahead over the throng, gave the River Island the feeling of being not so much the center of Karabas as its heart. On each beat the heart circulated its people and goods to keep its extremities connected to the whole. Lane inhaled deeply and felt himself flowing out of the vein as he reached the end of the bridge.

On his left, the upstream half of the island, sat the heavily fortified River Palace. The sandstone walls, characteristic of all the oldest Karabas buildings, shone yellow gold in the overhead sun. Inside the walls, a fantastic, wild explosion of curves, towers, walkways, ramparts, and roofs all of algae green marble so overwhelmed the view that the mountain range framed behind it seemed subdued by comparison. In front of the two-story iron gates of the River Palace sat the Island Fountain. It shot a single steam of river water in an unblemished arc forty feet at its apex and sixty feet from the gleaming green marble basin out of which it grew, to an identical basin back into which it was constantly returning without the slightest splash. The construction of the fountain was so meticulous that only in high winds did even a fine mist drift away from the jet. Today this perfect curve of water reflected the winter sunlight as though it were a solid piece of crystal.

Passing under the arc of liquid light and walking another few minutes ahead would bring one to the other edge of the River Island and the Lower Bank main bridge where Lane had crossed the previous night. But instead of continuing straight across the island, Lane turned right once more and entered the real heart of Karabas.

The Flat, as it was known, stretched down a thousand feet where the two branches of separated white water came violently together again at the sharpened point of the island. As its name suggested, the Flat was the largest open area of flat ground in all of Karabas. The triangular arena, from the tip of the island up to its widest point just below the lower

Island Fountain basin, had been leveled by generations long gone, giving the River Palace a commanding perch over the lower half of the island.

Down the long sides of the Flat ran two extremely long buildings known as the Alleys. Both three story buildings looked like structures so overly tall that they had fallen on their sides both because of their incredible length and the immense dull yellow granite boulders from which they were built. These stones made it hard to tell if the buildings were distressed from centuries of rough treatment by the elements or whether their original construction had been uneven.

The first floors of both Alleys were open to the Flat and vendors, and their customers filled up these shaded colonnades and spilled out into the crisp winter sunlight, squeezed together like tiny animals comfortable with their intimate proximity and glad for the mutual warmth. The second and third floors of the Alleys had originally been designed as warehouse space. Now these floors opened up here and there onto the Flat, twenty foot deep balconies jutted out from these holes, cantilevered over the crowds with beams added after the original construction. These precarious platforms were also full, not just now, but nearly all day every day, with people sitting, standing, drinking and eating the full range of Karabas cuisine. The heavy perfumed clouds from meats and meads dropped from ledge to ledge down to the Flat and set up odiferous regions as distinct as rooms.

During the summer months, endless sails of colored linen were drawn between the roofs of the two Alleys. These rainbow filters broke the heat of the sun and cast bands of crimson, cobalt, and ochre down on the crowds as they pulsed through Karabas's heart. Today, the bare taut wires for holding those sails ran for hundreds of feet between the Alleys, and Lane could hear them humming faintly in the breeze.

On a typical winter's day a few thousand people worked their way up and down the Flat. At the height of summer or on festival days as many as forty or fifty thousand men, women, and children, nearly all of Karabas, would pack themselves into the Flat. The sites of the garbage chutes revealed themselves only when the Flat was empty or when it became particularly crowded. Spaced unevenly along both Alleys, they created the only cleared areas two feet across in an otherwise unbroken sea of heads and hats. These chutes were holes big enough to accommodate a careless leg, dug down through the island to tunnels of water rushing beneath. The garbage dropped down through these openings was never seen in Karabas again and, if it did happen to surface in some other town far away down the mountain, the people of Karabas knew nothing of it.

Along the first floor of the Alleys, commodities of all varieties were piled high against the back walls. As the saying went in Karabas, "If it can be bought, it can be bought on the Flat." This was possible only because in these mountains of food, materials, furniture, clothing, and trinkets there was only one of everything. Each vendor stood in front of his or her goods and auctioned items to the immediate press of people. Buying a good meant paying for a slip of paper, signed by the vendor. The good was then delivered when the ticket was surrendered. These deliveries were performed by the youths of Karabas, who constituted the largest, though hardly the most lucrative, of the city's guilds. The prices on unusual items and goods in high demand fluctuated sufficiently within a particular day that side auctions on the paper itself were as much a part of the market life as the direct purchasing of the goods. The process worked well for Karabas. If someone purchased a side of beef and the prices then dropped, he still got the beef at a price he had been willing to pay. If the price rose after his purchase, he could always keep the slip or if he chose, sell it to another party and take the profit. Exactly for this reason, the notion of flexibility in one's habits and daily routines was commonly associated with amassing wealth.

Lane strode down the middle of the Flat, enjoying the sensation that whether consciously or unconsciously, the clumps of people parted to let him pass. He walked confidently on through as each group reformed in his wake. The Flat was the best place in Karabas to see its social strata thoroughly mixed. Nobles in their impractically tall shoes stood out above the crowd, the bald heads of the men and the short cropped hair of the women. Moving slowly through them, Karabas peasants shuffled past in open-toed sandals, their blues and grays clearly separated from the bright violets, greens, and pure whites of the taller nobles. These peasants were constantly swaying and twisting as they moved, skillfully maneuvering the children slung on their backs and hips so that the oddly shaped patches of blue and gray moved through each other in close quarters without upsetting the crowd's delicate dance of avoidance. Looking across the Flat, the uniforms of the guilds stood out. With little variation, the apprentices wore tan, beige, or cream colored linen shirts and darker pants, just as Lane did. The full guild members wore long black skirts and light grey or white tops. Evidence of the guilds to which these people belonged could be seen only at close range. Most of the guilds had insignias, and many of their members wore these signs stitched into their clothes either in the small of the back or over the breast. As a rule, the blacksmiths did not practice this habit, and Lane was similarly unbranded.

Lane moved away from the center of the Flat towards the right Alley, through a throng bidding on fur-lined footwear and then up a flight of stairs where he entered a scene whose colors suited him better. The tavern was crowded for a mid-winter afternoon, and its patrons were draped with reds, yellows, and oranges. These people were from that segment of society that served no useful purpose and survived in the Karabas culture because every culture knows deep down that it is incomplete without its disreputables. The Rapids had a levity to its tavern noise that made Lane nod approvingly as he stepped over the threshold. The great black beards on the men and the carnival makeup splashed across the women's faces made Lane feel at home.

Across the room and out onto the wooden beams of the balcony, Lane raised his hand in recognition. Cye waved from a table by the edge, as did the girl sitting next to him. They stood to greet Lane and, though this particular balcony extending out over the Flat had no railing to protect its customers from the twenty foot drop beneath, they both stepped lightly around opposite sides of their corner table. This dangerous absence of any railing served a useful purpose. It helped to keep away the desirable elements of Karabas.

Lane clasped Cye's hand and brought Cye to him to hug him with the other arm. "Good new year, Cye. Am happy to see you still."

Releasing and grinning back at Lane, Cye nodded, saying "The worst of the winter ahead of us my friend. But we have easy waters now for a moon or two."

Lane's eyes twinkled as he waved his hand and grunted "Aaah!" dismissively, then turned to Rose. Rose stood patiently, arms akimbo, where the simple blue fabric of her dress rode out slightly over her hips. Her long silky brown hair framed and matched her wide brown eyes. Lane looked down into her eyes for a moment, enjoying her confident patience. Leaning down, he tasted her lips, savoring some hard to place sweet subtle flavor and losing himself for a moment. Then he bit her lip a touch and pulling away, flashed his teeth, "Peach, my dab. Always peach to see you. Are hale?"

"Well with you. Well and hale and happy 'cepting this lip you just bit." Rose furrowed her brow in a pretend frown, then burst into a wide, lovely smile.

Lane pulled out a seat and gestured to their chairs as he sat down. Cye pursed his lips as he dropped into his seat and gave a sharp whistle to summon a server.

"It's been many days, dear." Rose's melodic voice contrasted comically with another friendly scowl as she leaned back in her chair until her head was out over the edge of the balcony. "Many days and no sight of you. Where'st been?"

"Working. Year end's busy at forge and they dona go forward without me." Lane gave Cye a conspiratorial wink as he said it.

"Now that both you designing stead of hammering away, still they've you at it like the furnace slaves."

"Grats for your concern, little Rose. But when you're the best, there's always ought to do, aye Cye?"

"Aye. There's no work coming for the lame horse to be put down."

"Still Lane, love. Haven't been around and I'm missing you. I work tonight. Soon in fact. But am off after midnight. Come my way. Or is my side too rocky for Upper Bank boys?" She grinned at him again.

He would have come anyway this evening, but he certainly wasn't going to let Rose ride him on that point of all things. He tossed his head and his eyes glinted. "They dona make waters too white for me. Will visit tonight so save some anjo."

"Truly, Rose. Your petting zoo is all tame animals you serve. Being dirty creatures doesn't make them fierce. Though they certainly make a mess on you." Lane laughed with Cye and Rose shrugged her shoulders and laughed with them both.

"Of animals, dist hear? They say they'll be a mountain python for the next Kamakura festival beast. That'll be better sport than year's past." Rose flicked her tongue in and out a few times in imitation of the snake.

"Will sport a python myself," Lane feigned undoing his pants, "that will scare grand and corzon alike." Cye and Rose both groaned and shook their heads, but they laughed with Lane when he put up his hands and lowered his head a little in mock apology.

The laughter subsided and Rose stood up. Cye looked around and produced another piercing whistle, waving impatiently at the server back behind Lane. Rose slapped his hand.

"Be light, Cye! She spends all day dealing with whistles. And I go ta the Tengo ta deal with them all night. Here are pieces for fixer." And she dropped a few coins onto the table by Cye. "Grats for the time," and kissed Cye on the cheek. "Later, love," and gave Lane a short strong kiss. Stepping away from the corner of the deck, she grabbed her long skirt on both sides and flipped up the back side for just a moment, exposing a shapely bare behind. She grinned at them over her shoulder as the skirt dropped down and wove her way back into the main hall of the Rapids, disappearing into the crowd. Lane smirked and Cye nodded, smiling and putting a hand on Lane's.

"She's genius, Lane. You're a lucky man."

"Aye. She's a peach dab, na doubt. She's a peach distraction from the pit when do need one."

"Can help, boys?" The voice of an older waitress came from directly behind Lane and her sarcastic emphasis on "boys" lingered in the air.

"Mead and a plate of salmon rusk and ... Lane?"

Lane spoke out onto the Flat instead of turning to see the waitress, "Opened anjo yet, madam?" Lane gave the "madam" the same slight emphasis.

"Na yet. But pieces make all things possible." When neither Lane or Cye reacted to this, she continued, "Glass or bottle?"

"Glass."

Her arm brushed past Lane to pick up several dirty glasses off the table, and then her footsteps retreated into the background noise of the tavern.

Lane watched a hawk soaring up the middle of the Flat, wings motionless and neck still. Not hunting. Just riding the wind. It rode a little above the level of the buildings and its repose in flight was so complete, it seemed as if it were still and the buildings were in flight instead. Up, down, Up, down. The hawk rose and dropped slightly with the wind currents, the world inhaling and exhaling with each shift of the bird.

Still watching the hawk, Lane ended the conversation lull with, "A fine first day in the pit. This year'll be shine for sure." He leaned back a little in his chair, smiling at the crisp winter air filling back in the invisible wake of the hawk. The hawk was rising now over the Flat, its wings still motionless. The world dropped away until the hawk was lost in the heavens.

"You were late this morn. Have a care. The Masters' patience is na without limit."

"What?" Lane turned his head toward Cye. "Will they work me?" Lane snorted and shook his head. "Do think na."

Cye sat quiet and serious and Lane was gazing happily out over the Flat again when Cye said quietly, "Victoria might have said so too. And she's cold now."

"Spot. She was mercury and exact. And she took her leads serious with na' a professional memory. Will miss her. But she didna always obey their rules. Tokada is all for Don's. Play that or meet the riff."

Cye shrugged as if to say "Maybe. Maybe not," but he stayed silent and Lane only stretched out his arms to feel the pull on his muscles. As he stretched he watched a few stray snowflakes drift down into the human kaleidoscope of colors on the floor of the Flat. He could tell Cye was concerned at his lack of fear, and that tension only further lightened his heart and brightened his mood. Cye actually increased Lane's relaxed state when he started up again with, "Sona hates you, Lane. He was sorely disappointed to see you back today. That cloud has lightning to spend on you for half a chance."

What a gulf there was between their views of the same situation. Lane's amusement increased at Cye's persistence and he moved his arms to lock his fingers behind his head. "No doubt he hates me. But a half chance will na happen.

That mangy bear takes himself and the pit too seriously. And he's na so white." Lane looked over at Cye, unclasping a hand and letting it fall on Cye's shoulder, which he shook softly. "Relax, brother. Fun or nothing. Life is bright." His eyes twinkled still but with a little more care he finished, "Otherwise, what's the point?"

"Aye. Life is bright. Still I'll watch for you and an extra eye for Sona will be worth the effort."

A hand came into view, placing a plate of crispy, brown dumplings, steaming in the frosty air, and a steel tankard in front of Cye. It was gone and then back directly with a crude, thick, glass goblet in which a rich raspberry plasma swirled slowly. A chuckle from Lane seemed to slow this swirling. "Da, Cye. Da. Will give an extra eye. But your worry would be better spent on your bit hunt." And as Lane continued to speak, the swirling stopped and in the deep red liquid, tiny pieces of pulp began to appear slowly on the surface.

‡ ‡ ‡

Twin cream colored dots flowed straight up the middle of the Flat toward the lower basin of the Island fountain. From above, one had a short tail, as the cream colored knee-length jacket he wore trailed out behind Cye, held up by a breeze running the other way down the length of the Flat. Despite the bite of the afternoon air and the extra teeth of the breeze, Lane's loping gate and lowered shoulders flaunted his ability to ignore aspects of the world that did not suit him. His hair could not entirely ignore the wind, but responded only enough to lean back from Lane's shoulders in synchronicity with Cye's train.

"Grats for the food and fixer, Cye."

"Genius. All my pleasure."

"The pit'll shine this year. Getting to our cards'll be fun with Don Weaver. And you."

"Master Weaver is solid indeed. Tall trees make saplings stand up straight."

"We will. As long as we get Spirit's worth the trouble, riding this year'll be twice as bright doing it with you." They had by this point passed beyond the first basin and stood under the arc of water. From above, their light forms swam through the liquid prism as Cye put his arms on Lane's shoulders. Then they embraced, released, turned, and headed off, Lane uphill toward the Upper Bank bridge and Cye directly opposite, down toward its brother, the larger bridge linking the River Island with the Lower Bank. Like bolts from bows, the figures moved off in their opposing directions in straight lines through the chaotic eddies of the Karabas crowds, gradually disappearing as a damp, heavy snow began to drop down on them.

‡ ‡ ‡

Stepping out of the dark stairwell into Cian's perpetual lamp-based twilight, Lane's gaze sped down the line of sconces brimming with oil to rest on a tall pile of animated rags. Light, as she was called by Cian's students, was many times Lane's age, and the creases in her face matched the layers of tattered clothes hanging down her body like patchwork feathers. Her tall frame was neither bent nor crooked despite her age and occupation. Lane had never heard her speak. Nor did he know anyone who had. The name Light was just a reference to her main responsibility, keeping the several hundred oil sconce lamps in Cian full and lit at all times. In fact, Lane had never seen a lamp unlit or unfilled in his three years below ground. He supposed that she did other odd jobs, mainly as he had never seen anyone else cleaning the main hall, lecture rooms, and dormitories, yet they never slid into the grimy disarray of uncared for things. Lane studied her face as he passed, and she met his gaze not with defiance, but with calm assuredness. Lane liked her unapologetic attitude and admired the way she could vanish from or materialize in a room, unnoticed by his classmates.

Passing Light, Lane headed down the main hall of Cian, a street lined with giant trees of stone. As he approached, he could see the grubbies getting their first real lecture from Weaver. Ten of them knelt attentively, stiff as boards, working hard in their rigidity to attract as little attention as possible. Lane circled the stage, making brief eye contact and receiving a subtle smile from Weaver as he passed the platform. Ahead through the rough wood-slated double doors to either side of the empty avatar's alcove at the head of the hall, the students left in the hump would already be deep into a combat class with Master Horn. Veering to the right, Lane approached a similar pair of old wood doors. He scratched his nose, produced a toothy grin, and then pulled both doors open.

In the center of one wall, a forge spat out light and heat through tongues of flame. Its smoke rose up the immense chimney, passing into the commercial forge above. The only other light sources in the cavernous room, nearly forty feet deep from the door and almost twice that in length, were two heavy bronze braziers. The room was, however, anything but dark. Lane basked in the bright, wild air that sparkled around him as he stepped over the threshold. From the floor to the ceiling along all four walls, the room was teeming with weapons whose polished metal refracted the light, splitting it up, changing and multiplying it so that each dancing flame was transformed into countless luminescent sprites.

The weapons hung in ranks three and four deep, packed in tight competition for visibility and in no apparent order or preference. Swords, daggers, and bows kept company with scimitars, hooks, and spiked greaves. Giant lances, javelins, spears, and jerrids lay crisscrossed thirty feet in the air with hair pins and darts. Sharp blades hung in tight formation with iron cudgels, maces, and morning stars. Many items crowding the walls were not even clearly weapons. Spiked shields made backdrops for collapsible crossbows. All the weapons were clean of blood and only those nearest the forge had their burnish blunted by the fire's endless discharge of smoke. Every object on the wall had a story, and their weapons instructor, Maya, seemed to know them all. Many had histories from far away lands and many bore insignia or crests of those men and women for whom they had been created.

A number of the walls' trophies were students' work that Maya and her predecessors had placed there, but whatever the selection process for this honor was, it was inscrutable to the students. The only apprentice creations eligible for a place among these swarming constellations were the senior weapons of students who had graduated to become part of the guild. Lane had designed and forged his pair of barbed spikes at the end of the previous year and was required to have them with him at all times for his final year in Cian. Surely they both would one day be added to this illustrious collection.

Around the edge of the room were a series of work areas broken only by the forge itself. Benches, tables, and anvils lay covered in the tongs, hammers, molds, and projects of the first year grubbies, those in the hump, and the seniors. Cye and Sona were bent over separate areas, both working intently. The mess around them had a vibrancy that suited Lane. The chaos of the space felt controlled and purposeful without the fetters of regulation and order. In the under-used center of the room, reserved as a practice area, Maya stood looking back at Lane.

Maya was much older than Lane, but not yet old. Not pretty, but beautifully passionate and striking. She had an air about her that mixed together delight and anger energy. A simple gray shirt streaked with the day's labors, and below that the traditional black dress of Cian's Dons presented a body fit and yet surprisingly womanly for her position.

Lane turned to drop his two rods next to the senior weapons of Cye and Sona, and then turning back to the room and Maya, he knelt for the required show of deference. As he opened his eyes, they connected with Maya's eyes, framed by jet black hair and dramatic eyebrows. Lane stepped forward and gave Maya a warm hug that she returned with gusto, then held him away from her to look him in the face.

"Welcome back, Lane. How are you? Good? Great! I'm excited to have you finally back for this year. Oh, some of these younger students make my head hurt."

"Hale, Don Maya, Hale. Am hale. It's peach to see you again and this year'll be bright." Lane paused and smiled at her, "If you can keep me busy." She grinned back and tousled his hair. Her affection was totally inappropriate, and he reveled in her disregard. Cye was waving a greeting from across the room, and Lane stepped towards him.

"Things are moving, Lane?"

"Aye and hale. Am feeling particularly fit today."

"Good..."

"Afternoon and greetings, Lane," Sona interrupted from nearby. Still bent over his work so that his hair flowed down around his head, hiding his expression from Lane, he continued, "Come you come for today's lesson? I'd thought these notions were too low and easy and simple for a natural?"

"Spot, Sona. Have come to keep Cye company, respect Don Maya and watch you muddle on."

"Master Maya."

"To you."

Sona turned towards Lane and though the hair still fell across his face, sharp eyes smoldered through the veil. After a long moment, Sona turned back to his work carving a wooden knife handle.

Lane turned away, fondling a thin steel disk hanging from the wall, sharpened around its edge. The cold metal stole the heat from Lane's hand. He held it another moment, then dropped it absently, letting it swing back to the wall with a harsh clang. Turning, he saw the two Wrens kneeling by the door.

"He goes eyeless together like clockwork dolls." Lane gestured toward the Wrens with his head, and Cye smiled. Indeed, the two lanky young men bowing their heads over their knees at the entrance to the room were choreographed by some unseen puppeteer, each motion so synchronized that one of them could have been genuflecting beside a mirror.

Maya waited until the twins raised their heads again, then moved to a low bench beside the roaring forge. The five students dropped to kneeling positions in a half-circle around the bench. The bench was covered with items as innocuous as a bowl, a book, a window and its frame, a pile of spoons, a candle all piled together.

"We spend our time in this room learning how to make and use weapons," Maya began, "but not all weapons are made in the end. For our first class of the year, I thought we'd stretch our minds a little bit." Maya's sentences came out enthusiastically, each one jumping in before the previous sentence had quite finished. "I've brought in a pile of things. Actually this is garbage I found behind my apartment this morning. These aren't weapons. Or at least they weren't designed to be weapons. But all of you are likely to eventually find yourselves in a situation where what you need cannot be crafted and must be found or improvised. Some of these things I don't know if they could be a good weapon." She held up the book. "I personally could always do more damage without a book than with one. This on the other hand," here Maya triumphantly produced a small silver spoon from the heap, "can be made serviceable." She bent to the rough stone surface at the edge of the forge, forcing both edges of the spoon's bowl across the rock, two score passes on either side. Holding it up again, where the spoon bowl had been was now a wide pointed head with serrated sides. The raw, frayed edges held on to minute hairs of silver that glimmered and danced in the forge light.

‡ ‡ ‡

The gold edged crimson tassel snaked through the weapons room, fluttering as it cruised towards Lane's temple. Lane watched it with a bemused expression, noting out of the corner of his eye an identical strip of material creeping low to the ground toward his opposite thigh. Waiting casually until the last instant, Lane lowered one hand holding the leather bound book Maya had pointed to an hour ago, simultaneously tilting his head back a few inches.

With two concurrent cracks the frayed fabric ends broke the air with the speed of their snaps, one end catching the space half an inch in front of Lane's nose and the other slicing a chunk of leather off the cover of the old book in Lane's hand. The Wrens, holding the other end of these discarded bell-pull cords, circled Lane on opposite sides. Lane jabbed playfully at one of them with the book, but they were well out of reach and neither reacted to Lane's antics.

Synchronized blinks of the four eyes were the only mobile features of their faces while they sparred. Raising their arms in unison, both lashed out again. Again, Lane waited calmly between them. This time the book deflected one of the assaults and Lane deftly caught the end of the other whipping cloth just as it snapped beside his waist. Tugging it as he grasped the rope, the surprised Wren found the bell-pull disappear from his grip just as he heard its report. Lane gave a friendly but patronizing smile to Wren and tossed him the book from his other hand. From across the practice floor, Cye and Sona witnessed this smooth exchange of make-shift weapons and Lane waved cheerfully to them, leaning forward without a sideways glance to avoid a strike to his torso from the other bell-pull.

Sona stopped for a moment, arrested by Lane's incongruous gesture, his hand holding a rotund pewter ewer frozen in the air. In that moment, Cye brought around a heavy chain-link butcher's apron like the long sweep of a cape. The metal weave caught Sona's hand and knocked the pitcher across the practice floor. Sona let out a feral grunt of pain, jumping back and shaking out his hand, now spotted with welts. Sona retreated toward the table, keeping his front to Cye and an inimical gaze on Lane. Lane smiled, shrugged, and then as the bell-pull he held wrapped its end around the midsection of Wren's rope, he pulled that second rope out of the fray. He waved again to Sona.

Reaching the table, Sona picked up the large window frame and came marching back into the center of the room. He bent down as he walked, and his juggernaut strides chewed up the window frame, spraying glass and wood in his wake. Straightening again in mid stride, Sona came up holding the two long ends of the frame, one in either hand. Sona and Cye began to circle again on top of the broken glass and wood debris, Sona jabbing here and there, his face dark and thunderous. Cye repeatedly avoided the makeshift wooden spears, deflecting and returning each attack with graceful waves of the heavy apron. Lane was now turned away. Sona tossed aside one shaft and bending down, picked up a triangular glass shard the size of his palm as he and Cye continued their slow spiral. With a flick of Sona's wrist, the glass shard leapt from his hand. Whirling end over end wide past Cye's head, the makeshift projectile flew straight toward the nape of Lane's neck.

Lane's attention came around to a warbling sound approaching him from behind. Time stretched out endlessly as Lane contemplated the advancing missile. He was used to the wait, but it was still tedious attending his muscles' response so long after his mind had chosen a course for his body. Without looking behind him, Lane brought a closed fist up behind his ear and jabbed across the backside of his head. The first two knuckles of his hand connected with the clear chip slicing through the air, exploding its substance, dissipating its energy, and covering Lane's back with a layer of glass splinters. Lane didn't even turn around.

Maya stepped into the middle of the floor and put an abrupt end to the session with a curt wave of her hand. "Sona, your use of the glass is excellent, but your aim is poor. The purpose of these exercises is learning and I don't want an inadvertent injury just because someone is not paying attention." At this last phrase she looked pointedly at Lane. "Intone tokada and return tomorrow."

The five knelt where they were, hands on thighs, heads down, eyes closed, droning out Cian's self-serving pledge. Lane was a few lines in when he felt a hand on his shoulder. Looking up without breaking his chant, he felt Maya wink, felt the squeeze of her hand, and then she passed out of the room. Lane continued to chant, trailing off at the end, watching her body move as she exited.

Lane rose and followed, out the double doors and back down the now empty main hall. As he passed into the entryway to Cian and was swallowed up by the darkness of the stairwell, he heard the clomp of Sona's boots behind him.

‡ ‡ ‡

The regular beat of boots on stone heralded Lane as he came again out of the stairwell darkness into Cian's artificial dusk. Striding through the entrance, he slipped the last piece of a meat pastry into his mouth, and dashed his hands together to dispel the flaky residue. Then seeing the residue still on him, brushed the buildup of tartlet shavings from his gray tunic, opened halfway to his navel.

Lane dragged his feet slightly to hear the scraping sound
they made on the unpolished stone floor. About half way up
the colonnade, the Wrens were cleaning up from sculpting
work. They had found parallel spots on pillars facing each
other across the arcade. What caused Lane to roll his eyes
was not the enviable fact that the Wrens had found such a
convenient location to do their year's work, but that they had
started at all. A month into the year and already at work
made them seem desperate, too eager to please. Lane didn't
bother looking to either side as he passed. It was premature
for even such over eager students to have produced anything
recognizable. The twins moved in silently behind Lane like
leaves dragged into the current. At the stage all three left their
senior weapons and climbed to the raked lecture pitch.
Weaver, Sona, and Cye sat, already talking.

Kneeling, the three newcomers lowered their heads for
only a moment as Weaver, Cye, and Sona continued their
dialogue.

"Tis nothing and na matter but a hobby, a little time
waster. Fun is all it is and so I do it."

"It's not a small thing, Sona. Just an hour a week like
that will pay off for you in some surprising ways a few years
from now. I'm very glad to hear you're taking your free time
seriously."

Sona inclined his head slightly in thanks for the
feedback, obsequiously serious.

"Welcome, Lane. Welcome Wrens. We were just talking
about how each of you does or might invest in yourselves
when you're not here in Cian. Lane, any thoughts on
improving your mind and body?"

"Do'na be too hard on fixer, nor too easy on pretty dabs,
and avoid working for fun."

"That's how to stay alive, in good health, and a good
mood."

"A genius investment, spot?" and Lane grinned.

Weaver smiled but shook his head in exasperation. "Wrens? I don't see you at the pubs." He left the statement hanging as it was.

"We inner listen"

"twice a day"

"every day."

"Exactly my point. That pays off for you everyday." Weaver stood as he continued. "For each person, what investment you need is different, but there is a part of each of you that is fallow, waiting to be cultivated." Weaver was pacing slowly now in the semi-circle in front of them. The session had clearly started, though it was odd that it had not begun with a more formal statement and genuflection. Lane didn't care. He loved listening to Weaver's smooth, even voice. As he was doing now, Weaver would often pace as he talked, adding weight to his thoughts with big waves of his arms. At times Weaver almost acted out the descriptions he was giving, stooping here, or jumping suddenly across the stage. Far from being a show, Lane loved it exactly because Weaver lost himself in the communication with his students, an hour long monologue sometimes, or a cross-legged discussion sitting in front of them, drawing out his points through a stream of natural questions and answers. The experience was so pleasant that Lane's attention wandered in and out of the specific thoughts Weaver was conveying.

"There is, for each of you, for every one of us, a right action to take at each moment in time. It may seem complicated, but this is always - always I promise you - because you're thinking about it. Each of our natures knows the way to go and it is only the contemplation of that direction that distracts it. Following one's nature sometimes has unforeseen or undesirable consequences. But those consequences are always mild compared with the tangled web we weave around ourselves when we step out of the path of right action."

Weaver had a way of making everything he uttered sound obviously and simply true, in part because his sincere desire to be understood was untainted by ego. Lane enjoyed that too, but more as a spectator than as an apprentice. Weaver broke the rhythm of his gestures to sweep the hair back from his temples, running his fingers down the spine of his skull. Lane made a mental note that a quick jaunt to the pub where Rose worked would buy him another month of fun when he wanted it. As Lane returned to Cian, Weaver had moved on.

"Situations have that same property. You just have to find it." Weaver paused, thinking to himself for several moments with his pacing frozen in mid step. Then he continued, "I'll tell you a story I heard first when I was not much older than you are now. It was my first year as a guild member and I was new to Jaichi, a walled desert city very far to the south. Over an afternoon of teas, the elder in that town's guild told me about one of the jobs of his mentor, the town's previous guild elder.

"Many years ago, Jaichi was besieged by a large army. Many thousands of troops. The siege was unwavering, but Jaichi was well provisioned, with several fresh water wells inside its walls and enough food to last for a decade. It was nearly three years into the siege and both sides seemed content to wait, the army outside eager for the city's spoils and the oligarchy of Jaichi certain they could outwait the siege. The weather was bitterly hot six days out of seven and there was so little rain that water for the encamped troops was a problem and the swirling swarms of dust were a perpetual irritant. After three years, it was miserable for those outside the walls, far from their home country or a reliable supply train with reinforcements or fresh goods. For those inside the walls the situation was hopeless in the long run, but quite comfortable for the moment. The people devastated by the siege with no tolerance for additional waiting were the business leaders of Jaichi. Each day marked significant opportunities lost, eroding social position, and another few customers from other cities out of the habit of dealing with them. One of the wealthy businessmen of the town approached the guild for help and the elder, a woman by the name of Tsuyu, took the job of killing the besieging general.

"For weeks, Tsuyu went to the encamped army as a peddler, selling dried fruits and strips of meat. The soldiers tolerated a number of these hawkers from Jaichi because in truth, they had less food than the people they were trying to starve and were glad to see the Jaichi food supplies diminishing, even at their expense. The general in question had, however, maintained a state of heightened paranoia through nearly three years of inactivity. He was surrounded at all times by a number of soldiers and slept out in the open under thick insect netting. There was no opportunity to get close, and because he even slept in his battle gear, there was no opportunity to use a projectile from a distance.

"So Tsuyu spent her time talking with the soldiers, getting to know them. Because she was already quite old at this time, the soldiers treated her as a non-person, neither male enough to fight nor female enough to lay. And this non-person status made it easier for many of them, particularly the older soldiers, to confide in her the loneliness and boredom they would not admit to each other.

"Tsuyu struck an hour or two after dusk at the end of the tenth day of a harsh and relentless sandstorm. The wind had finally dropped and an exhausted silence covered the camp below the city walls as thick as the coat of driven sand that lay over the men, their equipment, their food, and their tents. Surveying the scene from atop a rampart, and satisfied that the company below was at a desperate low, she pulled a long wooden flute out of her robe and began to play. One after another, the flute poured out songs from the soldiers' home country - sad songs of lost loves and better days, of good food and the family bond. The sliver of a moon had no power to light the scene below through the dust that hovered above the encampment, so Tuysu played on blind throughout the night. No response came, no arrows, no threats, no cheers, no singing, no crying. But in the morning as the dawn brought the first touch of color over the horizon to breathe life back into the siege, the sun found the camp nearly deserted. One by one and in small bands, most of the army had packed up and headed home, sick of the land and sick of eating, breathing and seeing nothing but dust and sand month after month. Many of the tents and mounts had been taken too, and the general woke to find the army's remnants in a sparse, undisciplined patchwork across the open field.

"The humiliation was too much for the general. Or perhaps the music had cut to his core as well. He dismissed the few soldiers who had stayed on through the night, most having slept through the music entirely. At dusk, the city inhabitants lined the ramparts to watch as the general, alone on the barren field, opened a slit in his armor and fell on his sword." Weaver continued to pace, lost in thought for a minute, then added "Every situation has an essence. Understanding that essence in the context of a patron's wishes is the core of right action."

Weaver began again, and Lane watched Sona following Weaver with his eyes in rapt attention. All of them were hanging on his words, but Sona seemed particularly immersed, all sense of the here and now absorbed into the tones, gestures, images, and reflections being woven in front of him. Weaver was saying, "The patron's will is, literally, our will and that bond is sacrosanct." Lane closed his eyes and tried out a future world in which he was teaching a similar class with his own version of the world built of his favorite aphorisms. He imagined being much like Weaver, only perhaps with fewer stories. His reverie was eventually invaded by the sound of his name, "...for today. Lane if you could stay after to receive an assignment, I'll see the rest of you tomorrow. Intone tokada." They repeated Cian's required pledge together as one voice with one rhythm and in one unmodulated tone. Behind Lane his four fellows headed for the combat room while Weaver rested on his knees opposite Lane, shoulders low, recuperating after his discourse.

His teacher was quiet for a minute, resting and seemingly enjoying the silence. When he finally spoke he said, "Are you ready for your first job of the year, Lane?" The question would have been rhetorical from Master Horn or Maya, but Weaver seemed genuinely interested in the answer.

"Da. And white is better. Do have energy to burn."

"Good, Lane. This is very good money for Cian. This patron has used the guild before. This person pays well and pays promptly, so keeping them happy is important." Lane nodded his understanding and waited for more. "The Spirit is called Sylvester. He makes tiles on the Upper Bank on Bellur road, including atarites for several past Kamakura festivals. The form of death is unimportant as the patron wants the Spirit's atarites contract for this year. As long as the body is never found and there is no evidence of your work, any method of dispatching him will do."

"Give me the patron. Knowing who will lever the play."

"You have all you need to know about the patron, Lane."

"Will shine for you, Don."

"I know you will. You've always made me proud with the work I've given you. You're a good student, Lane, and will be a great pride to the guild someday."

Lane flushed a little, fighting off a juvenile grin. He bent forward, closing his eyes, obeisance to Master Weaver, but also an attempt to calm the pleasure churning in his stomach. Lane knew that he deserved that praise and more, but for some reason it still left him giddy when he got it from certain people, including Master Weaver. The fact that even tidbits of praise made him lightheaded with happiness bothered and embarrassed Lane, making him feel childish and insecure.

Lane rose to his feet, glided down the stairs, and sauntered off towards the double doors of rough wood slats at the far end of the main hall to the left of the large statueless altar. The light from the candles in front of this empty alcove played along Lane's outline. He took large swinging strides, eating up the distance to the combat room with a pleasurable sense of power and certainty, resolving into an almost perceptible golden aura around him as he pushed through the swinging doors.

‡ ‡ ‡

Lane followed from a block behind, walking in the middle of the road. Secrecy was pointless when following someone with no suspicion. The large square shoulders he followed were draped with simple thick wool and stuck out because the head they supported was the highest on the road. A light afternoon snow, accumulated on Sylvester's uncovered head, had ceased for the moment and the day was cold and gray. Sylvester had drifted up beyond the part of the Upper Bank where Lane made his bed, into a quarter populated almost exclusively by artists and artisans. This section of the Upper Bank was cleaner than most. Many of the little stone houses and shops that lined this road had decorations across their exterior, the smoother buildings painted with geometric shapes and the buildings faced with indigenous mustard-colored clay embossed with interlocking designs across their walls. Sylvester's long heavy canvas pants had veins of color smeared across them and as he strolled, Sylvester would occasionally wipe his hands unconsciously across his thighs.

Lane had expected to follow Sylvester to his home or shop, if they weren't one and the same. Instead, Sylvester had lead them to a temple Lane had never been inside before. The main door to the small temple through which Sylvester entered appeared to be the only door to the building, and possibly its only source of light. The hunched structure, no more than three times Sylvester's height, spread out in a large square, constructed of massive blocks of masoned limestone. There were several windows, set with frames and bars upon their exterior, but the windows were filled with limestone blocks almost as though they'd been placed there with the original building and the architraves and bars had been the mistake. The crown of the building and doorframe were patinaed bronze, but without decoration or adornment of any kind. The sun, low in the sky behind Lane made the patinaed green of the door lintel purple, and Lane reached above his head as he entered the temple to brush this ephemeral tincture.

Inside, the temple was almost entirely bare. It had no furniture, no paintings, frescos, or mosaics. The people inside, no more than ten or twelve, sat on the floor or stood, all facing the statue at the far end of the room, as there was nothing else to see in the entire space. Lane's eyes adjusted to the sepulchral gloom and indeed, the open door was the only light source.

The statue in the temple's rear scraped her head against the ceiling between the last two timber beams that stretched across the hall. Bell, the avatar of Selfishness, was depicted in this carving as a middle aged woman, old enough to know the weight of years and still young enough to have the last petals of youth clinging to her hips, cheeks and breasts. She was shown bending over and away, her arm hooked across her chest to shield the last of her food from the wailing, emaciated infants tugging at the hem of her dress. Lane knew little of Bell's life, but frowned at the juxtaposition of these malnourished babies, frozen in the carved granite, looming several feet above the supplicants standing at the statue's base. Bell, one of the more recent additions to the Karabas pantheon, had been designated as the avatar of Selfishness when Lane was five years old. This particular district of the city, previously identified with the avatar of Hunting, had won the Kamakura's fall festival Atar game, though Lane could not remember the game that year. The quarter's victory entitled the district to be subdivided into two sections, one retaining its old temple, and one to receive the newest avatar if one were to be named that next New Year's day. It was their bad luck in this case to end up with such an undesirable avatar.

Even in the murky half light, Lane could make out Sylvester's tall frame, standing near Bell's feet. His prominent square chin highlighted a generous mouth, friendly when it smiled and kind even now in its seriousness. There was something in the way he stood that Lane could not quite place. A discomfort or perhaps an awkwardness, decidedly more social than physical.

After several minutes, Sylvester still had not moved. Lane had only been following him off and on for a few days, so it was entirely possible that Sylvester was the type to spend as much as a half hour in contemplation when he visited one temple or another. Still, it was hard to imagine what could occupy him, or anyone for such a length of time in such a depressing environment. Looking around, Lane noticed a dwarfish old man propped against a side wall, his head lolled to one side in a slovenly torpor. Lane approached the ancient midget, stopping to tower above him. The man's head was covered by tangled strands of ivory hair and a more impenetrable white bushy beard into which nestled venerable crumbs and food stains.

"Flood! Are you already cold, old tiny?"

The ancient wrinkled eyes trembled on the edge of another world, then opened to see Lane far above him. A deeply puzzled look came down like a curtain over the aged face. "Do know you, master...?"

"Of course you know me, Flood!" Lane crouched down next to Flood and lit Flood's face with his lucent gray eyes. "We worked the high house kitchens together." Lane's smile was warm, friendly, and earnest.

Flood's frown deepened and he said to himself, "So long ago. Too long ago. And you are too young for that," Then to Lane, "Are you sure?"

"Of course am sure! Used to strip fish with you late into the night. The smell was with us for weeks!"

"Remember stripping fish many nights at the high house..."

"Tell me a specific night at the Island Palace you remember old one," Lane interrupted.

Flood was quiet for a moment as a distant memory dragged his lips into an unconscious smile. From far away his voice rumbled out like the wheels of a cart on a paved boulevard. "Remember one night. They brought to the high house a huge tub of fish. Live fish in the tub. Many live fish. Maybe trout from down river? Some grand was visiting the high house and he can't eat but male fish. He can eat bucks but na does. Rams but na ewes. Tonight he wants fish. Got to get a few male fish for high dinner. Male fish?" Flood's gaze slowly refocused on Lane. "Male fish?" He smiled a mischievous smile. "All look same. Fish is fish." He looked at Lane sharply now. "You were there?"

Out of the corner of his eye, Lane could see Sylvester moving back up the center of the temple towards the exit. "Na. But will be next time, antique. Thanks for the story. Will remind you of it next chat." Lane laughed boisterously as he straightened. A few of the petitioners turned at the incongruous sound, but Sylvester was already through the door, framed for a moment in a blinding rosy glow, then swallowed up entirely by the daylight. Lane followed through the framed radiant threshold.

‡ ‡ ‡

The front of Sylvester's workshop was bathed in morning light. The sun's warmth penetrated the cold air, making a dew of the late winter frost. Sylvester's building was situated so remotely, at the extreme uphill section of the Upper Bank at the end of the road, it seemed like a poor joke on Weaver's part. The workshop was built directly into the mountain behind it, and the façade's only indication of the building's purpose was a triangular tile, three feet on a side, hung directly over the door. The tile was painted with a pattern not abstract but unidentifiable, like a giant puzzle piece. Through the reds and browns on the tile's background, thin arteries of gold leaf flashed in the morning sun.

Lane shifted his position slightly, relieving pressure on one of his legs. This part of the city, a cul-de-sac at its margin, was quiet nearly all of the time. The few shops along this road were also workspaces for artisans, except for a run-down storage structure directly adjacent to Sylvester's building.

Through the two rectangular windows on either side of a white wooden door, Lane could see a little of the cavernous interior of the workshop. Near the door stood a few chairs, two tables, and a kiln. Beyond that lay a labyrinth of stacked pottery, mainly tiles, that disappeared into the darkness of the mountain. Sylvester was sitting in front of the kiln, bent over something out of Lane's line of sight. Just as Lane was wondering whether there was any traffic at all on this far edge of the city, up the street came a well dressed gentleman, his head protected by a stiff, formal felt hat, his cape a dark amethyst on the outside, lined on the inside with a vivid green that shot bursts of color as his train waved along behind him.

The man did not hesitate, but marched forward to the end of the road, turning into Sylvester's workshop, where he knocked but then entered without waiting for Sylvester's reply. Sylvester was polite to the visitor, fetching a glass of something for the man to drink, and they sat talking together near one of the windows. Given the elegance of the visitor, Lane felt sure this visit was not about pottery. The Kamakura festival, at the boundary between the final gasp of summer and the birth of fall each year, was the only excuse imaginable for an artisan to receive a visit from, rather than a summons from, such a guest. The Atar game was the high point of the festival and though the pattern of the ceramic atarites played no functional role in the contest, it was, in a sense, the setting and stage for the festival's pivotal competition.

Another person was approaching up the road and Lane recognized him immediately, not by name, but by occupation. It was one of the gray sweepers of the city, gliding forward like a daytime phantom, oblivious to all his surroundings. Lane had never actually seen a sweeper not sweeping, nor had he seen one sweeper alone. The gray robed specter reached the end of the street and, turning, began again his recurrent task, pushing the unwanted flotsam of civilization back to join his company as it herded the city's rubbish down towards the river.

The regular whisk, whisk, whisk of the broom passed by and dissipated in fading echoes along the narrow road. Through the window, Sylvester was laying out a large rolled up paper in front of the gentleman, more animated than Lane had yet seen him, pointing around the sheet like a child at play. It seemed clear enough that Sylvester's sentence was tied to the money and, more likely, the prestige associated with the job of creating the full Atar board for this year's festival. Though why this position was worth the price of a head made no sense. Making, painting, and glazing five thousand tiles to be used for one afternoon seemed like a harsh punishment, not a covetable award. Lane wondered as a flash of green from the gentleman's cape heralded his departure, how much Cian would be paid for Sylvester's demise.

The echoes off the stone walls, this time of hard heels on cobblestones, set a rhythm to the pattern of facts Lane had observed. Sylvester was well liked by those with whom he interacted, but not well known even in this section of Karabas. Though he had no close friends, relatives, wife, or woman on the side, Sylvester was likable in his odd, quiet way. He was the sort of decent quiet person the world could use more of. It seemed wrong that he would be made to leave the world prematurely.

Sylvester was alone often, successful in his craft but introverted in his ways. His usual location was fixed and isolated and he often was there late into the night. There was no evidence he suspected anything was amiss, nor that he had the means to defend himself. This task was too easy. Trivial in fact. The whole situation was pointless in its insignificance and insulting as a result. Almost better not to bother.

The sunlight streaming in through the shop windows caught Sylvester rolling up the sheet again, a naïve smile on his stubbled chin. Sliding the tube back into its sheath, he turned and gradually disappeared back into the mountain's depths and a sea of his own artifacts.

‡ ‡ ‡

A thousand people stood quietly around Lane in the stone paved field, shifting from foot to foot, waiting for the ceremony to begin. The stone structures of the park were higher than the trees, as long as the surrounding buildings, but barely wider than the dignitaries who stood along their top edge. These structures appeared across the space like giant brick and mortar fins slicing up through the ground. Up the spine of each structure, stairs ran from top to bottom. Taking up much of the ground space between these two dimensional buildings, huge bowls of white marble scooped out of the earth lay scattered across the same area, each inner marble surface etched with tracks of crisscrossing contrasting black marble arcs.

Sylvester stood twenty paces from Lane, looking up at the tallest of the free-standing stone stairways on which the ruling family was perched precariously. These steps were broad enough not to be vertiginous but narrow enough that the entire procession was lined up single file along the structure's spine. Near the top, Cirrus, the first male scion stood with two impassive body guards above and two below him. Cirrus looked much taller than he had even a year ago, and though it wasn't growing in evenly, nor helping his naturally good looking face, he appeared to be trying to grow his first beard. Cirrus held himself maturely and cut the part of leader in his tailored tunic, jacket, leggings, and cloak. Still, Lane could almost smell the cocky boyish assuredness lurking just beneath Cirrus's surface. And Lane approved. Cirrus seemed like his kind of fellow.

Below these five, the regent stood leaving a step between herself and the prince's lowest body guard. Karabas' long-time temporary ruler stood with a calm posture, almost strangely so. Her plum-colored double-layered caftan ruffled uneasily in the breeze like a sail caught mid tack. Below the regent, the other siblings of Cirrus trailed down the edifice from oldest to youngest. Lily, the oldest of the deceased ruler's offspring stood still, her arms crossed in annoyance, her silver white close-cropped hair framing an elfin face gazing out over the river and down the valley. Ava and Leaf, both handsome and well-dressed, fidgeted by themselves and occasionally with each other. Two steps below Leaf, Weaver stood in a thick white dalmatic, tied at the waist with a jade-colored tassel.

Lane had never seen Weaver in his public persona before, though he heard often enough about his teacher's standing as the herald for the suzerain and, since the death of the suzerain and his wife, herald for the regent and first scion. A gong sounded, signaling the apex of the sun's journey, and as the ringing echoes of the gong's vibration died away, Weaver began to speak. His voice carried across the crowd, forceful and vibrant through the clear winter air.

"Welcome, citizens of Karabas and subjects of Cirrus, your lord. On the one hundred year anniversary of the founding of this astronomical observatory, your lord has generously established several new instruments which will allow us to determine the time of day and the position of the stars with greater precision..."

Weaver continued on about observations to be made from the shadows cast by tall spires and long edges of the thin brick structures into the labeled bowls of marble at their feet. Lane's mind and eyes wandered over the crowd and many of their eyes were wandering too. Lane himself couldn't say nor cared to know which structures were new to the stone field. The draw for the throng of people, and presumably for Sylvester as well, was the assembly in public of the entire ruling family. As if to underscore the significant nature of this confluence, two dozen guards surrounded the base of the step-topped structure on which Cirrus and his siblings stood. Each guard was dressed in dazzling emerald ceremonial dress, crossed and recrossed over the chest, waist and curled separately down each leg. In each man's right hand an elongated halberd stretched up over his head, culminating in a silver-tipped spike. Just below the spike, curved in a deadly smile, a silver crescent created the first and third points of the weapon, light flashing off each crescent as the hands of the suzerain's guards twisted slightly in the bright sunlight.

Weaver's voice dominated the gathering, melodic and reassuring. Lane's mind drifted to the sound of the churning water rushing past the edge of the field, passing under the Upper Bank minor bridge, rejoining its other half past the tip of the eyot, and from there on down the mountain to calmer passages. Lane's ears on the water, his eyes still on Weaver, he settled definitively on the only method for dispensing with Sylvester that felt right to him. It wouldn't technically fulfill the Cian assignment but it was more elegant, more interesting, more fun, and achieved the same outcome.

‡ ‡ ‡

Puffy white clouds floated across the blue sky of the Atar board. An equilateral triangle, itself made up of hundreds of smaller tessellating equilateral triangles, was decorated with the pasty billows floating inside and across the boundary lines of these inner triangles. And as the light flicked across the surface of this painted sky, it seemed that the clouds took on more specific shapes of mountain flora and fauna. Oblong stones of five colors lay strewn across the clouds, many of the triangles without a piece, and no small triangle holding more than one of the painted pebbles.

A cracked leathery hand reached over the surface, moving each of the nine crimson stones onto triangles directly abutting their current locations. The hand withdrew and there was calm again in the decorated sky. When another, smoother, younger hand cast out over the board it removed one of the cobalt pieces whose three directly adjacent spaces were blocked with other stones. With six cobalt stones left on the field, the hand then maneuvered each of these stones to adjacent triangles with an index finger, sliding the colored markers through the miniature heavens. The hand's counterpart approached the edge of the board and the two hands together snapped off the just emptied two outer layers of triangles from the right side of the board. The remaining board was smaller, but still equilateral in scale with the same number of stones upon it. A still younger, hairier hand soared over the pieces, moving the eleven golden pebbles into their next constellation. In one shift of the board two of the crimson stones and one of the lime-colored stones were trapped without egress, two against the edge of the field and one in a corner that had been an edge just a few moments ago.

Four men and a wizened little woman sat around the board. The smoke in the air clumped together in banks and waves, like an animated version of the clouds depicted on their game board. The board covered most of a heavy wooden table etched with the scratches and grooves of many generations. At the edge of the table, to the right of the female Atar player and directly below Lane's elbows, a jumble of the removed atarites lay in strips of decreasing length. Lane leaned into the game over a railing. His eyes ran over the Atar board with a practiced eye, reading the signs and portents of the stone patterns as they shifted over the cerulean background. Lane became dimly aware of the musty, almost moldy odor of the woman sitting by his elbow. In any case, Lane was used to the pungent clientele of the Tengo. Having been drawn away from his thoughts by this malodorous player, Lane straightened and looked over the extensive room for Rose.

The Tengo's short ceilings trapped the smoke near customers' heads, reducing visibility substantially. The night was young but already the tavern was packed and boisterous. The fires from the fireplaces, the heat of the kitchen in the back, and the press of bodies, all contributed to exile the outside winter drafts. Near the Atar game, a group of young girls sat on the edge of a warm hearth, one playing a simple melody on a guitar and the rest in song at intoxicated full volume.

The room was undecorated except for the foxes. On every available surface a rendition, often unsolicited, often amateurish, but rarely without some charm, could be seen of the Tengo's faux crest: two snow foxes with wide grins, up on their hind legs, front legs outstretched not to paw each other, but to rest on each other's shoulders for support. It was a friendly if undignified symbol that was nearly synonymous in Karabas with drinking to excess.

In the opposite corner of the tavern, Lane spotted Rose's hazy form. She was standing by a group of storytellers, no doubt listening with one ear and taking in orders with her other. Lit from behind, the thin textile of her dress silhouetted even more indistinctly the shape of her body through the material. As she turned and moved his way, he noted with approval that the front of her dress was cut down low over her stomach and he felt a pleasant sense of ownership as she headed his way through a chest-level sea of heads. Reaching him, she threw her arms around Lane's neck and leaned back, hanging off to look up into his eyes.

"Lovely, Lane. Good of you to come."

"Am fine for it anytime."

Rose cocked her head to the side appraisingly, then cooed, "You are as good as meat to eat."

"Others wait on their food from you." He gestured towards the table she had been hovering near.

"No one will go hungry over hardly minutes," and so saying, Rose dragged Lane a few steps into the hallway to the kitchen and shoved him against the wall. Her mouth on his, her hands went first to his ribs, then slid down and back, drawing his pelvis into hers as they kissed. Lane smirked as his lips swam across hers and twice as she fondled him, he sniggered so that she had twice to grab a handful of his hair to steer him back to her business.

Pulling away with her mouth but pressing her groin a little harder against his, Rose whispered, "If you wait til late, a little locking will be worth it."

"Have work tonight, little one. Regrets."

"Tonight? Why must it be tonight?"

"There's labor that's below me, but it must be done. Doing it's worthless, but avoiding it's worth less still. Better out of mind by doing it."

"If the effort is less than you, why do it t'all?"

"Cause...cause things are as they are. No matter. It's trivial labor. And can always find a way to make the work interesting."

"Well tonight the loss is yours love," and here again she pressed herself against him, this time clearly just to afflict him.

"If am still in the humor, will come back for you late."

At this she stepped back from him, smiling but with a raised eyebrow. "It's not clear humor will still catch me after hours."

"Will see."

Rose shook her head, gave him a last kiss, and disappeared down the hallway into Tengo's kitchen. Hanging on the wall opposite Lane at the edge of the hallway was a large, rough wooden sculpture of the Tengo foxes, leaning on each other in a sloppy, prancing, intoxicated triangle. The eyes of both foxes were half closed, the lolling tongues out not in a vulpine pant but in the insensibility of drink. The pair were happy, oblivious, and unwell.

‡ ‡ ‡

The door's white wooden mullions cut the moonlit frosty glass panes into repeating luminescent rectangles. Through the white veins of ice lacing the windows, the interior of Sylvester's workshop appeared as a bottomless corridor of shifting shadows and earthy colors. Once inside the door, the two tables were covered in brushes, tiny paint pots, and a range of ceramic tiles. The kiln door was open and though the coals inside smoldered darkly, the emanating heat wave was a second layer between the outside air and the depths of the work space.

Beyond the front tables and a few scattered chairs, the piles began. Up to the limits of visibility, carved out of the mountain rock, the cavity expanded into a cavern widening out behind the façade into an unevenly shaped, roughly finished grotto. The entire space as far as could be seen was a labyrinth whose walls were made from hundreds of stacks of fired clay goods. The heaps of pottery contained plates, cups, pitchers, masks, and bowls, but these were no more than occasional deviations among the thousands upon thousands of atarites. Each triangle of baked terracotta was painted, glazed, and dried, each a different pattern. The tile mounds were sometimes only a few feet high and in other places reached to near the roof of the cavern. The flickering candle light burning somewhere deep in the maze made the endless forest of piled earthenware pillars otherworldly. Nearer the candles the shadows wavered wildly around Sylvester.

In the midst of this sea of work, Sylvester sat painting an atarite. Several stools surrounded him holding a dozen paint pots. His legs pulled up on the bar of the stool beneath him, he rested the large triangle on his lap, laying a thin swath of ruddy plum across its surface. The cold had no power to reach this far into the mountainside, and his paint-speckled shirt was unbuttoned down almost to his navel. Reaching up absently, he scratched himself behind his ear, leaving a small vermilion mark by his earlobe. The enormous work space, shielded from the outside world by so much rock, was silent except for the whispers from Sylvester's brush and the occasional sputter of a candle overhead.

Lane cleared his throat discreetly, almost politely. Sylvester whipped his head around, freezing entirely as he took in Lane sitting on a stool no more than three feet behind him. Lane looked not at Sylvester, but down at the knife Lane was fingering, absently picking specks of dirt from under his nails. A moment passed without motion or sound, and then as though suddenly unstuck, Sylvester lurched to his feet and backed away, keeping Lane in view and knocking into a tower of still unpainted tiles. As he jumped from his stool, it teetered on one leg and the atarite he had been decorating slid from his lap to the floor with a crack, breaking into a puzzle of chunks. After a full wobbly rotation of the stool, it fell down on top of the ruined tile.

Lane looked up slowly at Sylvester, watching him. Reaching down and righting Sylvester's stool, he said, "Sit down," in a light, conversational tone.

Sylvester looked at the knife in Lane's hand, and then looked around the workspace. Finally he settled on a trowel in the pocket of his apron and grabbing it, held it out apprehensively, more like a ward than as a weapon. Lane sighed and stood up, placing the knife on the stool. He stepped toward Sylvester unhurriedly, looking directly into Sylvester's eyes until he could see nothing else, his lids unblinking as he closed the distance between them. Gradually he reached out and as Sylvester's hand began to inch away from his, he closed his right hand around the tool, felt it sticky with wet clay, and slipped it out of Sylvester's grasp. Placing the trowel down on a stool next to Sylvester, Lane turned his back, returned the three steps to his original stool, and picking up the knife, reseated himself facing Sylvester. Sylvester was motionless now, looking down at the trowel that had just vanished from his hand. Lane motioned with his knife for Sylvester to sit down as he had been. Sylvester blinked, but did not stir.

"They have a Judge who wants sudden sleep for you." Lane let that hang awkwardly in the air and Sylvester stood, looking at him blankly.

"You're a straight lead. And sleepy at that." Lane paused again, talking more to himself, but watching Sylvester for a reaction.

"Why this Judge wants you gone is bare. And you make the lead na game." Still Sylvester's expression was annoyingly blank. "Truly, can't learn na'thing on this lead with a Spirit like you such a donkey corzen hermit." Sylvester blinked again.

"Judge wants you quiet gone. He must want your atarites business. Though why can'na say." Lane paused, and still Sylvester played the statue for him. "As long as the Judge gets his end request, happy he. The details make no matter, but you will be gone forever. Can make that interesting with you. Have done so before. The Judge pays pieces for the results not the process, right? And it's more

game this way when a Spirit like you's too slow for chasing..."
Lane trailed off. The silence stretched out from seconds into a
minute and beyond. Sylvester was frozen, waiting. Lane too
waited, unsatisfied about what to do with his captive
audience. Back farther into the stacks, tiny rodent feet
scurried a ways, and then stopped again, waiting as well.

"You know these hands could put you under roses?"

"Yes. I know." Sylvester croaked out his response, loud
but hoarse and unsure.

"You know could hunt you anywhere and make the cold
a blessing?"

"Yes. I know you could."

"And want you to see the sun rise tomorrow?"

"Yes. I would very much like to see the sun again."

"Then leave. Karabas is riff for you now. Disappear
instantly. Take aught with you. Go silent. Never return nor
never send message back. Can you follow these rules?"

"Yes. Leave now. Tell no one I'm going. Never come
back and never send any word back."

"Then go. But," Lane paused here again and saturated
the man above him with a hard, humorless gaze, "doubt na
that punishment on breaking these rules would make the riff
game in comparison."

"I understand. Thank you." Sylvester turned to leave,
then turned back to Lane again. "Thank you. I don't
understand why you're giving me this chance but I won't let
you down. I'll leave immediately and..."

Lane cut him off with a sharp uncomfortable wave of his
hand. "Go now or the rules will change."

Sylvester opened his mouth again, looked at the grave
young face in front of him, closed his mouth again, turned,
and ran back up through the maze of tile stacks towards the
front of his workshop. The sound of those footsteps receded
until a door slammed closed and the footsteps were gone.

Despite himself Lane stood up suddenly to pursue his
prey, then frowned, shook his head, and forced himself to sit

down again. He absently picked up a paintbrush resting on a stool to his right, its tip stiff with a dried indigo paint. Staring down at the palm of one hand, he traced lazy patterns with the tip of the brush over the palm lines, leaving traces of the tint behind. The brush hand shook a little but the sound of a blithe tuneless hum set the tempo for the sweeps of the little stylus.

‡ ‡ ‡

The stalagmite grew out of the rough stone floor, up four feet to a sharp tip. Unlike naturally formed protrusions, this cone of rock had been left as the room had been carved out, the negative space of the area's excavation. This granite spike, roughly symmetrical otherwise, had a groove and lip cut into its chest three feet off the floor. A thin tongue of flame flickered a second tip from this stalagmite oil lamp just below the pinnacle.

The floor was uneven, unfinished. Many of the closest stalagmites were similar in shape, though their height varied from six inches to almost ten feet tall. In a number of places the oil lamps were carved directly into the floor, creating through all these fires a feeling that the entire floor was porous and opened sporadically to an expansive inferno beneath. The floor of the low, expansive room undulated, sloping gently up from the pair of wooden double doors towards the back. The edges and corners of the room were totally undefined, each rough, unfinished aspect of the room curving seamlessly into its adjacent parts.

Cye, Lane, the Wrens, and Sona knelt on the floor in the middle of the space, a short thick stone spike resting between the second Wren and Sona like a sixth apprentice. Facing back towards them, Master Horn was dodging from some invisible attack. Pointing into the empty space, shaping and gesturing with his hand, he continued to feint and block, explaining, attacking, and defending simultaneously. Occasionally pointing at one or another of his small audience and more rarely at the city overhead, his arms were windmills of activity, channeled into an intricate instructive performance. The oil lamp lights dyed the short sparse hairs on Master Horn's crown a jeweled ginger and his irises reflected the light like polished obsidian. On the dark uneven surfaces of the room the fifty dancing light sources created a shifting dusk, magnifying the many rock protuberances into projected phantoms on the squashed dome overhead.

‡ ‡ ‡

Cye's expression was calm and focused, his mouth relaxed at the corners. Cye's torso was covered by a thick white chiton, hanging over loose tan pants cinched tight at the waist. His shoulders low, arms hanging at his side, crooked at the elbow, Cye's waist glided through the room, his upper body floating along above it like a boat riding a current. The shadowy combat room circled behind him, Master Horn, Sona, and the Wrens passing into Cye's blind spot, behind his back, and reappearing on the other side. Without warning, one of his hands or feet would shoot forward, fingers out straight or curled into a fist, the ball of his foot the vanguard for his leg. The rest of Cye would flow after these assaults in a flawless dance that never left him off balance or overextended. Turn after turn he whirled in graceful precision to his personal music.

His partner stood in the middle nearly motionless. Lane could appreciate Cye's efforts and his technique. In fact, he envied Cye's craftsmanship. It was the next best thing to natural ability. As each of Cye's blows came drifting through the air towards Lane, he watched Cye's impassive expression.

Not angry. Not frustrated. Not even overly focused. Cye seemed unaware of his performance as he gave it and yet there was a thoughtful, philosophic character to his movements. Each motion carried a symbolic gesture. The cloth-on-cloth friction of each thrust, punctuated with twisting snaps, created a wonderful percussion to which they danced. As Cye's outstretched fingers neared his throat, Lane raised his hand to tap Cye's wrist, diverting the thrust just enough to send it grazing by the few blond hairs underneath his chin.

Lane turned slowly and Cye was already floating through the air towards him, not high above the floor, but a coordinated burst that did not use the ground. Lane's smile receded, annoyed that Cye had caught him a little flat footed, and he was forced to step aside as Cye came through. Two pairs of slim black boots continued through a forest of knee high stalagmites, lit from all sides by the oil lamp fires between which their harmonized soles moved with careful grace.

‡ ‡ ‡

On the other side of the room the spikes of rock grew to nearly shoulder height, the fires burned higher, and a threesome was performing a very different kind of ballet. Every move at every joint of each Wren's body echoed in the other Wren almost as though they were mocking one other. Their eerie coordination revolved around Sona, who stood in the middle, biding his time. Periodically he would let a compact fist jump from his loose fitting jersey, knuckles first, snapping at the end of the punch with such force that his body recoiled awkwardly whenever his hand connected with the air. This game of cat and mouse continued until the assailants were close enough that with a feint toward one, Sona whirled away again, turning and grabbing two handfuls of the other Wren's shirt. Sona heaved the captured apprentice around through the air, and his brother had to jump back to avoid being smashed by the swinging legs. Sona released his human cudgel in mid swing, leaving Wren to the terrain's mercy. Continuing around through the spin, Sona came lumbering back after the still upright Wren.

The lanky Wren stood dispassionately, facing him with his body turned sideways, arms up, legs bent. As Sona drove into him, Wren shuffled aside, striking Sona in his gut. Sona was turning around, thunder on his brow, when he was hit from behind, launching him forward into a short rock stump. He stopped with a jolt, arms outstretched on either side of the carved-in lamp an inch above the flame. For all his bulk, he rolled to the side and up on his feet again in a flash and was barreling back down on the two Wrens as though the shock to his body had been a nudge, not a blast. Sona's arms moved like seeking tentacles, hands and fingers reaching out not to rake or claw but to catch and hold. The Wrens retreated, respecting the space Sona was carving out with each grasp. What Sona's movements lacked in accuracy they made up for in ardor. Lane watched across the rocky expanse as the three bodies moved in and out of the shadows, passing behind and in front of the cones of rock. From a distance it looked like a slow motion game of chase.

‡ ‡ ‡

Sona, Lane, and the Wrens knelt in line near the center of the combat space. In front of them stood Cye, still sweating, holding the front of Master Horn's tunic in much the same way Sona had earlier grabbed hold of Wren. Master Horn pointed at Cye, gestured down the length of his body, and then indicated a spot four strides to his right. With a nod from his teacher, Cye heaved and nearly fell over as Master

Horn launched from his hands like a bundle of laundry, curled in mid air, landing with a roll back to his feet again in the exact spot he had indicated. He beckoned Cye to him, who then repeated the strange display, throwing Master Horn with seemingly no effect as again, his teacher landed unscathed. For several minutes Cye moved around the open room, throwing the clothes he grabbed as through they were uninhabited. Cye's face was wrinkled with humbled fascination as Master Horn calmly continued the lecture, even finishing a few of his sentences en route to his next landing. Lane beamed at the comical display and Cye's uncharacteristic confusion. Next to him, Sona and the Wrens' attention was humorlessly impassive.

In apologetic exhaustion, Cye threw Master Horn to the ground directly at his feet. Even here the older man seemed to bounce back up like a ball, obeying some natural law that did not yet apply to his students. At this Lane laughed out loud, clapping his hands with delight and tilting his head back to give his mirth full rein.

‡ ‡ ‡

Lane spun lazily, end over end across the room. The flickering flames beneath him created spinning constellations as his somersault continued. Supporting being flung was easier than it looked, but picking a place to land and doing it smoothly was that much harder. The undulating field of burning stones rushed up to meet him, and Lane curled his right shoulder into his chest to glance off the base of a tall spike of rock. Rolling over and then upright, Lane straightened his twisted gray shirt, now smeared with lines of black, singed in two places, and red along his right side from the scraping the latest landing had just given him.

Sona approached Lane and grabbing his collar and the waist of his pants, paused. Sona looked coldly at Lane and said nothing. Lane, fully aware of the effect of his insouciance on Sona, gave him another face splitting grin. Not until the ursine hands closed on his clothes did Lane realize that he was rocking slightly in time to a jaunty tune in his mind. As the weight of his body began to leave his feet, Lane participated in the heave, adding to the momentum. He felt Sona flicking his wrist as he let go of Lane, turning what could have been a simple arc into the wild gyrations of a windblown leaf.

As he tumbled through the air, nearer the ceiling than the floor, Lane thought a little ruefully that Don Horn had made recovery at the end of the journey sound like a matter of strategy and philosophy when it clearly was not. He could no more choose where to alight than Sona could aim where to place him. Letting Sylvester go had been a choice he could have made differently. That unwelcome thought was still forming as his eye caught sight during a revolution of a particularly steep waist high stone pinnacle toward which he was headed. Twisting as he could in mid air, Lane managed to curve himself into a crescent, pounding the ground with a painful thud as his body curled around the base of the rock formation.

Sona appeared above him instantaneously, and shaking his head to clear it, Lane saw that it was in fact Cye standing above him with lines of concern creasing his face. Sona approached and Cye stopped him with a word and a gesture, extending his other hand to Lane for support. The wind had returned to Lane's lungs, but he lay still another moment, watching Sona's pointless internal struggle. There hadn't been anything substantial Lane had done to justify Sona's hatred, and Sona's dark nature only encouraged Lane to make light of it.

Cye gave Sona a stern look. "He's your fellow Jack while in Cian. Act true."

Grudgingly, Sona put out his hand also for Lane to grab. Lane caught hold of Cye's and stood up, dusting himself off and cracking his neck a little by craning it to either side in turn. As he walked back toward the room's open center with Cye, well scratched but undamaged, he swung his arms nonchalantly. A spot between Lane's shoulder blades warmed from Sona's smoldering stare.

‡ ‡ ‡

The oil lanterns raised on pillars at the end of the bridge broke the spring evening with wide pools of light through which the population returned from the River Island to the Lower Bank. Many of the bobbing heads and rocking carts drove straight into the core of the Lower Bank, but a number turned downstream to follow the water's edge, lit along the way by the elevated lights. Skipping across lily pads of light on this promenade, the crowd thinned slightly at each intersection as the inner quarters of the Lower Bank diverted a little more of the human stream. Along the water, the Lower Bank buildings were old, grand, and shabby. The great stone buildings wore ivy up to the nostrils of their turrets and spires and age had overtaken these once opulent facades. In places unmended windows were covered, and dislodged roofing fragments lay at their building's base, untouched for a generation.

A smaller, newer, and more clearly maintained edifice interrupted the hoary structures. The temple to Empathy sat squeezed between two buildings many times its size. Peach blocks of granite created strong intermittent supports between which thick glass panes magnified the interior. The curved roof washing down around its edges, a soft comfortable hat of ceramic tiles for the temple. Two continuous benches circled the temple, one just inside and the other just outside the transparent walls. Both were dappled with people talking or sitting quietly in pairs. Four doorways, hung with rough tapestries splitting their medians, gave access to the temple's heart. A warm sandstone statue was situated forward of the center of the otherwise symmetrical temple. The carving stood three times the height of the tallest visitor, deep grooves of texture mapping the figure like physical brush strokes. Zain was depicted holding one hand to his cheek and reaching with the other to touch the spot where his mirror would have been. The haunting scene was read by Zain's devotees as one of the moments when Zain's disorientation is absolute, his ability to understand the people around him so complete it has left him lost as to which of these lives he feels so deeply is, in fact, his own. The simultaneous compassion and panic of the carved face was uncanny.

Outside the temple Lane, Rose, and Cye, having stopped for a moment, reentered the flow of people and continued down to the next intersection, turning left where it opened up into a wide boulevard. They moved toward the building, three streets off the Lower Bank river walk, that stood out from its neighbors like a blooming white wisteria in winter bracken. The white marble structure rose four stories tall and spread out over several acres. It had no formal walls or complete roof to the construction, but from a distance looked like woven marble, a dense intricate forest of bleached mineral columns curving together to make domes here and there, rising to the summit in a central crown. The meager lights of the Lower Bank grew in the reflections off the surface of Nagadith, putting to work even the faint glimmers of the distant stars thrown out across the sky above it. As it had no well-defined walls, Lane, Rose, and Cye could have entered from any point along the perimeter of the ancient building, but they passed as most did along the portico of intricately carved marble columns that led from the boulevard a short distance into the entertainment hub for Karabas.

As they entered, Lane shook out his hair and Rose slid the thick cobalt scarf she had wrapped around her shoulders down to tie it at her waist as a second skirt. The three figures stepped forward into the passing crowds that swirled around the calves of a forest of bleached marble trunks. The structure was built almost entirely from these supports, collectively rising to the walkways and spaces above, but allowing lights and sounds to leak through openings above and between them. The innumerable rows, halls, and open areas through which they now strolled were lit by a motley assortment of candles. Nagadith relied on its visitors for illumination. Cye stopped at the base of a marble column where several crude, colored beeswax candles already burned. Lighting a longer, thinner white candle he had been carrying from one of the fire-tipped wicks, he stood his candle in some still wet wax and they continued on.

"Well where will Lorna find us, Cye?"

"I set no more specific time or place than this field and this night."

"This is stone ground to hound one dab down, Cye." Lane waved his arm at the throng milling through the forest of columns before them.

"But we're zip hunters and the prey is na adverse to being snared."

"Have had the meat yet? Or is she still selling the chase to you?" Rose didn't turn her head at the remark, but whacked Lane across the chest with the back of her hand as they walked.

"Do you remember what the quarry looks like, Lane?"

"Straight. She is almost as serious and dazzle as you." Lane smirked at Cye.

"Shine. Just beat the bushes and when the hind comes out, we won't have to run her down."

As the trio stepped down from an avenue of columns into a wide hall with a higher cover and more occasional supports,

Lane pinched Cye's behind, and Rose, without breaking stride, threw out her arm at Lane for another playful reprimand.

A number of musicians had chosen to set up around the periphery of this open space inside Nagadith. As there were no organizing rules or even principles for the musicians, they tended to roost far enough from each other to reduce acoustic competition, but close enough to affect each other's playing. The result was overlapping local areas of harmony and coordination linking musicians across distances greater than any one instrument's sound could carry. This created waves of synchronization and melodic influence that washed across the acres of space and up the stories of the building. Tonight, in this particular space, all the performers within earshot happened to be playing horns or percussion instruments.

To their right just at the bottom of these few stairs, a young woman stroked a triangular shaped board, made up of varying sized metal triangles, with two rubber-tipped sticks. Despite the stocky stand on which this instrument rested and its apparent durability and strength, the sounds it emitted tinkled like tiny glass bells. Catching the young musician's eye, Lane fanned his fingers beside his ear and then moved them over his heart, indicating that her music was beautiful. She blushed a little and nodded shyly.

The gallery reached up to an inside dome above the second floor and the space was circled by a railless balcony at the second level of the building. Throughout this gallery the people swarmed and clumped around old benches and tables that were too large to have been hauled away by locals over the years. Here and there more temporary fixtures were strewn, such as the half dozen chairs in the corner, brought in by the party now using them. They might well be left for Nagadith, but the chances were good that before long someone would reappropriate them for another part of the building or just take them home. Through the throng the independent vendors pushed their way, selling warm viands and potent wines and spirits out of baskets and hip slung bags.

Rather than fight the crowd at the heart of the mall, Cye, Lane, and Rose kept to nearer the edge, strolling down the long side of the space.   The hall bubbled into regular transepts, dimly lit as fewer people chose to leave candles in those areas. By indirect light, the depths of these half rooms swam with indistinct drawings and phrases put on the walls with care in some cases and a casual hand in others. Occasionally, chalk images of rivers, trees, mountains, and skies would push through from the darker recess. Lane stopped Cye and Rose to point out a phrase written large enough and high enough on the wall to be seen from where they stood. It said "Sweetest savoring in affliction's jaws." Underneath the hand-printed letters in the corner of the transept, a heavy-set man thrust himself repeatedly into a young girl. She faced away from the man, leaning against the side wall with both arms outstretched, her skirt bunched over her back and her stringy brown hair almost brushing the floor, obscuring her face. One could never tell for sure here, but it seemed likely from her posture that this was a business transaction, not a spontaneous flight of passion. Rose cocked her head to the side a minute looking at the pair and then purred, but rather louder than was necessary, "Genius keying, boys. A master at work." The heavy-set man continued his pounding, unaware or unfazed, and the three of them laughed as they moved on, the grunts behind them drowned out within a few steps.

The trio talked as they wandered through the endless series of galleries, buying finger foods and glasses of spirit as their paths crossed with vendors. The atmosphere was boisterous, the liquor was strong, and the touch of Cye's arm on Lane's shoulder crystallized a feeling of perfection and balance that had been gathering inside Lane all evening. Even the spring night chill was banished from this place by the warm press of humanity. This was the cross-section of Karabas it was worth brushing up against. Several times they stopped to chat with friends they chanced upon. Lane knew few people well in the city and had no notoriety to recommend him to the general public, but among the rougher, more nocturnal natives of the Lower Bank, his face was a friendly sight. The seedy side of Karabas had been his cradle, crib, and classroom. Though his feeling of having outgrown it had suggested the Upper Bank for his sleeping quarters, this environment was a homecoming he enjoyed from time to time.

Sylvester strolled past Lane at the edge of his vision. Lane jerked around scanning the shifting crowd for the tall man. It couldn't have been Sylvester. He wouldn't dare still be hiding in Karabas, let alone dare parading through Nagadith.

"Have you spotted my hind, Lane?"

"Na. It was...na'thing."

They moved on together and Lane searched to recapture the balance of the previous minute, cross at having had it disrupted by something so stupid. He worked at it until his feeling of alignment reached a febrile pitch that required release and putting his long arms out around the shoulders of both of his companions, he tilted his head back and howled as they walked. The wail echoed faintly off the ceiling over the general din. Rose's smile when he brought his head back to neutral, happy to be with him and unembarrassed by his outburst, only fueled his recovered euphoria.

"Feeling peach my friend?"

"Am insiding invincible, Cye."

"That's a steel feeling. And feeling so takes you closer to being so."

"Am there!" and so saying he raised the hand holding Rose's smaller hand in his and spun her around, away and then back toward him in a smooth gesture that she gracefully accommodated.

"We're always in the middle of our expedition, never at the destination."

"And our expedition tonight? Will it continue forever too?" Lane gave Cye a grin to go with the teasing.

Cye smiled, opened his mouth to retort, and had to jump suddenly out of the way to avoid being bowled over. The doorway they were approaching was thick with smoke. Some of the inside rooms had less airflow than the outer layers of Nagadith and those with pipes, hookahs, and rolled tobacco gravitated toward these sections of the building. The smoke wall of the doorframe was pouring forth a stream of children on each other's heels, a marble cornucopia spilling frenetic fruit. The annoying parade was gone in another moment, and as there was never anyone responsible at Nagadith to chaperone the younger visitors, or to complain to about their behavior and lack of supervision, Cye stepped back in line with Lane and Rose as they passed single file into the gray cloud framed by carved white stone.

‡ ‡ ‡

Lane stepped through the dark haze of a white marble archway and over toward the round table at the center of the room. It took a few gentle nudges of his shoulder to stand so he could see the full surface of the table through onlookers standing three and four deep in concentric rings. All the candles in the room were on the table, so that the spectators receded to insubstantial phantoms around the seated players.

The table itself was no more than a square plank of unfinished wood whose supports were invisible from where Lane stood. There were nine seats around the wood slab, two vacant, the other seven occupied by players still in the game. Given the number of players still engaged, disproportionate attention was focused on one man sitting at the far corner of the table. Bent was hunched into the contest, his shoulders curved in, elbows on the table, and his chin in his hands. Absently, he tapped one of his pinned pieces recently removed from the board against the wooden surface, setting the game's tempo with a regular clicking sound.

The girl to Bent's right couldn't have been more than fifteen. Dressed in dirty over-sized clothes, her oval face painted with cosmetics and accented with food stains, she was frozen with her hand extended indecisively over the playing field. The Atar board may have been as large as four feet on a side when the game began, but now it was slightly under three feet wide and three feet long. The board design was an elegant silver and azure duotone aerial view of Karabas. The River Palace was certain to have been the center of the field when play had commenced, but now the center of the remaining area had shifted down river to the point of the eyot, and the Palace was halfway to the edge of the board. Strips of land and water as wide as Nagadith and twenty times as long lay discarded around the table in the jumbled earthquake of the game's progress. The Atar pieces positioned across the tessellated triangles were coins from different countries, making it hard at a glance to differentiate between some of the teams. With an extravagant sigh, the girl slid a small bronze coin to an adjacent space, thereby blocking in an identical bronze piece.

The rumbling started low and sparse, a distant thunder echoing around the edges of the contest. Then as the specters caught the nuances of the move, the rumbling grew into a stampede and then settled back into the insistent march step stomping of appreciation for her move. The play passed to her right and the rotund hill of a man who entirely eclipsed his chair carefully placed his ornately carved ivory pipe on the table and made his moves quickly, filling the vacancies the youngster had just created. All six of the square copper-colored coins in their disparate locations across the Karabas map were abruptly hemmed in. Four in the open, one on an edge, and one in a corner, all suddenly without adjacent triangles open to move to. It was going to cost the girl one of her own pieces to have opened this opportunity for the obese player that followed her, and with only five pieces left to Bent's ten, she had little hope now of even finishing second. Still, it was a beautiful move and she smiled, toothy and self-conscious, at the crowd's subsiding approval.

The elegant gentleman who had been playing the square coins rose ceremoniously. Collecting his six dead pieces and placing them on the side of the playing field, he performed a stiff bow from the neck first to the pixie who'd executed him so suddenly, and then to the other remaining players. Carefully sliding his chair into the table, he took a half step back, blending into the front row of spectators.

Around Lane the debts were being calculated, demanded, and paid. Gambling was so common to Nagadith that it became for its visitors a noise like the rapids outside, silent as it roars, and deafening in its absence. The implausibility of the sudden elimination of a respected player had, however, caused a few payoffs to rise above the steady wagering hum as pairs of individuals confirmed their odds and exchanged payments. Then the crowd, floating in the thick smoke, began speculating again immediately. The audience proposed and ventured on any and every aspect of the events. Next to Lane a shabby man was soliciting takers at two to three that the well tailored gentleman just now unhorsed would leave the room before any of the other vanquished combatants.

Two rows in front of Lane a man had revised his odds on the opponent who would come in second to Bent and was now taking money at two to one that the street urchin would place. Raising an eyebrow and focusing his attention behind him for a second, Lane confirmed that just a few feet back into the charcoal cloud a voice was taking even odds on this same urchin placing. Aside from a few Nagadith regulars who all used prominent spots on the first floor for taking longer term bets from wider audiences, wagers, odds, and pay outs were physically and temporally localized. This made odds discrepancies an accepted feature of the hazarding landscape.

And this feature created its own sport involving structuring profit from these inconsistencies, referred to by the gambling subculture of the Lower Bank as 'swelling.' Though Lane chose not to gamble on events he could not control, he did swell from time to time and was tempted now given the easy proximity to both risk niches. The money was inconsequential - it was the exercise of ensuring victory that was appealing. Then again, knowing it could be easily done satisfied the urge. A euphoric halo outlined the moments as they passed, blurring the edge between what is and what could be. Checking his pocket, Lane calculated roughly the upper and lower bounds on what he could have made, savored the provisory winnings, and then refocused on the shrinking board.

Bent's turn finished, his nine remaining pieces had each shifted to adjacent triangles, leaving the left and bottom edges abruptly free of tokens. Before advancing her coins, the precocious teen snapped off those same edges two triangles deep, returning the board to an equilateral triangle, now little more than two feet on each side. The increasingly myopic map showed no more than the bottom part of the Flat, from the River Fountain down a little past the edge of the Alleys, the blue and silver tones so detailed that the texture of the deserted stone expanse between the Alleys looked rough to the touch. This paring of the space left two of her pieces pinned against the new edges, surrounded on the other two sides by other players' tokens. She removed these two from the board with a juvenile sigh and slid her remaining two pieces into the only spots open for them to move. The chances were good that even in such a crowded room no one was bothering to bet on whether Bent would lose the game. When Atar was played at full size and Bent was only one of twenty members of Humility's team, his skill could be diluted by any blunders of his teammates. But Lane was sure that as a player for side board games such as this, Bent had not lost in years.

Underneath dark aristocratic brows, the hazel-brown eyes watched the board, blinking slowly and rhythmically. Rather than skipping from scene to scene, piece to piece around the board, the eyes devoured the whole scene at once, consuming it more like a painting than a page of text. In the thirty minutes Lane had been watching him, Bent had not once raised his eyes from the field or in any way acknowledged that there was anyone sharing the table or the space with him. The intensity with which his gaze lit the table and the patient perfection with which his plan unfolded around the other participants' fumbling moves warmed Lane and resonated in his gut. He caught thoughts about Sylvester's flight creeping up again and struck them down before they could distract him. Bent's precision was inspiring, and responding to it, Lane let loose another unrestrained howl. A silent howl only someone that good could understand. A howl only Bent could hear. The howl reverberated inside of Lane and he knew that Bent could hear it too.

With only three players left in the game and one candle sputtering its last moments of wax, the onlookers pressed forward toward the center of the space. Behind Lane a few teeth-clenched pipes amplified the surrounding atmospheric tobacco effects so that first the black shapeless backdrop to the host, then the insubstantial onlookers, then the table and its light, and finally Lane himself was drowned in the thick slate-colored haze.

‡ ‡ ‡

Lane, Rose, Cye, and Lorna strode on energetically through the stark marble surroundings of Nagadith, unconsciously choosing the clearest paths through the endlessly tiered complex. Cye and Rose were intent on their discussion with Lorna, who was inappropriately dressed.

Lorna's smart linen pants, spotlessly clean riding boots, deep violet silk vest and tight cream undershirt was a fashion statement lost on the vast majority of the Nagadith population and certainly out of place with dwellers of the Lower Bank. Cye was attentive to her, but there were streaks of grey in her hair and she was so intense that when she spoke the muscles clenched in her face, making her look too thin and severe to be comely.

For Lane, his current rapture made meaningful participation in their conversation impossible. He flew, skimming over the experiences of each passing moment whose lightest touches sent periodic pleasure chills shooting up his spine. From time to time Lane found they were stopping to talk to a friendly face. Many times these others knew Lane, nodded to him, or smiled, looking for recognition and acceptance. But generally they wanted to talk to Cye. Not that Cye said much to them. He would greet them. He would give them a compliment or ask them a question to show he remembered them. He shook their hands and clapped their shoulders. He listened when they spoke. It was nothing special, but in return the friends they stopped to talk to were transfixed while Cye paid them attention. Not that their sycophantic attention to Cye was entirely misguided. Cye was in a class by himself and worthy of their admiration, but their transparent deference still had a pathetic edge to it.

Cheap courtesans were a common distraction around Nagadith, sprinkled into the darker niches and quieter alcoves of the building. These women enjoyed the implicit protection of the Lower Bank population. Not because their services were seen as particularly necessary. But Nagadith was sacrosanct to its visitors and they all considered themselves caretakers of this last standing structure of the golden age of Karabas. Nagadith's self-organizing custodians had no formal rules to uphold but the implicit rules had evolved over time into a canon no one disputed or transgressed: do not hurt the building, bring what you need, and no one has the right to obstruct or control the behavior of other visitors. This effectively made Nagadith an oasis free from the organizing influences of the more disreputable parts of Lower Bank society.

Lane brushed his hand over a carved marble column as they began moving again, caressing a twisted braid of ivory serpents stretching up into the floor above and feeling a few individual scales with the tips of his trailing fingers before it slipped away behind them.

"That canna be. How suzerain seemed and how his wife seemed has na compromise with what you say."

Lorna frowned at going over the same territory again, "Appearances as they may be, I say again she guided most of his major and minor decisions."

"If he was so private weak, in public why did he present so wise?"

"There are many ways to rule well. Her advice may have been his structure. Perhaps our suzerain was a figurehead on purpose."

"It's ancient history. We were little urchins street playing when they were still alive. When they were still in power. When it still mattered."

"No, Cye." Lorna pounded her thin fist emphatically on the air in front of her. "It matters now. If the suzerain's wife shaped Karabas policy for years and gets no credit even in memorial, then we will all repeat our oversight, never giving credit where it is truly due."

"Is it possible she didn't want tribute. Perhaps she understood her role, the essence of her nature, just as suzerain may have appreciated and lived in line with his."

"Perhaps. But the evidence is heavily against it in my opinion."

Lane found Lorna's view tedious and was ready to try to end the banter when he saw a familiar tuft of shock white hair at knee height further down the wide hall they were traveling along. "This is opportune. Game for sure and an answer straight for you." Lane pulled them up around Flood, crouched against the wall next to a beggar three or four times his size. The two were talking quietly to each other, both heads lolled back resting against the wall behind them. It wasn't entirely clear whether Flood was simply talking with the vagabond or whether the collection hat full of coins in front of them was some sort of joint alms request.

"Greetings history! It's me!"

"Apologies son. Misplaced you..."

"It's me. Lane! Worked the high house refectory with you!" Lorna opened her mouth to speak and Lane put out his hand at waist level, palm down. She closed her mouth again and crossed her arms.

"Proper? You're na as old as me.... You seem too little for so long time."

"Spent long nights you and I, Flood. Am slighted if you dona remember me." Lane paused a moment and Flood shifted uncomfortably where he sat but was quiet. "Do you remember this? A guest came to the high house who would eat no dabs, only men and us told..."

"...told to dig through a barrel fish looking for the males..."

"...and as all were the same, picked some na mind..."

"...and told chef all male fish for sure! Do remember such night. And maybe do remember you better now. Odd can no picture you then there. Mind plays strange on me now." Flood shifted where he sat again, visibly frustrated with himself.

"Proper remember!" Rose, Lorna, and Cye wore masks of bewilderment. Rose mouthed to Lane, "What do you do?" Lane grinned, enjoying the performance and pleased with the effect of his bravura. "Flood. Were talking just before on Karabas's dear departed suzerain and his wife. Remember you again on his high house. Which held rule? Him or her? Which made choices and which acted the choices? Suzerain puppet? Or did she play the proper wife?"

Flood's face smoothed over as the underlying muscles relaxed. He was falling back away from them in time so that when he spoke it was from a distant place and his voice sounded more natural and more confident than it had a moment before. "It's na one or the other. It's na that can't remember. Nor is it that could'na tell. It was both. Was around long enough to see a thousand tiny examples, happenings. From her view, decisions she made for him she loved but she thought him weak. Help him? Yes. But get her way too. She knew he was enlightened to take her choices. And she let him have his harmless illusion of leadership." He paused, witnessing some scene before him they could not see. Lane's companions were slack jawed, and Cye in particular was mesmerized by Flood.

"And yet. The suzerain knew he was wise to let everyone help him do right. Knew he was strong to get right choices done to take credit him alone. He loved wife and took her choices when good, and humored her thoughts on him." Flood was quiet for a minute until his eyes refocused on the four people standing before him, blinking and squinting as though newly out into the sunlight from a cave. Finally he concluded, "So was both. Na one or neither. It was both."

Unable to contain herself, Lorna stepped forward as she burst out, nearly treading on the little man in her enthusiasm.

"Are you saying you know this because they both personally told you this is how they felt before they died, or are you saying this is a guess you had from your privileged vantage point as a palace peon?"

"Vantage of the invisible is powerful." Flood seemed cool to Lorna's jab.

"Gentle be, Lorna."

Lane laughed out loud a short merry burst. "Na worries for him, Cye. Flood will na remember this conversation tomorrow na how."

Flood's leathery face tilted towards Lane and it looked like the old man might cry. The relative giant beside him who had until now been effectively asleep, opened his eyes, glared resentfully at Lane, stirred ever so slightly, then closed his eyes again.

Lorna was leaning into the seated pair as she launched a counterattack on Flood, but Lane was no longer listening. His other ear was saturated with Rose's warm breath. She was asking about Flood, something about how funny the little man was. But in the presence of the hot moist air on his ear and the brush of her velvet lips against it, he could hear her words no better than Lorna's. Her sing-songy speech rippled through his mind like an undulating breeze through his hair. These sensations thundered above the lesser noises of the world. This intimate air was fanning the fire of his earlier ecstasy like a careful forester breathing through pursed lips new life into her coals. If there had been an irritant in his thoughts, it was burning away. Lane could feel the glow of his body, could feel his skin heat up enough to light the expansive hall. It consumed him, then the people around him, the building, the city, the world. He was lost, immolated in the pleasure of the rightness of it all.

‡ ‡ ‡

The five final year apprentices knelt attentively on the dirt stage. Weaver, as he sometimes did, had been talking in a melodious voice without break or variation for nearly an hour. He was a first class orator, but maybe too proficient. The presentation was often so polished that the content seemed secondary, and it was hard to stay focused under such conditions.

Lane's hands rested palm down near the top of his thighs. A tan linen top hung off his frame and down to the palms of his hands, covering the top of his cream-colored pants. He knew the still air was, as always, a little on the cool side, but he felt a little hot. Not the seductive hot that slides a person creeping toward unconsciousness, but the unpleasant hot that manifests itself as minor dizziness. Another apprentice might have suspected impending illness, but Lane had never been sick. Not once. The air must simply have been a little warm just then.

Weaver had been talking on ethics, but Lane refocused his attention as the topic changed abruptly.

"...which reminds me, Sona, please stay after my talk, your second job is ready to be specified." Sona gave a staccato nod in response and Weaver returned to his theme.

"We must be particularly trustworthy given our profession. Trustworthy for the guild, for our patrons, for the society in which we live and work. When trust is betrayed, everyone suffers. And for our guild more than most, the rules are inviolate. Breaking, even bending, one of Cian's rules is a violation of trust for all those parties." Weaver's posture, intonation, and gestures conveyed the impression that he was not lecturing them but talking with them. Sharing thoughts as though they had just asked the questions to which these were his impromptu answers. Lane missed a few sentences watching the craftsmanship and sincerity with which Weaver delivered his messages.

"Karabas, without explicit knowledge, suffers Cian to exist. If Cian had no place in Karabas, Cian wouldn't continue. Could not continue. Karabas has not found and closed Cian because we have rules and we follow them. These rules guide us to be expedient extensions of the will of others, not wild animals loose in the city. Our obedience to our patrons and our prohibition against acting without a patron, these things ensure we're a functional part of society. It is precisely because our rules protect us from being policed by others that we must so rigorously regulate ourselves."

Lane shook his head discreetly, trying to clear it. His sense of being overheated had become noticeably unpleasant, ushering in behind it the first faint swirling echoes of nausea.

If that wizened scrap of an old woman had fed him something rotten this morning, he would take it out on her hide. And if that breakfast came up during Weaver's talk, he'd give her his feedback with gusto. Forcing a smile, Lane straightened his head. He had the constitution of a mountain goat. This would pass without incident because that's just how his body was built. It bothered him that he was even thinking about being ill.

"It's the nature of our business to be secretive. Secrecy does not however imply anarchy. The true test of honor is how you behave when your actions are unmonitored. Cian's rules and the mandate that we comply with them is what separates our vocation from a street fight, from a brawl in public, from a juvenile power fantasy. This is the root of your education: you are not here to learn skills, but to learn a profession, a way of life, a calling. Integrity, honor, persistence, discretion, these are the foundation and essence of tokada."

There may have been some intervening sentences, but Lane next heard "We must be feared but never vilified by the societies in which we work. From this we derive two of our basic rules: no mercy, no torture."

The torpor drew down again over Lane like a thick blanket and it was all he could do to remain upright. So close to swooning, Lane's mind raced across his body, up one limb and down the next, looking for the condition. Even an identifiable symptom. But the more he tried to nail down an effect, the more elusive the symptoms became until he could not have sworn to any particular affliction but knelt as he did in catatonic anguish. A thought flapped through the periphery of his consciousness a number of times and each time he beat it off as a feeble person might fend off a bat with a broomstick in an enclosed space. With a final dodge and lunge, the idea popped into his mind's center stage. That burning feeling sapping the strength from his muscles and the chills doing their work on his exterior, was his body responding to something Weaver was talking about. This realization was itself a balm, taking the edge off the ache and sharpening his mind back from the blur it had become.

Lane's first lucid thought on rising back out of the murky bog of his distress was that he hadn't even really been paying attention. He almost never did. These lectures crossed the same terrain a dozen times along similar paths so that by now there was little of the landscape Weaver hadn't given them a thorough tour of before. On reflection, there was no chance that this sudden infirmity was just a mental response to one of Weaver's sermons. Lane's body would never turn tail over a stream of words, whatever words they might have been. Furrowing his brow, Lane made the effort to refocus on what was passing.

Weaver's dark brown eyes drilled directly into his as he came back to his sight. Weaver had locked his gaze on Lane as though the two of them were alone in the hall. There was no doubt that this tirade was being delivered for his personal consumption, and when he tried to smile back at Weaver, the smile would not come.

"Be proud to be part of Cian's traditions. Trust these traditions. They have worked for as long as Karabas is old. The traditions are wiser than you are. Wiser than I am. And they will guide you along your path, even if that path takes you to your end." And so saying, Weaver turned away.

"When I was your age I was given a task and one of my constraints was that no one other than the target was to be harmed if at all possible. I had only two nights left to finish the task, through delays of my own making, and I found myself in a position in which a serving girl would have to be harmed, perhaps killed in order to complete the task that evening. Could I have come back the next evening? Perhaps. At the time I told myself that the risk of exposure was too great for the patron. I told myself that the patron's completion date was too important to miss. I told myself that the patron's request had been 'if at all possible,' and so I dispatched the girl. In retrospect I could have been more accurate in my report to my master, but with the deed done it seemed right to align the report with the requests of the patron. Though he said nothing, my master knew. He knew before I knew. And I doubt I would have survived the year had I not gone back to make a more complete report to him on the choices as I had seen them at the time and as I saw them after the fact. The traditions were my guide. They showed me as I drifted to the edge of the course and they led me back to the faster flowing heart of the stream. My master and I..."

The sonorous voice faded away, dissolving with the speaker's face until Lane was back in that labyrinth of tiles, listening now with a horror he should have felt then to the sounds of Sylvester's escaping footsteps. A cold draught was slipping through his veins like an icy venom of poisonous thoughts - self administered. Lane's mind felt jammed. Like a bell tower clock with a loose timber blocking the gear's rotation, the tension mounted as the minute hand kept repeating the changing of the same minute in an endless spasm and jerk. He'd heard this all before. He'd heard this all before from Weaver. He'd heard this all before more than once before. Why now did it sound so different?

Externally his face was frozen, abnormally still. Looking straight ahead his gray and usually luminescent eyes were wide, but dull and defocused. Beads of sweat covered his brow and temples, occasionally breaking into brief tiny streams down his cheeks or across the bridge of his nose. Lane's head rose and fell just a fraction too regularly as his diaphragm contracted and expanded with an overly controlled depth and speed. The lids of both eyes fell down, curtains over his vision, and then rose again out of habit. Inside the gray iris the black pupil took most of the space. The empty center of the eye pulsed subtly in size to the rhythm of the strained respiration.

‡ ‡ ‡

The stale air sat heavily in the pyramidal space. Dust motes hovered in the air. Dust so thick that where weak planes of light broke through the floorboards below or beams of sun poked holes in the patchwork roof above, diaphanous curtains and posts appeared, breaking the attic area into a puzzle of shadow pieces. The wood floor panels and ceiling timbers had no section open as an exit. No outlook to the outside world. No identification, view, or sound for context. This wooden container could have been anywhere.

Lane's body lay stretched out on his roughly stuffed mattress. No covers, no pillow, no movement. His lower body shrouded in darkness, clothes blending the limbs and torso into the background, arms crossed on the chest almost visible, and a line of light drawn across him at an angle near to bisecting his face. Gray eyes open, staring up at nothing. Nothing. Blink.

This cannot be. Impossible. There's no point getting up until this is figured out. Lane had felt this way once or twice before. But previous times had been from being intensely cold. It was beyond numbness. More a distancing from the sensation until it could be observed without pain. Like remembering a condition rather than undergoing it. How bad is it really?

The sounds of the workshop door slamming shut behind Sylvester echoed around Lane, and it sounded like the definitive crunch of a guillotine. Then his memory dragged him up a mountainside. Gray clouds. Day is almost done. The man in front of him swoons in the snow holding a broken leg. The haze washes out the detail of the landscape below. Karabas reduced to a cluster of protrusions breaking the white blanketed surface of the highlands, the sprawling city massed up around the branch and rejoining of the thin snake of water coming out of the mountains. This wretch will not survive the night.   Cannot move, cannot summon help.   Work is accomplished.   Finishing him would be abattoir work not fitting this calling. Stepping lightly down from rock to rock, skimming effortlessly over their icy surfaces, back the short steep way to the city. Leaving the deed undone and the target in agony.

Virtuosity fades away.   It's not good.   Not good?   It couldn't be much worse.   Lane hasn't broken his own rules. But Cian's?   No mercy, no torture.   Who cares about their exact rules. Just get it done. Don't be a slave to their details. That seemed right somehow.   Until yesterday. Maybe it will again once sleep comes. But it still won't fix Cian's rules. It won't make Cian flexible or understanding. It's all so stupid. In both cases nothing stopped Lane from doing what the rules say he should have done.   There just wasn't any point.   He could have. But where is the fun in that?   Where was the challenge? He's too good to do it by the rules. But then why not do it right?   They're going to kill him for this!   Not motivating enough?

Maybe it's not too late. Maybe it can be fixed. No. Not now. No reason to think the mountain didn't do its job, and Sylvester has been gone weeks now. It could take months to find him.   Even more maybe.   Leaving Karabas now for months... inexcusable...he'll be the one being hunted...by Cian.

So do the rules really matter? Of course! To him? Of course. They define the discipline. They are the admirable part of what he's learning to do. They are the context that makes him love it.   Then how can Lane not have noticed before? How can he have violated that context? What about him made this lunacy possible? It is so frustrating! In both cases he could have done his job. Done it right. By the rules. It certainly wasn't for lack of talent! He didn't because...why? Because he was lazy? Because he was scared? Because he'd gone soft and allowed himself to like two of his targets? And liking them too much, couldn't bring himself to finish them?

Maybe so. But liking people is no crime in Karabas. Even liking the target is no crime against Cian. True, but being soft is a crime and people who are soft deserve nothing but contempt.

The scar of light across Lane's face was waning yellow as it inched along. Day was ending and the sun was leaving Karabas behind. The still musty air had been recycled too often and Lane's breathing labored. Like drowning. Though it would have helped his lungs to release them, he could feel his arms still locked across his chest. As though he were falling down an endless hole and becoming inured to the vertiginous descent. Paralysis in freefall. Dust continued to settle on Lane, a gossamer shroud building on the body, draped down over the mattress, spilling across the entire floor. Only the eyes remained free of the dust. The irregular, reflective cleaning of the lenses. Blink.

‡ ‡ ‡

Tongues of flame licked the leather of Lane's black boots as he shuffled over the rocky terrain. Long arms and longer legs came at him from all sides. Punching, grabbing, sweeping. Turning as he dodged there was no safe spot from which to regroup. No clear space in which to break and reform. The Wrens surrounded him with a flurry of silent blows. Hard to enjoy this morning.

Perhaps it was darker than usual in the combat room. No. Perhaps it was that the Wrens were wearing black, blending into the ambient charcoal background. So. Just distracted right now. And. The sweat was thick on his face. A soaked spot on his tunic between his shoulder blades lifted and then stuck again as he waved his arms. He could see the droplets jump from his face as he jerked aside. He could feel the water weighing him down. Had he ever sweat like this before? The water weighed so much. It seemed the Wrens were forces of nature, driving toward and through him without expression or experience. Did they never tire? Between the two of them they had connected on Lane only a few times in an endless sparring session. But it was endless. He needed a rest. A few minutes to dry out. Shake off this malaise.

Lane stumbled backward onto the upsloping edge of a rock cone, nearly twisting his ankle, and taking a foot in the chest as he recovered. Rolling across the rough floor. Almost a break in itself.

‡ ‡ ‡

Lane bent over slightly and held his hand up, palm out, fingers spread. A request masquerading as a command. A yard beyond the gesture, Cye wound down to a stop and stood patiently, bending forward and backward gently from the hip to stretch while he waited. With his hand still raised, Lane looked up and saw a puzzled look on Cye's face. A worried look? The air in Cye's eyes lanced Lane and he forced himself to straighten with a smile, waving Cye on again. His lungs cramped in his chest, his organs spawning a dreadful anxiety. Or the other way round. Cye flowed forward in seamless continuation of his earlier motion.

A fog enveloped Lane's mind. Each sensation came to him at the last moment, appearing through the mental mist. He knew each perception was coming but couldn't grasp or handle them until they were nearly past. It wasn't just that it was harder to think. Someone was holding the news up so it kept coming too late. Moving should have cleared his mind. Should have sped up the news. But it didn't. The more he moved, the more disoriented he felt. He kept pace with Cye, but barely. He took advantage of his awareness of Cye's rhythms, anticipating the moves before they happened.

Otherwise Cye would have worn his knuckles down on Lane's chest and face. The more he watched Cye, the stranger it became until...Cye wasn't really trying to hit him! The realization came through the haze to strike him like a runaway horse crashing through the milling crowd of thoughts in his brain. Cye was just practicing his form. Cye didn't expect to hit him so he was focused on himself instead. Had it always been this way? Robbed. Winning isn't winning if they let you win. Robbed of the implications of victory. Deflated.

Cye made eye contact as they moved over the treacherous landscape, but Lane could see now it wasn't with him Cye was sparring. Carefully crafted turns, strikes, bends, blocks, rolls, jumps and kicks. All a little slower than necessary. Building muscle memory. Lane stepped aside again, putting a tall stone sooty spire between them as Cye continued to go through his motions.

‡ ‡ ‡

The silky black hair waved like a curtain lifted softly by a breeze. Sona's shoulders were off just enough. Lane had nearly missed it. What was this! Thin powerful fingers of dread were tightening on his throat. He choked another ragged breath down. Impossible! He'd let it go again. Focus! Sona's stance was recovering and the window was gone. Too late and too rushed, Lane threw his arm into the gap. Too fast for Sona to react. Almost too fast to see. He watched as his fist constricted and twisted, pounding into the billowy white shirt hanging loose down over Sona's developed pectorals. The fist sank into the fabric, smashing to a sudden halt on the chest's sternum.

The shock of the impact ran from wrist to shoulder. Then he flicked his eyes to Sona's. No reaction. None. Not a flinch. Not the slightest facial tic. Whatever illusory progress

Lane had made out of his bog of dismay vanished. He was sinking. He had to pull himself out. He had to back away. Arms flailed in panicked uncertainty.

Why was Sona not dismantling him? Couldn't he see? Lane lurched back again in defense. Sona moved forward again, but cautiously. It must be obvious. He was drenched with sweat. It was hard just to keep his footing. Sona couldn't be cutting him a break. Impossible. He thinks it's a ruse? How could that not have hurt Sona? There's no give to the sternum. Bad form? Lane was just having a bad day. Just a bad day. Sona's not impervious. Very durable though. Has he always been like this?

Sona strode forward impassively. Despite the scars on Sona's skin and the dirt on Sona's clothes, something adamantine about the figure's core shone through. The beating of Lane's heart rang in his ears and he imagined it was the crashing sound of the footfalls of the approaching juggernaut.

‡ ‡ ‡

Cian's Doyen, Master Horn was there somewhere. Pushing him. Pushing him harder than he'd ever done before. Lane was beyond seeing the head instructor. Who knows how he was doing. Not well, certainly. He couldn't even really feel the blows anymore. They reached him late and dissociated. Distant, muffled thunder claps of pain.

The thinking was killing him. Stop thinking! Easier said than done. Impossible to do if you're thinking it! Lane felt like punching himself and smiled weakly as he weaved. That would be quite a scene. Have to focus! Exactly. No. Concentrate, but don't think. How?

The desperation only served to exacerbate Lane's confusion. The more he wanted to go with the flow, get back to how it used to feel, the more he thought about the fact it didn't feel that way and the worse it got. The feeling that it would forever after be this way, that it would never again be like it was, mounted in his gut. The rising bile spilled into his mind, the horror at his loss cresting the walls of his intellect and washing through his spirit, corroding everything it reached.

Lane was brought back from the edge of panic, but not by the automatic movement of his limbs. It was what they were responding to. And it couldn't be just a chimera created by his madness. Master Horn's attention was different. Though he couldn't look up to see it, he felt again this new intensity from Master Horn. Or was this how it had always been? Why would he drive Lane so differently now? What was he trying to get? To prove? To find out? Does he know? That thought tore through Lane, blinding him, then releasing him to a stunned pause broken again by a loud rumble of pain.

‡ ‡ ‡

It didn't look bad. His brown pant leg rolled up above his right knee, the bottom of his thigh gave no visual confirmation of its throbbing ache. The pain helped. A strange unction that brought clarity and even a little soothing. Massaging his thumbs into the spot above his knee he attacked the bruise to revive it, but also to keep the pain coming. Leaning back against a wide-based rock stalagmite, he stared down at a finger of flame dancing in its ground hole near his other knee. His left side lit, his right in relative darkness. He raised his left leg, masking the light from his face.

No one was watching him, for which Lane was grateful. This was the first time he had ever been hurt down in Cian. Hurt enough to sit down anyway. The stabbing in his lower thigh was still there, but the alarm was winning its way back into his core. He was no longer himself. Nothing now. Maybe he never was? Even the transgression against Cian was minor compared to this horrid person he could not see how to unbecome. But they are the same. No they're not...how? It was all jumbled up in his mind. Tied in intricate knots that tightened every time he struggled against them. He jammed his fingers into his thigh until water collected in his eye sockets and dripped down his face. Harder and harder until the pain was white hot. Just pain now. No relief.

He leaned back, gasping. The pain too short-lived a palliative. Arms fell loose at his sides in defeat. With a booted heel he pushed some loose gravel and dirt into the nearby burning oil pool. It guttered, sputtered, and popped out with a small sucking whoosh.

‡ ‡ ‡

Lane passed from the clean late spring light into the murky inferno. The forges blasted out heat from both walls that crashed on his bare skin, unprotected by a coat. The heat waves came on as a story of extremes told to him by a stranger. He coughed intermittently as he moved down the center aisle of the giant foundry, passing through billowing black clouds and making no attempt to cover his mouth or suppress the fits. Charred crooked shadowy shapes fed the fires fuel, air, and alloys, or dragged themselves in aimless paths across the open spaces, baked insensible. Arms raised to bring the hammers clanging down, metal on metal on metal, a din Lane did not hear but knew must be there. He remembered those days and understood now that he had never really left. Never really escaped.

Back by the last forge he slowed dully in front of Slate who gave him the queerest look. Confusion? Surprise?

Suspicion? Slate said something. Lane's gaze was blank and he shrugged slightly. Slate's expression grew still stranger and he might well have said atypically more but Lane drifted past him and closed the door.

The black hole gaped up from the floor, drawing him like a shade from the half-life of the lost back down into the ground. The spiraling threshold held the light for a turn or two, then all was black. Insensate, Lane continued down and the world disappeared. By tradition this brink that separated Cian from the city above was unlit, even by transported light, and this suited Lane now. The sensory deprivation was comforting. A mirror. A justification. A break from living.

Down in the main hall he squinted until his eyes readjusted to the lamplight. The achromatic surroundings rose above him, around him, and increasingly behind him as he was marched down the avenue by the stone pillar sentries lining the arcade. Occasionally, Lane noticed a sharp, probably constant pain in his right thigh. Not enough to stop. Not enough to even favor the other leg. Just enough to notice. The empty play of chiaroscuro from hundreds of lamps on the intricately carved surfaces of the enormous grotto pierced Lane only to pass a faint ghost of sadness through him as he rounded the empty stage and headed for the arsenal.

At the double doors he paused before pushing on the interlocking faded wood panels. Everything was fine. Normal. Mundane in fact. Lane faintly nodded his assent. Business as usual. And in he went.

The other apprentices were there and already at work. They turned, and Lane greeted them all with an abstract wave of his hand, a dreary smile screwed to his face. He stood, waxen, momentarily unsure where to go, and Maya approached him and grasped him though he could not feel it. He waited until it was over and felt a gloom deepen in him for having missed her touch. She was talking excitedly. Pointing. Waving. Smiling. Lane nodded just to keep her talking. Etherized by her warm breath and their disconnected communication, he wandered off at some point. Wandered toward an open table to find his tools and a half finished project he dimly recognized upon it.

Lane tried to work, but his eyes rambled haphazardly around the room as his mind alternately sagged and cramped. A pile of slag lay under his table, a drab remainder of the work he'd done, quietly building up at his feet. The layers of colorless weapons hung by innumerable posts across the walls, their banners, hilts, crests, and emblems etiolated by the weak lights, smoky air, and by long subterranean disuse. He noticed he'd caught a finger on a serrated edge of an unfinished piece waiting to be ground smooth and polished. He wiped the blood on his pants. The other students moved quickly about their tasks. Industrious. Positive. Vigorous, all four. Maya was working on something too and for a moment Lane wondered what she was creating. The brazier nearest him was low on wood and the flame, licking the side of the shallow basin, seemed like it was trying to consume its container. The sepulchral silence elongated the moments into days. It was time to go, apparently, as the others were leaving.

Lane began to float out on the tide, but Maya stopped him. She wanted something, though she seemed pleasant. His paralysis was complete and she held her conversation with a helpless spirit. She put back her head to laugh and the paler skin beneath her chin and down her neck seemed in the shifting light to have the dead, beautiful luster of polished wood. Lane watched her squeeze his hand again and then he drifted from her, a banished wraith.

The room fell away behind Lane. Nothing had happened. Nothing bad. Nothing unusual even. Cian was clearly manageable. Lane felt fine. He brushed the ashen earth surface as he passed the stage, disrupting the parallel tracks of the last broom dragged across it. He looked at his dirty palm as he stepped on, then dropped it by his side undusted.

Halfway back down the avenue of titanic double columns he stopped at the foot of one. Everything was fine. He ought to work a little. Get something done. A little more than half a year left and he'd done little yet on his sculpture. Lane could imagine raising an arm to grasp a low hanging protrusion and starting the long climb. But his asthenic condition prevented the slightest twitch of his muscles. He stood stupefied as a minute went by. And then another. He could not reach out to start the climb. Could not even turn his head to scale the massive carved pillar with his eyes.

Lane realized he had started walking again only as the black pall of the stairwell closed in around him. No sight, no sound, no sensation even from his footsteps. In his numbed state it was possible he was no longer moving, stuck halfway up the staircase. It didn't matter. The blackness waned as he reached the apron room and Lane was almost disappointed.

The forge continued its relentless cycle of consumption and production. Lane sailed slowly through the byproducts of heat and smoke. The phantom workers appeared and disappeared as the black clouds broke and shifted. So tired. He appeared and disappeared as well in the noxious atmosphere, fading in and out, a figure, a silhouette, an oblivious shadow, and then gone.

‡ ‡ ‡

The sky overhead was clear of clouds. The warm day had become hot as the long afternoon wore on toward evening. The clatter of humanity mixing with the roar of the rapids irritated Lane as he walked slowly over the main Lower Bank bridge, leaving the island. He watched a crowd of urchins near the center of the bridge as he passed them by. A handful of these half naked waifs screamed and called as they tossed branches and bark into the violent white river, watching to see their objects resurface downstream. Their naïve pleasure in the activity irked Lane, sour at having to share the scene with their baseless contentment and structureless game.

Coming off the bridge, Lane plunged into the labyrinth of Lower Bank alleys and passageways. The harsh daylight glare over the water was replaced now by the long trapezoidal shadows of tight packed buildings and a musty atmosphere in the many pockets of the city where no wind reached. He had no destination in mind. Nothing more specific than walking off his frustration. Something about moving harmonized with the undirected hostility hammering out a bitter tuneless melody in his head. That Cian's masters could put him in this state, that they had put him in this state made Lane clench his hands in furious resentment. He consciously and deliberately released his hands without resolution, just to give his fingers a rest.

The heat was just enough to keep the streets quiet except for a few grungy peasants shuffling across his path from time to time, their bodies nearly scraping the walls of the buildings in unconscious attempts at invisibility. All ignorable. All irrelevant. Lane's vagrant pacing through the intestines of Karabas was cut off.

With one foot in mid swing into the intersection of two back alleys, he froze as the cats came pouring through. Dull adobe buildings two and three stories tall crowded the negative space between the structures, blocking out the sunlight. The deep shadows cast carpets of gray across the packed dirt alleys and rippling silently over this came a rolling wave of charcoal cats. They ran on effortlessly, pressed together too close to distinguish, in a company that stretched from wall to wall and down the long alley. Padding by on thousands of muted feet, the beautiful procession looked neither left nor right as it passed, focused on some distant goal. The eerie evenness of the feline current was broken only by the subtle swells of countless rolling shoulders under coats of midnight silver.

Lane was probably in no danger. They seemed in fact not to notice him at all. And yet as they surged noiselessly down the dusty Karabas passageway, he felt himself frozen into a heightened state of attentiveness, waiting for the sign to bolt. He had heard about the cats before but never witnessed them himself. They were rarely seen in the city and when they did come it was for food. Dogs, city cats, birds, and even small children had been known to disappear under this silky tide, never to be found again, in any condition. On they came so that their speed must have been an illusion. There couldn't have been this many. Not hunting in the city. The thought of being hunted, of being the prey and not the predator, grew like a lightning cancer in his mind. To be food to an endless army of tiny beasts. There was his skeleton bleaching in the summer sun on a ledge high in the mountains above Karabas. Stripped clean of flesh by a million feline teeth. Lane became aware he was holding his breath and, in wondering whether to risk a soft exhalation, realized they were gone. Then into the empty alley, sadly mundane once more, Lane's foot fell.

He paced again through the city, but the cadence of his righteous anger had been broken by the cats. The problem resolved to a matter of blame. Lane's animosity toward Sona was in rare form, but there was no way to connect Sona back to his predicament. And in that same way, there was even less opportunity to lay the responsibility at the feet of Cye or the Wrens. It was obvious that Cian had set him up. Somehow Masters Horn, Maya, and Weaver had colluded to tempt Lane into betraying himself and breaking their rules. It was all part of the deviously circuitous path they lay out to justify eliminating each student before they could graduate. Lane had stopped walking and realized he was looking at the ground. Raising his gaze, he saw he had come to the cul-de-sac at the end of a minor street, where it widened into a small square.

The square had more life to it than the Lower Bank had shown Lane so far that afternoon. Chasing a tiny dog holding a shiny object in its mouth, a few children ran around the square repeating something over and over in choruses of high pitched aggravating screams. Two women sat together in a doorway, sifting wheat through a broad wicker sieve, talking over their work in a conspiratorial huddle. In one corner of the square, a few toothless old men were shuffling their table with an in-progress Atar game a few feet over to bring it back into the dwindling sunlight. In juxtaposition to the dilapidated buildings and the threadbare citizens, the far end of the square was dominated by a strikingly involved and towering temple. Lane knew now where he was.

He had been to the temple for Determination a few times as a child. Not exactly for devotions. Lane just liked the space. Or he had as a youngster. He had not been inside in many years. Lane felt suddenly torn between annoyance at having brought himself here unintentionally and a desire to see the temple's statue again. The outside was tiered in five levels, each level increasing gradually in height as the building receded from the plaza so that the back of the building was nearly twice as tall as the front. Each tier consisted of many caryatids and telamones in a tight orderly formation, shouldering the tier above them in a range of formal poses. The temple's stern, around seventy feet high and three times that far to the back, could be seen from the square, crowned with a final ornate gathering of stone statues. The dizzyingly detailed edifice might once have displayed ivory stone but now was dark and streaked with the dirt of generations.

Sunlight was just abandoning the last sliver of the square as Lane passed through the wide entrance under the carved phrase "Strength for the Impossible." His eyes needed only a short pause to adjust to the half light filtering in between the thousands of limbs of the temple's human balustrades. From inside the basilica, the forms along each layer of the outer walls seemed alive, silhouetted against the twilight, motionless in their endless task of support. Though on the outside of the temple it had always seemed that the figures faced outward, the teeming stone audience in five successive balconies surrounding him on all sides now produced a powerful feeling of being watched and judged. Lane closed his eyes, attempting to regain the vitriolic passion that had fueled him all day. It was there, tantalizingly just out of reach. A comforting fervor biding its time in the back of his mind. He reclenched his hands into fists by his sides, but the rage didn't come back with the gesture. He let them go again.

The vaulted ceiling rose progressively from Lane to its pinnacle at the semicircular end of the temple. Around the apse of the structure sat a ring of devotees. Most looked drawn and haggard and two were collapsed from lack of sleep, lack of food, or just from mental fatigue. Inside this ring, crouching at the knees and bent in the back to fit into the space, the colossal figure of Sarn was even more imposing than Lane had remembered it. The figure's stance was almost frightening. The statue was nearly as wide as it was tall and though disproportionate in fact, the effect was to give the effigy a preternatural solidity.

Sarn leaned on a shovel whose enormous head bit into the floor of the temple, further intensifying his aura of hardiness and producing a disruptive tension for those in meditation at his feet. The pose of the figure was iconic in Karabas, indicating the first scoop of earth in Sarn's lifelong struggle with the elements. Many, many generations back in the youth of Karabas, Sarn had purchased a piece of land from the suzerain on the high side of the Upper Bank. At that time the houses and buildings had crowded up to the crest of a saddle point in the land, but beyond that ridge no houses were built. Sarn had made a sucker's purchase, a cheap price for a huge area of land on the far side of the saddle point. The views of the valley were magnificent from there, but the mudslides, rock slides, and periodic avalanches from higher up the mountain made permanent structures there senseless. Lane knew the type, the Lower-Bank-born palace servant with unachievable fantasies of belonging on the Upper Bank.

For two years Sarn did not miss a night, but after full days as a groom in the palace stables he would toil hour after hour on a protective wall that had grown to be five feet high, two feet thick, and nearly one hundred feet long when the avalanche washed it away. Any levelheaded person would have deserted the project as hopeless, but Sarn, still too poor to have the aid of a horse, spent the next eight years, night after night, relentlessly erecting a new wall, designed to shield his land from cascades of earth and snow. He began the new wall at a shallower angle to the stream of debris and he built it ten feet high and ten feet thick. It had expanded to well over a hundred feet in length when a mud slide uprooted the lower half. At this point only a simpleton would have spent another night out on the range. But after removing the rest of the stone wall, Sarn dug in his shovel and began swinging the crest of the hill over, foot by foot. It took him over forty years to move that ridge over in an arc that displaced it by a foot at the top and just over two hundred feet near the bottom. Before Sarn died he had time to assemble only one meager house for himself, but that area was now packed with buildings, the prime real estate on the Upper Bank. When asked once what gave him the strength to continue after so many years, with no break and no reward, Sarn's answer had been, "I've committed to finishing, so continuing is easy. It's giving up that would be hard."

Looking around the disciple's ragged ring, Lane felt an uncomfortable urge to participate. To be one of them for an hour. At least to have their focus and sense of purpose, whatever it might be. But he had no patience for temple devotions. He had never taken the time to practice them. Fishing in his pocket he found a few coins, just a drink's worth. He stepped through the ring of seated figures and dropped the coins on a broad chevron-shaped bronze plate. The clang of the metal disks on the patinaed surface was suddenly abrasive in the silent room and Lane quickly backed out from under Sarn and headed back down the hall. As he neared the exit, it struck Lane that the temple was somehow different than in his youth. Dirtier perhaps? There were certainly fewer petitioners and they seemed more desperate. Sad.

Lane burst back out into the day to find the day gone and the night poured thickly over the city. The bile had entirely slipped his grasp and left only a sullenness in its place. And to this Lane held tightly for fear he would lose that as well. Somehow even that was not secure, and the desire to see Rose had crept in while he stared blankly up into the darkening sky, mixing up the spitefulness and the loneliness into an infuriating swirl. In a wooden movement he turned, directing his feet downhill and away from the river, into the bowels of the Lower Bank and toward Rose.

‡ ‡ ‡

The neighborhood nearer the Tengo had an unpleasant flattening of the buildings. Many of them were squashed down or sagging, many of those then reinforced with odd materials to prevent or slow further decomposition. Either no buildings in this area had been built over a single story tall, or those grander buildings had been the worst hit by this local phenomenon. Shoddy construction maybe, or a rash of low quality building materials. There was no excuse for the broad, squat buildings around Lane to have been, from their conception, only a single head above the locals. Lane stopped and backed up to look down a side boulevard he had just passed.

From a little more than a block away it was clear that the street brawl was waxing, not waning. A few young men on either side circled each other lashing out across the separating patches of darkness. The street was unlit but Lane could see enough. He found himself watching his body from the outside. Watched it not move. Not dive into the melee. Why not? He wanted to throw himself into the violence to forget, and to remember the white-hot anger he had so recently lost. That's not true. He wanted to want to join the dance of knives flashing occasionally like fireflies calling to each other in a field. But he couldn't feel the desire. He just knew he used to feel it and it had abandoned him. Lane's shoulders slumped, embarrassed by his own behavior. Why not join in? Afraid? That's not possible. Slowly, hopelessly, he turned and shuffled on.

The roofs were so low that Lane could nearly see across them, making the narrow roads feel like connected ditches cut six feet down into the ground. This left visitors exposed, hemmed in by buildings up to their eyebrows, leaving their heads open and vulnerable. The trench he was traveling in came to a "t" at the Tengo. The building was a large brown square decorated on this side of the structure by a dozen unevenly spaced wooden buttresses and two rough mismatched plaques baring the inebriated snow foxes crest. Occasional meager portholes leaked light out into the furrow, suggesting the interior as somewhat less dismal than the external gloom.

Lane stepped down two steps through the side door, taking a blast of smoke and sound full in the face. The straighter hairs on his crown brushed the ceiling of the pub and Lane bent reflexively as he passed under each distorted timber. The dingy smoke, with no higher altitudes at which to collect, loitered about the establishment. At this young hour the Tengo was still relatively uncrowded and Lane had little trouble swimming through the yellow-gray haze and pockets of a cappella song toward the two girls sitting at the near side corner table. The residual feeling that being with Rose would help ease something for him expired just as he opened his mouth to speak.

"Greetings, Rose. Greetings..."

Rose introduced the plump animated woman sitting with her. The woman had a round reddish face, flushed with health and a juvenile zeal. She had her hand extended to Lane, fleshy fingers pressed tight below the first knuckles with oversized gilded rings. Lane took the chubby hand in his and shook absently. He had missed her name and had no interest in trying again to get it. Reflexively, he said his name back to her.

"Missed you, dazzle." Lane could not connect with the feeling, but the sounds came from his mouth sounding easy and relaxed.

"Hail Lane love. The cure for your absence is your presence, my sweet, and even chance appearances may pay tiny trophies."

"Time for me is deluxe and knotty, Rose. Am here now, na?" He grinned a boyish grin that was not his.

"Time can'na be so knotty that you have na home. Give me directions and'll dog you down. Without, must wait your turnout and no way to see you vexes me."

"Relax little bird. Do miss you. Did come. Do always return, spot?" He kissed her hand with a flourish and then dropped into the dwarfish chair beside her. It, like hers and all the other furniture in the room had had its legs shortened to compensate for the low ceiling, and these makeshift seats were particularly irritating when getting in or out of them.

"You are not the type to pine, Lane. Independent bird is you, flitting from tree ta tree with the wind, crowing from time ta time as it suits you."

Rose's posture was casual and calm, but Lane could tell she was annoyed with him. All he wanted was a few quiet minutes with her, not a verbal sparring match in front of this heavy stranger. Not that he was going to apologize for his behavior.

"Spot. All bright. Only thought to show, see you, hear news and all."

"Concerning information...imagine the company came into the Tengo yester evening..."

Rose's rotund companion burst in before Rose had finished her thought, "Leaf! Fourth scion of our suzerain!"

Lane's exasperation that he could not be alone with Rose was increasing, but his mouth continued on its current course. "Youngster Leaf? But he's thirteen - no more, spot?"

"He's small too! Came in here last night and came in with a playmate. Got here somehow we dona know. So wild. Obviously what could we do, we had to serve him, them, but if he'd been hurt in here...dona want to think what the regent would do..."

Rose cut her back off. "Actually visit was quality. The regulars connected to them directly. Good kid but grave but maybe grave helps him take others earnest too. No harm was brewing last night for the lambs."

Rose's friend jumped in again energetically. Something about the terrible wrath of the regent and unendurable punishment connected to events that turned out not to have occurred. A band was tightening around Lane's chest. The already claustrophobic space was getting denser by the minute. The trickle of incoming people had become a stream, cramming the bodies into unnatural proximity. The noise, the drink, the unbreathable air, all in search of a brief reprieve from the equally noxious world outside. Lane was still working his lungs against the atmosphere to relax the invisible press inside him when Rose's friend stood to return to work. Odd that he had never noticed her serving at the Tengo before.

His relief that she was leaving turned into an unpleasant twisting in his stomach as Rose pushed away from the table as well. Lane's hand flashed out to grab her arm faster than he had intended and she flinched in reflex response. The haze and half light accentuated her curves and her soft eyes, trusting but momentarily startled. In a simple ochre colored shirt and long brown dress, a ratty white apron folded down over her waist, she radiated for a moment the exact warm tender beauty that he had come to be near. He was glad at least their audience had left.

"Na yet, Rose. Stay while."

"Have to work too love."

"A few minutes. Just game." He barely managed to muster a lame smile.

"Not always able for game on your schedule. Long break's done and busy shift begun. Rest here and will come rest with you when can. Later we'll leave together."

"Perhaps." The two feet between them might as well have been blocked by an iron portcullis. She did not really see him. She was talking to someone else. Someone he could not fathom ever having been.

She was already turned halfway to depart and then slowed to say, "Are ill, Lane?"

"Na. Am peach. Only tired maybe. You run."

"Proper?"

"Proper. Have much to think on. Go. Will've time together soon, Rose." At this she gave him an exasperated look. "Proper. Run."

He heard his last phrase hovering in the air calm and smooth as she stepped back to kiss him but her lips, like his words, reached him only as a discordant hollow echo. She spun away and waltzed off with her characteristically carefree steps, her bouncy departure reigniting his dormant rage. Lane stood abruptly, then hesitated as his maddeningly targetless temper tried in vain to attach itself to Rose as she disappeared into the crowd. Weighed down by his black mood, Lane dragged himself through the packed room toward the door, squeezing past hot sweaty revelers, trying to escape with a minimum of accumulated muck. Somewhere before the exit his ire found its home, prompted perhaps by his revulsion at the streaks of humanity collecting on him as he struggled to get out.

He had failed himself. Lane staggered, gripped the doorframe, nearly fell, and then heaved himself forward into the dark. He knew it. He had known it. But to be this angry at himself couldn't be sustained. A cold chill passed through Lane and he shuddered violently, momentarily interrupting the regular lug lug of his strides.

To be asleep. To not have to think. What wouldn't he give to have a break. But the thought of the vulnerability of lying somewhere fast asleep immediately ruined the desire. They routinely killed students for misdemeanors. And his transgressions had offended the very core of his discipline.

Karabas was strangely dark and quiet. Ominously quiet. The maze of alleys and byways leading circuitously back up hill toward the River Island should have had other travelers so early on a summer night. This made the sudden noises particularly unnerving. A door slammed. The tinkling destruction of a thrown glass. A desperate feral dog's howl viciously truncated. Lane picked up his pace.

Though he reached the river without incident, his apprehension continued to mount and his training told him not to ignore the dread that dogged him now. Halfway over the bridge with the rapids thundering under him, the sense of alarm overwhelmed him and he stopped, turning several times to survey both ends of the bridge. Not a soul. Not a sound. Even amidst the din of the white water below him, some sound seemed to be missing. He turned again, seeking. Seeking for someone, or something tracking him. Cian. It was the idea of passing Cian that had raised his uneasiness to a fever pitch. He could go around, out of his way. Go down the Flat and over the Upper Bank downstream bridge, then back upstream to his nest.

Rejecting the idea on principle, he started forward again, steeling himself for whatever waited ahead. Avoiding the building was absurd. The building was not the problem. Lane was furious with himself for feeling afraid. To abandon bravery too. He would have nothing left. Keep going. As he passed under the River Island fountain he felt himself followed by impersonal eyes hidden behind the high walls of the palace.

The effort to cross the Upper Bank main bridge nearly made his steps a march. The maelstrom inside him swirled wildly, driven by a foreboding he could not shake and the self-reflected wrath at all his weakness. The pounding of his heart drowned out the violent churning below him, and to keep moving forward he had to focus on the distance, ignoring the mammoth building just off the end of the bridge.

Once off the bridge he was forced to acknowledge the structure, walking as he was across its mouth. Enormous doorway gaping wide as it always did, smoke curled out around the edges and inside all was black except for the red baleful unblinking eyes of the furnaces. They were watching him hungrily. Patiently. Someone had promised them his body once it was limp, and it showed in their evil stares. He looked up and away but it did no good. He could still feel their lustful scavenger's gaze eyeing his carcass.

Above, the smoke from a few of the chimneys bloomed into the sky, immediately feathered into the abnormally cloudy desert sky. He was past the door and the wide boulevard continued into the Upper Bank. He felt his lungs begin to burn and released a stalled breath with a silent controlled exhalation. There! Another step and he would have missed it. Lane's body had no visible reaction, the tiniest bulging of the muscles in his jaw, as the indistinct shadow of a figure slipped out the door of the forge at the edge of his vision, disappearing to fall in somewhere behind him as he kept a measured pace on up the hill.

‡ ‡ ‡

Over Maya's long soft sweep of black hair, Lane could see the unfamiliar student, working at one of the weapons tables with his back to Lane. Nothing clearly wrong with him, but still it was unusual that Maya would allow another student to share her space with the seniors. And with no explanation. More than unusual. The student turned to look directly at Lane, and Lane quickly refocused on Maya.

The lilt of Maya's voice gave a certain pleasantness to everything she said. Though she was around a decade older than Lane, there was something about her to which Lane was drawn. Her intelligence, yes. Her lust for life, sure. Her devotion to her work, definitely. That she was beautiful was part of it, but only part. The foreign markings of her dark skin and fine detail of her features were unique. There was something else though. Maybe it was just as simple as the way she treated him. As someone rare and special.

He felt his end of the conversation lagging and jumped back in long enough to keep Maya talking. He pointed to a small steel disk in his hand, then at the workbench in front of them, and then at the wall above them. He had lost track of the topic of conversation and was thankful just to be able to get through each new minute undetected. And still, Lane's desire to confess to her was an almost irresistible pressure. Tell her his transgressions against the guild. Then it would all be over, either way. It would be so easy for her to guess, if she hadn't already. She knew him so well. The waiting was agony and the thick veil separating him from life was worse. He couldn't feel. He couldn't see. He couldn't participate in his own life. And when will it end? When they know and he has nothing to hide. Or when he's dead. Same thing.

That dark featured student kept looking over at him.

Lane's heart ached looking at Maya. She was wonderful but she wouldn't understand. Inside she was a hard person. The determination he loved about her left no room for compromise, no room for flaws of this magnitude. Maya hadn't made it to her current position with compassion and patience for the massive judgment lapses of her students. She would turn in Lane to Master Horn. She might enact the punishment herself. The intensity with which she currently defended and praised him had a darker side at least as fiery.

The unknown student was approaching them. He had a strong, arrogant stride and as he walked he was vainly brushing specs of dirt off his clothes, his face, and his bare muscular arms. A little too polished and perfect. He stopped directly beside Maya but then hovered silently, waiting.

"Genta, meet Lane. Genta is a second year student who is doing extremely well in his learnings and finally excelling at weapons design."

Lane put out his hand tentatively, though if she had been absent he might well have not. As their hands met he realized he had nothing to say to this person.

"Ta be a fellow Jack as Lane...it's an honor ta meet you! You've set unreacheable expectations for all Jacks in the hump."

Lane had even less to say after that. It seemed impossible that this kid could be a second year student in Cian. That he had been here a year and a half with Lane and he'd not noticed him - not possible. But whether this person's claim to being a Cian apprentice was true or not, Maya seemed satisfied with his response.

"Indeed, Genta, Lane has set an extreme example but it is anyway worth aspiring to be the very best."

What the actual meaning of their words were, Lane couldn't guess. If they saw those things in him it was an illusion he didn't knowingly produce and one he couldn't reproduce on command. Some combination of raw talent and a sort of skill for leaning toward his strengths had kept him in a winning way. But how different was that from changing the rules to ensure it was a game at which he could succeed. And doing that didn't make him a genius. Maya must be able to tell the difference.

"Being a Cian Jack is straight so no chance for distinction." Lane's pause was an awkward silence that he filled with "Grats just the same."

Genta seemed content and excused himself. Lane turned away from the retreating figure but Maya wouldn't let it go.

"Genta is a very fine student and also so you can enjoy that he and so many students look up to you though ultimately you deserve it."

This was even worse, so rather than say anything, Lane just managed to set up a grim makeshift smile on his face. Maya patted his hand and continued on with whatever she had been talking about. This supposed second year back at a table across the room was decidedly out of place, though Lane tried not to think about any dark implications to his presence.

Maya must have transgressed against her institutions at some point. And she would have toughed out the consequences. There was something so incongruous and so appealing about the juxtaposition of her femininity and the steel of her skeleton. She would have stoically endured an emotional tempest indefinitely rather than confess to stop the storm. The masses are reduced by each mistake they make. Only the truly great conquer their mistakes. Lane liked the sound of that. That was just how the world should be. The idea appealed to him but it wasn't real. That's not an answer. Just something to say when you don't understand. Though they sat together with their knees almost touching, the isolation was impenetrable.

Behind Maya and hidden from Lane's view, Cye was shaping a piece of steel. The steel on steel on iron anvil rang out rhythmically. The individual sounds were pleasant and crisp but the series became an exhausting demand like the insatiable crash of a battering ram working through a barrier.

‡ ‡ ‡

The long dirty tongs pecked listlessly at the barrel of vermiculite, pulling out bunches of the dusty strands and dropping them carelessly next to the barrel. Slowly, clump by clump, the edge of a disk was exposed, a few inches across, bulging in the middle, and tapering to a thin edge around its circumference. The dull gray metal floated idly in the vermiculite and Lane poked it directly with the tongs making a deadened click upon its surface.

The furnace opening in front of him blasted out its infernal breath and from its fiery coals, Cye carefully pulled his work with another pair of tongs. Though Cye was still early in the process with his first piece and Lane was nearly done with his second, he felt behind, and seeing Cye's piece exacerbated the feeling. Cye's tongs clipped the tang of an eight-inch piece of metal still only roughly shaped. He had refolded and re-forge-welded this piece already several times and only now seemed content with the particular orange glow of the steel as he held it up for a moment to examine it. Then he lowered it gently to his anvil and began to hammer it again. Starting at the point and moving gradually back down the length of the steel bar, Cye continued shaping it into a delicate blade. The blows fell with eerie regularity. Subtle variations of the hammer angle kept the face always perfectly flat to the bar's surface, respecting the nature and behavior of the hot metal, creating slight variations in each resulting clang. Lane watched the bronze, sculpted arm sweep the heavy mallet like a painter's brush, waiting for some dent or ding in the metal, some roughness left in the hammer's wake. But Cye was perfect. Lane had spent endless hours, often fruitlessly, trying to grind out those imperfections. He had never seen Cye do more than a surface grind. Not once.

Lane tried to tear himself away from Cye's meticulous labor, but he had no interest in his own. He wanted to talk though he couldn't interrupt Cye at this stage. Seemingly sensing what Lane needed, Cye began a stream of friendly chit-chat as he hammered, never looking up from the pliable steel cooling and forming in front of him. Lane pulled the annealed disk from the barrel of insulation and dropped it on the table in front of him. The lifeless surface was slightly irregular and the center of the disk nearly as thick as his thumb, making the object heavier and clumsier than it ought to have been. It hardly seemed worth continuing with it at all.

Cye's blade was transforming as he stroked it with the hammer. Its bright orange glow had receded first to a cherry red, and then to a gray similar to the piece Lane was finishing. But unlike the lackluster disk before Lane, Cye's steel continued to change, darkening stage by stage until it was ebony. And as it cooled, out of the black surface rose a hypnotic intricate natural pattern of light-etched swirls. The surface itself had been worth the work and the fine variation on the surface caused by the non-ferrous materials used in the original steel suggested an unusually strong, light, flexible alloy.

"Isn't that tang oversized? Too big for a handle cover it seems."

"Na. It'll be shine. Na cover for this one, the tang is the handle. Feel." Cye pointed Lane to a very rough piece of metal, roughly an awl with a thick spike and a raw steel backend with no covering for the grip. Lane hefted it, twirled it experimentally between the fingers of his right hand, nodded appreciatively, and reached to hand it back to Cye.

"Bright. And dazzle."

Cye was already hammering again so Lane dropped it back onto the table he had taken it from. Lane waited a moment with a lump in his throat, looking at Cye. Then he turned away and pulled the salt forge casing a little farther out of the furnace. The salt charge was molten without popping and bubbling, the right temperature to start the stabilization process. Clamping the disk with the tongs on the top and bottom of it center, he dunked the disk, tong prongs and all, into the liquid salt. Cye's puzzled look refreshed the lump in Lane's throat.

"Na tang to hold it by? That will na mar the normalization?"

"Na. Gives indents on surface." Lane tapped his thumb and forefinger together demonstratively with the hand not holding the tongs to show how the disk might be held. Lane felt simultaneously pleased with himself for such a clever recovery, and stupid for not knowing a decent way not to spoil the disk surface during the salt stabilization.

Cye nodded appreciatively in return.

After another minute, Lane withdrew his object from the bath. After air cooling it would need two more rounds of the same, so he just held it in the tongs, tracing random patterns in the space in front of him, watching it cool. Cye had just reheated his blade to the forging point again and was moving it back to the anvil. There he carefully laid it with the spine of the blade on the anvil surface and the edge facing up. Sliding it into the chisel attachment at the end of the anvil, he chiseled the tip off with one smooth stroke. This left the tip, counter-intuitively, angled up towards the edge. Cye never made a mistake, which pinned Lane between feelings of envy, admiration, and contempt. Cye was so conscientious, never brilliant, but so unshakeable. Like with forging. Forging was both an art and a science. Cye might not always be inspired in his works, but he had bothered to spend the time to learn the mathematics of metallurgy, one of Lane's many secret weaknesses. Rather than shore up his knowledge gaps with hard work, Lane relied on finding creative ways to avoid complexity or to sidestep his inevitably inadequate execution. He coveted the effects of Cye's methodical nature and patience but disdained the process that produced them. Purposefully, Lane jammed the disk back into the molten salt charge without looking at either to check if they were ready.

Cye had hammered the tip down toward the spine by now. This allowed the grain to flow into rather than across the tip. Cye was chatting away again about what he was doing, sure that Lane knew all these details, not noticing Lane had little to add to the conversation. Had the tip been cut originally in the forward direction, the soft core metal would become the edge material at the point. The lower carbon soft core would not harden sufficiently to hold an edge. Bending the point backwards from the front ensured the hard jacket steel curved around to form the edge. The amazing thing was how obvious these thoughts were to Cye as he rattled on about them and how completely he assumed Lane knew more than he on this and every subject.

This admiration drew them together and it made Cye the only person to whom Lane could really confess. Would he understand? Not entirely. But at least he would understand the context. And Cye would never expose Lane. Maybe he would even say Lane was making too much of two minor deviations. On the other hand, maybe he would push Lane to expose himself, do the right thing. That would be just like Cye.

Cye had started up the foot peddle grindstone, turning his black blade over and over, examining it for imperfections. Gingerly he would put the piece briefly to the whirring stone, then cradle it again, reading it for any hidden flaws.

"That must be a bright shrive to so little grind. Can file my spears to toothpicks before getting them clean. Recent early work has been sloppy so end work becomes a chore." Lane paused a moment, then added, "Very sloppy."

"Na, Lane. The issue is na how much we grind, but how worth grinding it is. Creativity and talent cut strange riverbeds but always lead to the ocean. Would trade with you in a heartbeat."

Lane flushed, mumbled "Grats," and turned away so Cye would not see his face. Try as he might to repress it, a grin flicked across his lips, shining out a few times like the sun peeking through the clouds for a moment on an otherwise momentously overcast day. Lane lived for that churning in his stomach that followed on the heels of praise and admiration. He hated that he loved it because it was a weakness, but he craved and responded to tribute like an intoxicating drug. Cye wouldn't understand. He wouldn't believe Lane capable of his offenses. Lane could never risk losing that kind of praise in exchange for so little relief.

The disk was fully annealed and cool to the touch, sitting now on the workbench in front of Lane. With a painter's brush, Lane began to apply a coating of clay, working from the middle and stopping an inch from the edge. On a whim, he had added fine shale from the floor around his anvil to the mixture of red pottery clay, water, and mineral salts and it brushed on now chunkier than he was used to. The added shale did seem to help prevent air bubbles from forming between the clay and the steel surface. Flipping it over he repeated the process on the other side of the disk. Normally he would have finished with thin clay strips over the whole length of the blade. But as little sections of softer material in the hardened edge wouldn't be useful on such a device anyway, he skipped them.

Lane sat with his head in his hands, back to Cye, waiting for the clay to harden. Telling Cye wouldn't help anyway. What hurt wasn't the guilt. It was that they might find out. And what they would think and do when they did find out. Telling Cye wouldn't fix that. Nothing would. Except telling them. Lane shook the thought off. Pain was something to experience, control, and fight through. This was just a different kind of pain. Same process. Only Lane was treading water in a dark ocean, with no help or land in sight from horizon to horizon.

To break his rumination he clipped the disk with the tongs and held it into the main forge again, watching as the gray edge warmed to a faint glow. As the glow became a dull cherry red, he withdrew the disk and quenched it immediately in a water trough by the workbench. In his dark mood the "krok!" of an edge cracking seemed inevitable and Lane was surprised that the hissing steam came and went with no other sound. He held the disk underwater, trying to drown it, but it rested quietly and patiently in the grip of the tongs, comfortable under the water. Irritably, Lane brought it back to the workbench and scraped off the clay with a file. The variable cooling rate under the influence of the clay created a harder martensite edge with a flexible pearlite center. But it looked terrible. It wasn't polished, but it was more than that. Lane felt utterly disappointed in the disk. It was too heavy, too thick, just plain ugly. Working hard with grit and water to clean it up wouldn't change the fact that it was a failure.

Cye put his hand on Lane's shoulder and leaned in to see how it had come out. Lane turned it so Cye could see the face and edge.

"Genius, Lane. May see?" Lane shrugged and dropped it into Cye's open palm into which it fit exactly. Cye hefted it, rubbed his thumb pad over the thin edge, held it between his thumb and forefinger as Lane had suggested earlier, then handed it back. "High impact, short to medium range? It's artful well done. You've just left to polish?"

Lane nodded. Cye clapped him on the shoulder again and moved on. Cye was always supportive. He had been a good friend for three years now. But it galled him that his closest friend couldn't see the pain he was in. If he couldn't see the pain, Cye might as well live in a different city. Lane would be no more alone.

He looked down at the mottled metal surface, covered with burned clay markings like leftover scars of a disfiguring disease. Anything less than perfect was a disappointment and this hunk of steel was far from perfect. He held it balanced, his thumb on the top center indent and his forefinger on the bottom center indent. He jerked his wrist slightly to watch it spin in place. Then with a sudden leap it left his hand, cutting through the warm air of the weapons space with no arc, as flat as if it were sliding along a pane of glass. The gray blur passed over the center of the room and buried itself up to its center in a table leg on the far side. From where Lane sat it looked like a strange gray mushroom growth on a worn smooth tree trunk.

‡ ‡ ‡

The surface of the reddish brown liquid was too thick to respond to the warm summer breeze. It lay impassively in the white bowl, still near the brim, black pepper shards incompletely incorporated into the tomato base. The other two white bowls were nearly scraped clean by oversized spoons slid unceremoniously into the crimson-splashed basins. The full soup before Lane had an evil, noxious aura. Another bite of it and his stomach would reject the few he'd already choked down. It wasn't entirely because of the acidic sauce, but that wasn't helping either. The waves of nausea ebbed and flowed so frequently that a constant queasiness would have been easier to endure.

Cye to his left and Weaver to his right sat jabbering away, enjoying themselves. Cye had a glass of last year's anjo wine in his hand. Lane looked past his bowl to the stem of his full glass of anjo, as unpalatable as his soup. The usually inviting raspberry pulp wine was revolting now. Weaver's tumbler of clear liquid, a distilled version of the same raspberry base, while free of the pulp, looked equally unappetizing.

It must be the soup. Maybe there was something poisonous in his. Some miasma rising from the bowl that had lowered his state from bad to wretched. This was worthless. Sitting at the same table with himself was worse than the soup.

Lane imagined yelling for help at the top of his lungs. No. He imagined yelling just to get their attention. No. He imagined them just stopping for a minute and noticing he was sitting where Lane should have been. Even worse than them not noticing.

The Root was full of diners, which was usual for a summer evening. There were hours of daylight left and a warmth the desert night wouldn't steal away until the daylight was gone. From their table the flight of wide stone steps could not be seen, so the high stone walls on all four sides made the grotto feel like a shallow well. A few tables away, the trunk of the whole arbor rose out of the ground, as old as the city and so far across that three men could not have linked arms around it. Up twenty feet, the massive gnarled pillar spread out demandingly and without limits, a garden cancer. In a hundred foot radius to the very walls and then on up the walls without respect for natural forces the leafy growth spread. And this unchecked expansion had been aided by generations from Karabas. A haphazard pergola had been constructed, a few supports at a time, so that there was no reason or order to the maze of timbers supporting the patchwork trellis, itself almost completely obscured by the giant vine. Even the seating was staggered and mismatched so that many adjacent tables were at disparate heights. The only consistency to the area was that each support timber in the bower had a sconce, a vase of sorts, hung at around shoulder height and filled with water, though it seemed no two to the same level. And the thousands of tiny white buds and flowers above them made the entire garden reek.

"But why would she purge it?" Cye clearly loved this sort of banter with their mentor.

"Wouldn't you say she has some history of removing things she does not like, Cye?"

"Dislike does na justify the slashing of such a core tradition."

"The past suzerain loved Elldoe. He did more than include it as a traditional part of some ceremonies and celebrations. There were events in which the Elldoe defined the ceremony, not the other way round. Is it possible the regent now rejects it just because the suzerain was so fond of it?" Cye was quiet, thinking.

There was no point being here, and nowhere better to be. At least being somewhere alone he wouldn't have to pretend. Feigning his normal behaviors was as painful as the thought that he had betrayed them and himself in the process. To be asleep. Unconscious was the only state in which he could stand himself.

"The regent shepherds traditions like the suzerain's scions, serious and thorough. Maybe better than the parents, proper?"

"For the most part, yes, that's true. It is still the case that she has pushed Elldoe out of every major event. Where else have you heard Elldoe in the past few years?"

"Cirrus may revive it. All say Cirrus will lead like suzerain revenant."

Weaver gave an eyebrow shrug and said "Perhaps," in a way that seemed more like "I wouldn't count on it."

Lane was caught between a conversation in which he could not bring himself to engage and the Elldoe itself with which he could not connect. The old ebony-skinned man sat on the far side of the grotto and Lane could make out little detail on him. The other, a similarly dark woman who couldn't have been more than half the old man's age, sat near enough to their table that Lane could see her breathe as they sang. In high, soft, ethereal voices, singing to each other in a dead language only maintained through these lyric poems, the two midnight singers were oblivious that anyone else was in the cavernous pergola. Supposedly these Elldoe songs were all tragic stories of loves that could never be. The songs were tragically endless at any rate. Somehow the two managed to create unbroken streams of sound, whether they were words or not. And the sconces hummed in response to their noise. The resonating sconces, tuned by their water levels, were a cheap trick. The fact that the trick was an old one just gave it the veneer of quality. Lane could hear that the sounds the two of them produced, directly and indirectly, were beautiful, sad, sublime even. But he could hear it like he could taste the food. He knew it was good for him, but it made him sick anyway.

Youths in offensively bright matching teal outfits swarmed their table at some invisible sign. The bowls and spoons were whipped away and Lane exhaled a sigh through his teeth, relieved to be free of the soup. Faster than any sense of good service could require, the table was covered again in food. A score of small plates overlapped each other and hung precariously off the table, each pinned down by fried sweet breaded fruits and vegetables, sugary and cloying. Lane was dizzy with desperation for the meal to be over. Sick at having nothing better for which to hope. And on came the waves of meat, slapping down onto the tabletop until the sugared accompaniments seemed pleasant by comparison. The meats were jammed up to the hilt on thin swords, carried point down between tables and then the carrion slit down in chunks over the diners small plates using sharp knives. There was no reason or discrimination for the waterfall of flesh that had begun. Whole hearts, whole livers, whole tongues, whole brains, nothing seemed to be off limits. Chicken, cow, fish, lizard, goat, no animal was safe. And no consistency even in presentation or taste. Some of the food reached them nearly raw, still dripping blood. Other bits of the meat were petrified with smoking or charcoaled through their core. The fare even tried to hide behind itself, one carcass appearing wrapped in strips of another.

"Lane, have I ever told you my 'guard' story from when I was just your age? I'm sure I've not told Cye."

"Na never do think."

Weaver was so grand, so imperturbable, it made Lane proud to be near him, envious of him, and yet ill-at-ease. Cye and Weaver always seemed so comfortable together. Maybe because Cye had that same noble aura about him. Even the way he leaned forward to hear Weaver's story and the flashing of his dark eyes made his attention seem generous. Whether Lane had heard the story before was hardly important with such an audience.

"In my final year as an apprentice I had need to get into the well-fortified walled compound of one of the local warlords. Part of the task was to leave no signs of entry or exit, so the front gate was out. It would have made the process easier if a bribe to the sentry at a smaller door on the side of the keep would have paved the way. I asked around about him at the guild and was assured by two of the instructors that he was an old gruff bear of a man who could not be bribed. It had been tried before and had spoiled otherwise well laid plans. For weeks I walked past that keep, irritated at the notion that the clean solution was not available. At that age I counted effort as costing me nothing, so I went instead over the top of the keep one night, with more annoyance than I had hoped for, and did accomplish the task to the guild's satisfaction.

"Many months later, just after the New Year and my graduation, as I prepared to leave town, that same irritation about the sentry came back, though I had no reason at that point to enter the keep. That last evening, with a heavy pack over my shoulders I stopped by the side gate of the stronghold, just to see the man. He was a large man indeed, gruff in demeanor perhaps, but considerably younger than I had been expecting. I bluntly offered him several pieces for entrance into the place and after a long pause between us, he agreed. I paid him, but when he opened the door I declined, having nothing inside worth entering for. I turned to leave and was halfway down the street before he called after me, 'Say me one thing. I've been at this post since the old guard died four years since. Why is this the first time anyone's come to visit me for entry?'"

Sometimes Weaver would give commentary on his stories, but tonight he sat and watched as his disciples lapped up the dregs of the anecdote. Finally he finished, "Our vision is full of things we think we see for not having looked directly at them. Wouldn't you say, Cye."

"Aye, Master. Painfully so."

"But you did a great job recently. Good tests are never about whether you knew the only answer ahead of time, they're about whether you can figure out a good answer in time."

"Had a bit of luck in where to look s'all. Could've missed Spirit all together."

"But you didn't."

The admiration and respect sloshed over the table, back and forth before Lane, repugnantly saccharine. Though to be fair, Lane and Weaver had created similar scenes in front of Cye. Before. The humiliation of having so completely disappointed Weaver made it impossible for Lane to even look him in the eye now. The idea of basking in the warmth of his praise again was a delusion. Not that that was Cye's fault. Fair or not, it still disgusted Lane in the moment.

Lane looked away. The young black vocalist sat cross-legged with her eyes closed, focused on her tone, the words, her breathing, the sympathetic vibration of the innumerable water sconces, something. She was no beauty, but she had an unblemished purity as attractive as beauty. The layers of colored silk swirled around her body tighter underneath with looser waves hanging above them. Her chest and diaphragm waxed and waned rhythmically, so steady, almost monotonous. Before Lane's eyes she grew old and dilapidated. Her checks sagged, her back curved, her breathy singing became raspy and harsh as her infirmity increased. The hideous press of time crushed her into a second infancy in the space of a few heartbeats and in a few more she crinkled and cracked like ancient parchment flaking apart in crispy black and colored shards. The bits winked out or were blown away until the ivy-backed stone bench was bare and the grotto silent.

‡ ‡ ‡

The sun was dipping into the mountains and a rosy glow was failing slowly between the teeth of the distant massif. Though their footsteps were still receding, Lane had already lost any sense of where he was relative to Cye and Weaver. They had probably walked off together but Lane couldn't bring the image of their parting back to mind. The jagged rocky fangs hovered disconnected in his vision, the world inexorably swallowing up the last of the daylight. His feet were moving. He could not make out whether they were taking him towards his resting place and wondered if his feet had some plan he did not know.

The uncharacteristically warm desert evening was being invaded by an alien fog rolling down the mountains along the river gorge, rolling so low to the ground that he could see over it almost until its leading edge met up with his aimless path. The wall of gray advanced quickly toward him, wiping out the city as it marched. As the fog began to curl around Lane's legs and smother the long shadows cast by the fading sunset and the first of the night lanterns, it seemed to Lane that the shadows rose up around him. They towered above him grim, formless, and terrible. They bent in, surrounding him, reaching out their spiny fingers on tendril arms to crush the life from his body. Encased in a patient numbness Lane felt them grope at and into and through his body. He did nothing. He imagined the feeling of his life force being extracted from his chest by the insatiable fingers, a tiny weed plucked from a crack in an otherwise pristine stone staircase. His feet keep moving. Then as suddenly, the giant shadows were gone, extinguished by the oncoming gray blanket draping Karabas with damp lifeless uniformity. Lane's limbs weighed him down, exhausted and disappointed. And on he walked.

The fuzzy edges and textures of the city bloomed and wilted around him at a distance of ten paces. The fog entered his body on each breath, layering his insides with a dirty white nothingness. Saturating him with nothingness. Lane wanted sleep as he had never wanted it before. He brought himself to a stop but could not fall to the ground. Looking at his feet for an explanation, he saw them toed up against the first in a series of wide stone steps. The stairs rose up and were smoothed into the fog so that nothing else of the building was visible. From out of the cottony air above the stairs, a large black hand of carved obsidian commanded Lane to stop. Beside it the point of a black dagger pierced the mist in frozen defiance.

It could have been the hand of Dawn, guarding the front to the temple of Loyalty. But that was on the Upper Bank and he hadn't crossed the river yet. Had he? Dawn stood waiting to die protecting the retreat of the lord she served though he had just betrayed and deserted her. Lane could not remember the details of her life and wondered what her face might show. And then he was suddenly glad he could not see it. If there was only a way to hide from himself in the fog. To creep off a distance and curl up on one of the steps, fading away as his body left the scene. But his legs would not allow him even to sit and he was moving again.

The last gasp of daylight was gone and now only the dimmest visual impressions of the world made it ten paces through the thick vapors. Death was a solution. No pain, no worries, no confusion, no fatigue could survive death. Death comes to everyone in the end. Why not use death like a tool. Make it convenient. Lane can't be killed. He can be - death is an easy thing to arrange. Death is the ultimate surrender. Exactly. Defeat happens even to the greatest men, surrender does not. Surrender cannot be as painful as the fight. Stop. Please.

Lane could see nothing specific before him. The little ambient light was so diffuse that nearby forms were turned into mere suggestions. Disgusted with himself for his failures and his weakness, Lane fanned his arms, wildly clawing the space before him, catching nothing but handfuls of clammy air. His attack wore itself out and by degrees Lane found himself motionless again, wrapped in gray obscurity. Or was he moving? It was hard to tell.

Muffled by the fog, Lane could hear a set of clanging hand bells calling the guests to a nuptial ceremony and feast. It was midnight already? Remote sounds of nearby events gave an otherworldly quality to the laughing, calling, joking, shouting, and running around Lane for he could not see the people as they passed him. Or perhaps as he passed them. Without seeing them there was nothing to mark or distinguish this event, so the sounds came to Lane like echoes returning from past celebrations. The distant crashing destruction of bottle after bottle filled the air as guests arrived, toasted the couple from a new bottle of spirits, and then dashed it on the terrace, crunching over the broken glass as they entered the hall. The site seemed to be moving in Lane's direction for the stench of the mixing spirits draining down wet steps and soaking into the earth was becoming palpable and vile.

Lane had no interest in joining the crowd, but he was drawn to see it. Their talking surrounded him but wherever he was they had moved away. At least they couldn't see him. A wall moving at high speed nearly knocked him onto his back. It was a high, old wall whose massive stones were so overgrown with algae and mosses that at first Lane had mistaken it for a hedge. He could hear the voices near him now and reaching out he dug his fingers into the damp vegetation to find a first climbing hold. The material had the wet, fleshy feel of raw fish and Lane had to sink his hand nearly to his wrist to touch the stone beneath. But as he raised a first foot to begin the climb he realized the voices were behind him and the shattering glass on the outside of the wall. On the inside now? He turned, his hands dripping tiny lumps of the black inner moss, moving again toward the sounds.

But they were receding now though Lane craned his head to follow them, the sounds becoming so faint they merged with memories in his head. So faint his ears rang in straining to hear them until all he could hear was the silence.

Though Lane could barely see them, his feet continued to shuffle forward and he wondered if he had lost the trail of the festivities or whether his feet had betrayed him in following their own course. The atmosphere was taking on a strange pearly glow, lit by the full moon as it rose up out of the valley to the south. The visibility was no better but Lane had at least moved from the dank smoky lung of an idle furnace bellows to the luminescent blindness of cotton swaddling.

Neither knowing nor caring where he was, Lane drifted on through the whiteout, protected from a bottomless despair only by a thin layer of insensibility. Step after step his life continued and step after step Lane wished he could check out. Stop the clock. Start again at the beginning. It was no good. No matter how he twisted and turned inside his head, the ache was still there, raw, inescapable, unrelenting. His face hurt with contorted clenching.

Hanging his head, he saw himself perched at the edge of a three foot step above the rushing river, packed in with glowing whiteness as though a moonlit blizzard were frozen in place around him. As the spot was protected from the main torrent by a number of high water rocks upstream, the calmer rippling water, freckled with indirect moonlight and hazy through the fog, reflected a distorted image of a tall, wiry youth back at Lane. He pictured that youth not reflecting from the surface, but lying at the bottom instead, strangely peaceful. He pictured the youth with closed eyes, blue skin, and a calm face. Lucky.

His rigid mask of facial muscles cracked and gave way, and jealousy, horror, and hot tears burned his eyes, further blurring the vision. Silent quakes wracked his body until they had spent their energy and subsided. Surrender is not less painful than the fight. It is. The pain is not the issue.

Surrender is unacceptable. All this pain? Any pain is worth obeying the lines you will not cross. Temples pounding, near fainting from the effort, Lane willed the waves to show him something else. Through the fog and choppy water the familiar corpse slowly became vague and amorphous. Then darker. Browner. Mottled. Decomposing into a submerged boulder laid out beneath him. A swell disrupted the boulder apparition, carving a form in again. Back. Long low, curved on the sides with the frigid liquid rushing over it. Flat on the top and brown. Just a stone. The length of a man.

‡ ‡ ‡

Across the room a woman's gaunt face held Lane transfixed. The visage painted cherry and mustard, outlined and highlighted disembodied between the backs of the heads of two men, floating between twin black bushy manes. Her face was thin. Too thin but not sick. A grim blankness haunted the surface of the face that beneath seemed hollow as a funeral drum. With dark eyes like deep dry wells, she returned his gaze unblinking and Lane had never been more invisible.

The Rapids was crowded, as it always was after midnight during the summer. The regulars packed the balcony and the main room, snarling their greetings as they passed each other in the shifting mob. The whole scene was unwashed, sordid, and treacherous, peopled by the undesirables of Karabas who wore frantic outfits and swaggered to hide their fears. In the tight quarters physical contact was inevitable. Hands grabbed hands, clasped shoulders, fondled rears, and still wherever he looked Lane saw one hand on a weapon and the other on a pocket or purse. The Rapids' raucous atmosphere was ruined by the overtone of hysteria in the voices and the fey and wild exchanges of its doomed visitors.

Lane hovered at the edge of a clique to which he unofficially belonged. The group had no idea he was standing there, which was just as well. He had a second glass of spirits in his hand that he had been nursing for much of the evening. Standing here, here in particular, without the aid of a tonic was unimaginable. But the stuff sat poorly in his stomach and Lane had become increasingly worried that he might become dependent on these spirits to keep his own spirits afloat.

The clique circled tightly two rows deep around a giant of a man. Bann stood a head taller than the next tallest in the clump and with his arms outstretched in gesture he was wider and thicker than he was tall. Heavy black breeches and an open massive, black coat framed an epic bare barrel chest of rolling muscles and shaggy black hair. Above the coat collar a knotted mass of black beard spread out to the shoulders, up both sides of the jaw, met on the crown and then exploded down the back of the head in one solid dirty tangle of hair. A wave of heat crashed through Lane and he nearly lost his balance. Small gold hoop earrings. This was some half-man mountain monster wandered down into Karabas. But there was an enviable fire in his eyes.

The huge beast bellowed and laughed, roared and commanded, buffeting his audience about in the storm of his voice. Lane's comrades would from time to time grab him or each other to keep their feet, repeat a thought, or bask together in the presence of this force of nature. The room swirled again as the harrying of his personal demons drowned out the distant thunder of Bann's passion. Preoccupied as he was, sensations came to him fractured from far away so there was little left with which to engage. Do they all feel so isolated? Could this be the normal state of things and each person puts on their best face for the duration? This cannot continue. It can be made like it was before. Never. Not possible. It can be made whole again. Fine. How? There is nothing to hold. Nowhere to start.

Mixed in with the bobbing sea of heads across the room, Sona's face left a blurred trail across Lane's vision. Sona was looking at Lane. Watching him? Signing? Sona fit in here so well where hard, cold, and swagger were the fashion. The bits of Sona that came through to Lane were broken up, making deciphering the situation hopeless. Lane turned away to make it stop. He closed his eyes and the sound receded, leaving Lane in a distracted relative peace.

A thud and a bolt of pain from the back of his shoulder reached Lane deep in the torpor into which he had slipped. He could feel his body dropping into a defensive stance, spinning towards the blow, his steel stakes out and pulling heat from his hands. He felt the jerks as he lunged forward or leapt back and the collisions as his weapons or his body met resistance. He tried to close his mind to the feral actions of his body but the heavier hits to his limbs and torso forced their way back into his thoughts. A few times he heard the crash of metal on wood but he was spinning now so wildly that what part he played in these sounds or which others were involved was impossible to tell. In fact it began almost to feel as though the violence he defended against were his own counterattacks.

Lane's berserk gyrations came to a piecemeal wrenching halt as one by one a vast crowd of unsympathetic hands clamped down like vices on his limbs. The captivity was worse than the wounds he could now feel, and he heard a series of growls mixing into the heaving of his chest. A thump and roll on chilly stones. The hands were gone.

Lane pulled himself into a cross-legged position, holding his lowered head in his hands, feeling the damp sweat on his fingers as they interwove with his hair. The cooler air out on the Flat felt good on his skin. He shifted slightly and his insides groaned, creaked, and moaned from the recent damage. Lane wondered idly if he had, for the first time in his life, broken a bone somewhere. A ruddy liquid of blood mixed with perspiration dripped slowly down his scalp and off his forehead, making a tiny pool just in front of his crossed ankles. The cacophony in his mind seemed to have been bashed out of him as he could hear far away footsteps and voices echoing back and forth down the Alleys of the Flat.

Had he even hit Sona? Lane had a flash of empathy for Sona and imagined sending some projectile his own way. He deserved it for the way he treated Sona. Had Sona even been the one who hit him first? It could easily have been someone else. And then he went after Sona. Did he? Had he even been fighting with Sona? Had anyone, in fact, really been out to hurt him? Things get thrown all the time at the Rapids. Would Sona really have missed so badly if he'd been looking to injure Lane? What had possessed him back there? Lane took a long slow breath, trying to clear out the past few minutes. His ribs ached with the effort but he kept expanding his lungs until their absolute limit, then exhaled, hissing a little as the pain gradually subsided again from his diaphragm.

Lane raised his head. The Flat was empty except for a few groups down toward the point and a pair just entering the right Alley farther back up stream. The evening was beautifully clear and as he leaned back on his hands, the dome of sparkling lights overhead felt unnervingly close. He watched them glimmer for a minute, wishing he knew how to find some of his favorite avatars in the chaotic map of twinkling pinpoints. He lowered his eyes to the Rapid's balcony, jammed with people to near the unrailed edge, and as he gingerly stretched his neck, he wondered whether it had been his acquaintances or the locals that had separated him from the place. And for that matter, whether whoever it had been had carried him down the stairs or simply thrown him from the balcony.

Lane rolled forward onto all fours, wincing on so many accounts that he could not localize the pain. The pounding he'd received and the gashes that still bled were as bad as he'd ever had and he teetered as he stood, unbalanced from the throbbing of his unreliable muscles. He turned around once hesitantly, unsatisfied with any direction until he was once more facing The Rapids. Though he couldn't say why, he knew that he had passed beyond something inside himself and he continued to turn until he faced the hectic imposing silhouette of the Island Palace. With a tentative first step the hunched, uneven figure began to limp its way steadily back up the way he had come.

‡ ‡ ‡

Lane stood forehead deep in Karabas, looking down the last few feet of the alley at the side door of the Tengo. The moon was gone now and in the early morning the feeble starlight left the crevice between the drab, ramshackle buildings shadowy and insubstantial. No one had come or gone in half an hour. He knew. He'd been watching it for two. Or maybe he'd just been too absorbed to notice some coming or going. Presumably Rose was still inside. Why was he standing here? Rose couldn't help him anymore. Then why was he standing here?

From either the fight or the fall, a long gash across the top of his hand continued to bleed at his index knuckle. He put it to his mouth to lick away the blood running down toward the base of his thumb. A lonely breath of rushing wind pushed around him and broke out of the narrow street. Lane hugged his arms into his chest against the sudden chill and felt the blood and salty sweat drying into brittle scales on his shirt. The air was still again, but Lane left his arms wrapped around his ribs.

It would be nice to go in. Just for a minute. Just say hi to her. Nice has nothing to do with it. Nice is part of the problem. Lane stood immobile, immersed in the darkness, and watched the door swing halfway open. A plane of warm yellow light cut across the transverse street like an off-axis lambent curtain. A hand held the door open for a dozen heartbeats and then changed its mind, receding back into the tavern. As the door closed, the luminescent swath winked out again. Lane's hand was up again at his mouth and he sucked absently on the bloody knuckle.

At some point Lane realized how far away his mind had wandered. And that it could never return all the way back to this place. He could never be again, should never be again the boy Rose thought she knew. He squared his shoulders, swept the hair back that ran down both temples and cheeks, and held the pose a moment longer. Then braced for the stiffness of recovering muscles two hours unmoved, he made an efficient turn on one heel and forced his body into motion with little outward sign of the limp that had brought him through the Lower Bank. His tan pants, torn and stained, swung on North through the dark passageway, methodically, silently, leaving a trail of faint perfectly spaced footprints in the dust.

‡ ‡ ‡

A bead of liquid ran slowly down Lane's arm from his shoulder to his hand, disturbing individual hairs as it ran its course, clinging for a moment to the end of his second finger, and then dropping onto the first plank of petrified wood at the edge of the Lower Bank main bridge. Lane looked down but could not find the tiny splash or tell the color of the liquid.

Stopped momentarily at the mouth of the bridge, he felt his legs and the muscles in his back seizing up from the double soreness of exhaustion and injury. Ahead, the bridge leapt the star-dappled rapids to the River Island in a shallow arc, framed by a colonnade of golden treetops, fiery palms marching two by two toward the Palace. A steady wind kept pace with the rushing water below so that the bitumen-fueled flames all leaned sympathetically downstream. Lane stepped out onto the bridge and the thunk of his boots on the bridge decking was almost entirely lost in the gurgling roar of the white water beneath him. Now on the bridge the trails of black smoke from the torch pillars interrupted the fresh mountain air in waves, pushing an astringent charring sensation through his nose. The sky behind these tracks of smoke was a degree brighter than the black it had been an hour earlier.

Lane stopped again near the middle of the bridge. Each muscle in his body, tight as a bowstring, felt ready to snap under the strain or pull apart the adjoining body parts. He tried to lean over in a forward bend to stretch out just enough to get himself home but the posture was impossible in his current state. Instead, he hung there half bent in the flop of a marionette discarded over the edge of its puppet stage. Carefully, gingerly, Lane pulled himself erect once more and looked around, torn between his debilitating physical condition and the pleasant last hour of a clear summer night. He opened his mouth a little and could taste the fine cool mist from the torrent below.

It actually took the intervention of his hands to get his legs moving again, but Lane began walking as steadily as he could, gritting his teeth in an effort to move without hobbling. By the time he had reached the end of the bridge and was a little way onto the River Island, he had to stop again. It was counterproductive but he had no choice. The top of the left Alley had been appropriated as the Temple to Shrewdness, only one of two on the eyot, with five wide steps leading up to the middle of the first floor where a series of openings led into the temple. Lane dropped down on the steps, resting back on his elbows and staring blankly at the nearby palace wall. The oversized yellow bricks used to build the outer wall of the palace looked an uninspired gray brown at night. The marbled green roofs and gilding along the window frames and steeple pinnacles were similarly dull, catching and reflecting only the first glimmers of dawn and the last twinkles of the

nighttime stars.   Lane watched the series of inlaid waterfalls
jet out from holes in the fortified walls and fall several stories,
only to be recaptured by jutting lips lower down the wall face,
sucking the water back into the palace. Placed strategically to
be beautiful and yet to leave few enough handholds, the wet
external surface of the ramparts might as well have been made
of glass.

Turning his head to look up the island toward the
Upper Bank, he started slightly, then realized the civet leaning
in to look at him from a few feet down the third step was
cleverly carved from the same quarried rock as the stairs. He
had seen the small animals before, but had never before
actually stopped to examine them.   Scattered around the
steps, resting, watching, thinking, waiting, he was surrounded
by a company of stone viverrine. Quite a few of the creatures
seemed even in their frozen states to be studying him. A mink
and a mongoose two steps up were turned toward each other,
nose to nose in conspiratorial conference about Lane. A row of
weasels and otters on the top step, silhouetted by the night
sky, flicked their ears occasionally as clouds rolled by behind
them.

He was ready to move on, whether or not his body was.
Standing reaffirmed that the agony of the blows was
continuing to evolve into the dull dual aches of soreness and
stiffness.   As he stepped down off the temple he saw at the
end of the bottom step an oversized polecat carved from
mottled limestone and a much smaller ferret carved in stark
white granite sitting side by side on their haunches. They
were openly staring at Lane. They were gawking. He snorted,
turning away from the inanimate figurines, and continued his
push across Karabas toward his bed.

He might have met someone from the Rapids again as he
passed across the Flat, but he did not. As he left the River
Island over the Upper Bank main bridge, he was reminded of
how he had once so enjoyed these moments of isolation.
There was something powerful and magical in being the only

one about. The pre-dawn glow and the crisp freshness of the air created a poignant bittersweet atmosphere.

Several figures were leaving the gigantic Karabas forge just past the edge of the bridge. Slowing his pace a little, Lane let the night-draped soot-covered characters turn away from the bridge and move out of sight. He passed the foundry and the small world it unknowingly sat atop, repeating the left right left right of his stride with increasing effort along the main thoroughfare into the Upper Bank. Something about his pain made the closed up shops and dwellings seem mundane by comparison. Not bad. They were appropriate and occasionally beautiful parts of Karabas. But they were all so sadly unexceptional. Perhaps he appeared unexceptional to them when the owners of those shops passed him on the street. Not if he could help it. Though of course at times going unnoticed was crucial.

Lane had never paid attention to how far up hill the temple sat he had appropriated for his sleeping quarters. Though he recognized each turn, alley, and sign along the way to his destination, his fatigue elongated the distance so that several times Lane caught himself still or even looking for a place to lay down and had to flog the energy back into his mind. So it was an enormous surprise to Lane when on turning the final corner past a bakery whose goods he thought little of, the temple shared between Addiction and Madness came into sight and he was immediately overwhelmed with a desire not to go to bed. It helped that the pain of Lane's beating was fading into the pleasant aching exhaustion of a long period of extreme exertion. But it was more than that. Though he could not finger what exactly had happened, he could feel his will stirring within him. It was weak, but its embers had been fanned and he wanted to give it a chance to catch fire again.

From the inside, the temple was many-sided, but at least it had corners, edges, and walls. From the outside the temple bristled with wooden spars sharpened to rough points at their ends, jutting out at random angles over the complete external surface, entirely obscuring the underlying architecture. In the dark purple of the coming dawn, the temple was a sort of overdone gigantic morning star, jammed into the ground up to the top of the handle. The frenetic crisscrossing quills of the building looked unassailable, and for all the times Lane had scaled the inside of the temple, he had never gone up the outside. But at the top there might be as much as another hour of that intense alone-in-the-world feeling before Karabas woke, stretched, and shook awake the little beings sleeping on its great hide.

The shadowy outline of Lane stepped onto a waist-level spar and began to climb. Silhouetted by the purple dome of the sky, the arms and legs of the figure appeared and disappeared, swinging haltingly up from beam to beam. Several times the body stopped, its torso emerging from the root of the poles, fighting to free its lower half from the tough leafy undergrowth that encased the building and hid the details of its construction. With a final rest and then a jerking heave, the climber's outline disappeared onto the top of the building, ringed with close vegetation and up and outward pointing spikes forming a thorny crown to the building.

Though hidden from below, three of the jutting spars crossed just at the roof's peak, forming a perfect perch. With his legs on either side of one spar and his back resting between the other two, Lane could see most of what there was to be seen of Karabas just by turning his head. The slumbering city spread out beneath his dangling legs in all its haphazard glory. Except for the River Island, little of the city had been planned and it showed from above. Housing heights and styles changed abruptly from one quarter to the next. Streets ran towards each other until they were so close and so parallel as to be entirely redundant. Still, seeing the city as a single entity gave it a unified life that seeing it street by street could not. The rolling patchwork of colored structures spilled down the mountain, rushing along with the river that from where Lane sat looked like a satin ribbon, shimmering and returning many muted colors as its context changed. This perspective, combined with the time of day, created a sense of ownership over the world, laid out as if it were for Lane alone.

Lane was steeling himself, but for what he could not say. Waves of emotion passed through him so powerfully that each brought its own climate, flushing him with exhaustion, chilling him with some core dissatisfaction he could not finger, warming him again to the tingling point with the overwhelming experience of being alive that came even from, maybe particularly from, the ache in his heart. The riptide of his mind pulled him around and down, this way and that until the disorientation was physically painful. He drew out one of his thin steel spikes and held it point down like a pen over the palm of his left hand. He imagined pulling the sharpened tip across his palm, cutting a straight path of brighter red through the grime and dried blood that already covered its surface. Slowly, without breaking the skin of his hand he released the tip's pressure on his palm and put the spike away again.

The only way forward was through a performance he was proud of. Do it right. To be the man he thought he was? No. To be the man he is. Be true to his nature, not some ideals. But as long as you're in the game respect the game, excel at the game. Respect those ideals or get a new game. Then come clean with Cian in order to start the game clean again. No. Scared? Fighting back to great is harder than coming clean. Maybe. Maybe not. No more excuses.

Looking east and south over Karabas, the background mountains blocked the rising sun, but the heavens were waxing a rich salmon color above the teeth of the ridge, washing out the stars with a promise of coming warmth and light. There is no goal but redemption and no path but true action. If he can do anything, can win at any game, then win at this. Show your colors. None of this removes the suffering. But it makes the suffering bearable. It makes the suffering part of the challenge of the game. But it doesn't make Cian the best game to play. Enough. Cian is the game to be played and it will be won.

Far below in the plains beyond the base of the mountains, a fire line of sunlight had been burned and was advancing. Moment by moment, league by advancing league, it marched back up through the foothills breathing vibrant colored life back into the shaded world. Karabas lay still in relative darkness, watching and waiting as the vanguard of day hiked up the slopes to wash over the city.

‡ ‡ ‡

The raised dirt stage was bathed in the perpetual yellow half-light of the encircling oil sconce lamps. Toward the head of the hall, beyond the reach of the last pillars, the illumination drained away. The diffuse lighting allowed no sharp shadows, but the final alcove was darker than anywhere else in the hall. And more empty. Its deep shade making the future avatar niche seem particularly unfilled and unfillable.

Lane knelt between Sona and Cye, water from his recent cleaning still trickling down his neck and back. Not wanting to be caught caring, he had not looked closely, but several sideways glances had uncovered no fresh battle scars on Sona from the night before. Sona's silky black hair hid a cheek, his neck, and part of his right arm but it was not Sona's style to hide scratches when he had them. Cye looked forward, waiting for lessons, or life, to continue with his unnatural calm. In front of the three of them the two Wrens sat impassively. Unlike Cye, their impassiveness was not an active stoicism but a reactiveness idling until the next stimulation. One of the Wrens had a small patch on his tan tunic, and for a moment Lane's mind sprang to this as some point of purposeful differentiation between them. Of course, with a patch present, the most meaningful difference between them was the patch itself, which was unenlightening.

Between the Wren's shoulders, Lane watched as Don Weaver knelt facing towards them, a flowing black blouse tight at his neck and wrists, tucked into the waist of a long black skirt spread out around him so that he seemed to be growing out of a black mound rather than kneeling into one. Clothed in black, Don Weaver's healthy olive brown complexion stood out rather than looking whiter by comparison. His expression was bright and intense as he examined their faces and, like Cye, he seemed in no hurry whatsoever to begin. The silence had lasted so long, Lane began to wonder if this hush was a test. Or perhaps this stillness was the lecture for the day. Though what there was to learn from doing nothing for an hour was not clear. Lane had already twice determined to speak and then immediately suppressed the urge when his mentor began without a preamble.

"Everything is inevitable in retrospect." Don Weaver let the thought hang again for so long that Lane wondered if that had been the entire lecture. Then again, without introduction, "The point of view that events unfold just as they should is not an emotional cushion for painful circumstances. It is a point of view that allows you to play a part in the world and make meaningful choices in the world without fighting to change the river's current. Because you will find that every ounce of energy you throw at redirecting the river's current will turn out afterwards to have been part of that river's natural course. Predestination is nonsense. But the world will only support certain event streams, certain dances, and appreciating how to be a part of the event stream, to work within the dance, will save you from enormous amounts of wasted effort. Or worse."

Lane clung stubbornly to Don Weaver's thoughts, but remembered better why he so rarely captured the specific ideas Don Weaver was distributing. These talks often were as unclear and ambiguous as their tone and delivery were smooth and simple. Focus. Not focus. Just listen.

"Two men once lived on a vast savannah in which trees were few and far between. Each man had the privilege of owning a little land on which a single large banyan tree grew. The first man was content with his tree as it was. He used it for shade, had built a small shed near its trunk in which he slept, and ate its figs when they were ripe. The second man was more enterprising and saw in his banyan tree more than it could make for itself, and so he cut the tree down to make bowls, idols, furniture, and building lumber from it. He may well have made a handsome profit from his labor, but working hard on these projects at the height of the summer with no shade to protect him, he developed a fever from the heat one day and died during the night." Don Weaver paused, smoothed his skirt out around his doubled legs, and then finished, "Make choices. They do matter. But see in the world its predispositions so that whenever possible you work with these tendencies rather than against them.

"These biases and inclinations exist inside you as well as outside you. Inside you we call these factors all taken together, your 'character.' In some of your jobs, you will need to be a different person in order to execute your task successfully. You may need to be someone very unlike who you are now in order for others, perhaps even the target or the patron, to help you achieve your aims. You cannot pretend to be this other person. Pretending is transparent. Pretending runs against the grain of your nature, and that tension is as clear and as painful to watch as the misuse of a banyan tree. You must find the part of you that embodies this person you must be and be that part of yourself for a while. If you can do this you will not need to pretend, you will be this other person without effort. By not fighting against your inner tendencies, you will accomplish your objective. Being someone else for a few hours is not an alternative to pretending. It is the only alternative. If you want to survive the job."

Lane's persistent attention to the moment was uncomfortable but his physical and mental fidgeting was so beneath him that it refueled his resolve to stay focused. Stop thinking. Even these thoughts of focus were mental laziness.

"An ironwood tree was rooted near the edge of a great river and around its feet grew many willow reeds. And when the wind would blow all the reeds would be bent by the wind and the ironwood tree laughed at them with a deep booming laugh and scolded them for being so small and weak that a gentle breeze could change their shape. And it would show with pride how it remained firm as the wind blew, not a twig would budge for the drafts. Then one night there was a terrible storm with clouds so thick there was no light from the stars or moon and wind so strong the little willow reeds were bent over nearly touching the ground. But in the morning when they raised their heads again, the ironwood tree lay uprooted on its side among them, its broad roots now hanging lifeless in the air. And even then, the willows noted thoughtfully, even on its side, the ironwood had not changed its shape, not by so much as a twig." Don Weaver paused again, his head up, but his eyes down, thinking about something, perhaps the tree. Lane looked around without moving his head and envied the patience the other apprentices showed, drinking in Don Weaver's lecture, pauses and all.

"It is a general and obvious truth about life that if you cannot bend, you will break. The challenge is to figure out how flexible to be on each facet of your life. I will tell you a story about Karabas. A story most people either don't know or choose to forget.

"Karabas has had a monarchy for many hundreds of years. What is conveniently forgotten is that it has not always been the same bloodline. About four hundred years ago, the ruling family's hegemony was waning. They had become weak and soft, insensitive both to the politics of the period and to the needs and traditions of the city. There was a man named Toko who had become the commander of the Karabas defenses and was much loved by the soldiers of Karabas and the people of Karabas generally. Toko was young, dashing, friendly, intelligent, and fearless. The corzons loved him because he had had lowly beginnings in a dirty quarter of the Lower Bank. The soldiers loved him because he respected hard work, achievement, and loyalty and because he had worked his way up through the ranks from the local militia through a post he had won with the Palace Guards. And the merchants and artisans of the Upper Bank loved him because he epitomized much of how they had come to think about the Karabas they loved. So one morning when the royal family woke to find guards in their bedrooms inviting them to leave the city before nightfall, the citizens of Karabas were on the whole very satisfied with the outcome when Toko stood before them that evening to assure them he would see to it that the city continued to run smoothly."

Don Weaver turned his head slightly to look between the Wrens at Lane as he continued. "Toko had chosen to spare the lives of the ruling family, which was foolish, from a certain point of view," and at this Lane flushed a deep red, experiencing the heat from his neck as fast as he could comprehend the implied accusation. He clenched his jaw waiting for Don Weaver to finish the job. Wishing he would get it over with.

"But in this particular case there was a daring statement to be made as well. He had said effectively to the people of Karabas 'I do not consider these people a threat as I know that you prefer me to them.' And by so doing, he reinforced this feeling in their own minds so that there was afterwards no talk, even in the back corners of bars late at night about the return of the original family." Lane forced himself to breath slowly, confused. Had this lecture not been directed towards his lapse with Sylvester? "Now for centuries from father to son, the suzerains of Karabas have remained attuned to the spirit and needs of the city. And in return our city has adopted their bloodline as though it was meant to be. As though it had always been. As I began, the city has chosen to forget that it was ever otherwise." Don Weaver was no longer looking directly at him and was at least outwardly relaxed.

"Do you believe Toko was an unusual man?" Don Weaver left the question floating among them too long for it to be rhetorical. Though it was clear the question was loaded, eventually Sona spoke, "You said he was tempered and exact, dazzle and genius and worked the suzerain bloodlessly. Such stone work must be unlikely unusual."

"I agree, Sona. I would not claim that Toko was other than a very unusual person. Maybe a few people a decade are born with the set of talents he had. But the society knew what it wanted. It was ready for Toko. It made Toko. If Toko hadn't been willing to fill the role, the city would have found another person or another way to accomplish its aims. But in these larger issues, the river knows which way it runs, and in a ravine, no single boulder will change its course."

Lane realized in a dizzying flash that he had roused himself in some way. Perhaps more awake was not the issue. But he had just been listening. Intently. Without dissecting or categorizing but still listening carefully. Was that useful? It felt better. But in the act of noticing, he found his footing gone. These thoughts had snatched away the perspective, a moment of dreamlike hyper-clarity.

"I've heard it said that this piece of history hinged on a momentary lapse of reason by the King. To have chosen to give Toko such power, command over all the forces of Karabas, could seem shortsighted in the extreme. But such a statement misses the point. The King's choice to do this was a symptom of the problem. It was no accident that it happened because it was part of the same tide of problems and the underlying current of required changes. It was in that sense inevitable that the King chose to hand control of his troops and then his city to someone who would turn the sword on its owner."

Don Weaver let this rest uncontinued and Lane hung onto his personal silence as tenaciously as it appeared Don

Weaver was gripping his own. Lane clung to that silence until the frustration with a question and the battle between 'who cares' and 'he's wrong' had grown and blistered to the breaking point. "But Karabas adored Toko precise. You said the city's love was na abstract. They loved him precise for him and how he moved them, proper?" And immediately, Lane regretted having spoken first if only because he had blinked in a contest he perceived, even if the others didn't, even if Don Weaver did not intend it as a contest.

"Of course it depends on how you choose to look at it, Lane. When you go to the temple of Beauty, do you pay your respects to Anna or what she stands for? Well, perhaps not you, Lane. But if you did pay your respects at a temple..." Don Weaver shared a smile with everyone but Lane. "When most people enter Anna's temple, they think of Anna. They speak to Anna. But Anna is a lightening rod for their thoughts. She is the finger pointing the way and the finger is real. It is often easy or important to focus on the finger to understand the direction. But the pointed finger is not the destination, it is merely a guide. I can imagine an avatar for Beauty that was not Anna, though this person would point somewhere slightly different from where we are used to Anna pointing. Yes. They, the city, loved Toko. But he was the incarnation of what they wanted. He was the pointing finger, not the thing itself."

Don Weaver waited again. The irritation ground into Lane. He could see Don Weaver waiting for another question for which he already had a prepared, purposefully ambiguous answer. Lane found Don Weaver's stories enjoyable if not comfortable, at least relative to these pauses between them. Waving away a series of thoughts, Lane shifted slightly in his kneel and resolutely held his tongue.

Finally, "It is not an accident that the strong survive and the weak are discarded. Are there other ways the world could be? Perhaps. Maybe the world tried out other ways as well. But those other ways were inferior, the survival rule was strong and has ruthlessly wiped out all other rules. The guild does not need to graduate, cannot graduate ten students every year. Which students will move on? The tall ones? The funny ones? Clearly, it must be the ones who are most fit for service to the guild. That is the version of strong that matters for you. Masters in Cian have a stick against which our appropriateness as masters is measured, as do all people in all places in all the aspects of their lives. How could it be otherwise? If you were guaranteed a graduation, you would not be an apprentice. If I were guaranteed my job, I would be useless as a teacher. Toko was stronger than his King. He was better in the ways that mattered in that situation. The rules are set. There will always be a cycle of winning and losing, birth and death, new replacing the old. The stick against which you will be measured is set by the circumstances, not by you. You cannot redirect the river, particularly while you are swimming the rapids. The river is inevitable, the path you swim is not."

Lane saw himself from high above rushing forward on crests of white water, bobbing and dodging sharp rocks slicing the water like monstrous jagged teeth half submerged in a torrent of saliva. And then in closer and closer until the foam pounded around him, swirling, sucking, and shoving so that keeping his head clear took all the strength he had. Being drawn forward into some inevitable mouth. He tightened his pectorals reflexively, shaking off the vision and seeing again Don Weaver's engaging face floating before him over the two tan shoulders of the Wrens.

"Have any of you actually tried to swim the rapids?" asked Don Weaver. Lane looked from side to side. He had never tried. Water was not his element. Apparently his fellow apprentices felt similarly. "The more you know about the water, the less work you have to do to survive. In the face of powerful forces it is not only true that fighting against them is futile, it is also the case that you can use that power to your advantage if you move with the flow of the force." That had to be the least practical statement yet from Don Weaver today.

"Down the mountains and beyond the desert are great steppes covered with waving grasses higher than a man and dotted with semi-mobile palaces of the nomadic satraps who rule those lands. One day a number of lords, vassals to the local satrap, set out to hunt, packing with them weapons fit for gazelle, boar, and even tiger. As was their custom they began the hunt at the edge of their camp by the day's first light, asking their magus for his guidance. Instead of pointing them in a direction, or telling them for a type of animal to watch for, the magus announced that they would return that evening without a kill, but leading a wise man who would become their mentor.

"The lords thanked the magus politely and enjoyed their laugh as they rode off, bows strung, eyes scanning the expanses of grass for signs of animals passing. The day ended without the sighting of so much as a kite in the distance and the party turned, disgusted, to head home. Within minutes, they came upon a pool of water and sitting beside the pool was an old man in tattered clothes fishing with a simple bamboo shaft for a pole. As they approached, he stood to greet them and they saw that his pole hung with twine at the end of which dangled a nail and no bait. In an irritable mood, the lords pointed down from their short stocky steeds and laughed at the poor man for wasting his time. The old man accepted their derision humbly saying only, 'The fish meant to be my supper will find their way to me on their own and the rest will not. I would rather enjoy the afternoon than work trying to compel these other fish into doing what they are not meant to do.' One of the hunters drew him out saying 'Then why even use the pole, old man?" And the old man replied 'Asking the fish to make it all the way into my basket here without a little help might be asking too much of the fish.' All the satrap's vassals were laughing so hard they dismounted to lay by the bank, eating a little and watering their ponies. As they were remounting to leave, one of them pointed across the pond to the old man who was pulling a large fish off his nail and putting it carefully into his basket. The lords conferred quickly and then approached the man again and said 'Sage, we apologize for our previous behavior. We were told that today we would meet our mentor and bring him back with us. Will you come?' And the sage stood, laying his fishing pole carefully aside on the ground, and bowing to them again humbly mounted behind one of the hunters, saying 'I would be happy to come with you as all things please me. And do you see? You don't even have a pole with which to fish and you have filled your basket today as well.'"

Don Weaver's gesturing hands returned to neutral, cupped into each other on his lap. The other four apprentices nodded slowly and individually in what Lane assumed, and hoped, was just annoyingly feigned agreement and appreciation.

"There is nothing more worth learning than to learn to act as an agent for forces already at work. Executing the will of the patron, using rather than resisting the flow of life and the events around you. That is the essence of what Cian requires of you." Quite opposite to the gravity of the words, Don Weaver looked and sounded nearly exultant. The afterglow of his tone and his radiant face did have a contagious effect and Lane struggled not to be overtaken by it. The moment lasted a long time and unlike a fading echo, Don Weaver's appearance of irrepressible satisfaction grew.

"Let's take a break for an hour to work on your carvings. As you all have completed your first assignment for the year, I will be passing out your second assignments over the next two or three weeks. Cye, please come see me in about half an hour. Lane, if you would, stay with me here for a few minutes." The five backs curved down in slow coordinated deference. Lane straightened as the others drifted off, feeling more removed from Don Weaver now that the Wrens were not between them.

"How are you, Lane? You've been quiet lately."

Lane shrugged, "Am hale enough. Mind is in foam lately," then feeling that this wouldn't do by itself, added "Dabs," and produced a guilty grin, trusting Don Weaver would misinterpret the source of the guilt.

His teacher smiled back widely, "We're not boring you here are we, Lane? I worry about that sometimes."

"Na. Cian's na bare, Master Weaver."

"Good. You finished your last assignment exceptionally cleanly. The patron is very pleased. No signs of struggle - no body - as though the Spirit left town, which is just the sort of impression the patron was looking for."

Lane watched Don Weaver's face intently for some twitch or momentary tick that would tell him where the conversation was going. Nothing. Lane inclined his head slightly, "Spirit was sleepy. Did the work exact. Work was na white. Na stone."

Don Weaver in turn studied Lane for too long. It didn't look like his mentor was waiting, but like he was thinking. Deciding what to do. There was no way this would go well.

"You have more potential, Lane, than any other student I've ever had."

Lane's stomach lurched wildly in uncomfortable pleasure. His body's disobedient hysterical response to the praise mixed in a noxious way with the tension in his gut, producing a swaying queasiness that nearly overpowered him. Rigidly controlling his appearance to compensate for his internal pandemonium, Lane closed his eyes slowly, opened them again, and inclined his head slightly, mumbling, "Just a Cian Jack. Perhaps do appear tempered because of these straight bare Spirits."

"You know that's not true, Lane." Don Weaver was studying Lane again. Waiting to see something? Some weakness, maybe. "Would you like something more challenging for your next assignment?"

"Proper? Da, Master." Lane's body was purposefully exaggerating his certainty.

"Even if the significance of the project heightens the consequences for an imperfect performance?"

"Da. Am na nerved to work shine, Master Weaver."

"I know you're not, Lane. And I was sure you'd say that. But you'll understand why I needed to ask. Your final assignment will be Cirrus, next suzerain of Karabas." Lane's pupils dilated in his otherwise frozen face. "Cirrus would turn eighteen early next spring. On his birthday, he would become the suzerain. The patron wills that Cirrus not see the onset of winter." Lane was silent and motionless - halted both internally and externally. "You have seen Cirrus in public? You know what he looks like?" Lane nodded again slowly. "Cirrus must seem to die of natural causes, Lane. The body cannot disappear. Small suspicions will be magnified because of the sudden death of both of his parents." Lane was suddenly glad he wasn't kneeling directly in front of Master Weaver. "Do you understand the constraints of the project, Lane?"

"Da, Master Weaver. Cirrus must be under roses before winter with na pointers to the work."

"Good. The patron has hired me to do this job, but I'm willing to let you do it because I believe in you, Lane. I wouldn't be offering this to you if I didn't think you could do it." Lane's stomach did another wrenching flip. "But I have to be clear again, Lane. The stakes are higher. You will not survive a failure here." Master Weaver paused, but Lane had nothing to say. "It is entirely against the spirit of your training at Cian, but if you need help, Lane, come ask me for it."

"Won't fail you, Master Weaver."

"I know, Lane."

Lane lowered his head in the obeisance, an image of his hands still spread across his thighs, knuckles pale, digging ever so slightly into his legs, burned into his eyes as they closed. Strong clean hands with a few faint scars over taut muscles and no dirt under the nails. And only the slight blur on the mental image gave away that the hands were shaking.

‡ ‡ ‡

The direct morning sunlight was still fresh on the River Island and already it was seething with people. A strong current of bodies ran both ways along the top of the Flat, passing before the gates of the River Palace and trickling off one of the two main bridges. Eddies in the flow of humanity happened just below the gates, around both of the Island Fountain basins, and in the streams heading down and back up both Alleys of the Flat. From above the birds saw the lower part of the Flat as a prismatic arrowhead, outlined by the Alleys and colored with bolts of rainbow fabric stretched across the market expanse. Floating along in the circulating crowds, Lane and Cye strolled aimlessly together.

"Weird lead from Master Weaver for you. To na know even how stone or how sleepy the work might be."

"Spot. That's what's so stone about it. In fact, I don't know for sure the Spirit exists. The Judge isn't even sure the Spirit exists."

"Well if he...he?"

"He."

"Well if he exists, like what does he look?"

"Judge does na know that neither. Spirit would be eighteen to twenty years. That's all I have to go on."

"Has this maybe person a name?"

"You know I can't give you his name, Lane."

"Do know that sure. Am saying 'Has Spirit a name at all?' You na know what he looks like, na know where he is..."

"He has a name he isn't using and may na know is his...if he exists at all."

"And if he does na exist? Then what?"

"Judge believes Spirit exists. Let's hope Judge's wise in this way."

"It's rocky to give you a lead with na clear success."

"I have from Master Weaver that this lead is na small thing. Jacks will rarely pick the lesson from which they learn the most."

"It's still rocky unjust."

The hot air lay increasingly heavy on the Flat as the sun continued to rise. Without a breeze the brilliant colored cloth sails sagged across the Flat, oppressed by the effort of blocking the direct summer sun. The crowd thickened and slowed as the morning wore on. Even inside the River Palace's open courtyards, the little figures working and passing through moved at substantially less than their winter pace. Along the wide ramparts of the River Palace, broken only by the two donjons in the center of the side fortifications and the third taller keep rising from the head of the island at the back of the palace, helmeted guards leaned against the walls and positioned themselves in the shade of the towers.

"And final lead for you? Is it too bare again? Na'thing to learn from again this lesson?"

"Na precise!" Lane laughed roughly. "Am na sure even where to begin."

"Be thankful you know even the look of your fox and where to find him."

"Spot. On flip, once you find your Spirit you can dispatch him straight. Spirit of mine can na go missing and must sudden sleep from a natural cause."

"Proper? Your Spirit is old enough to meet the riff alone? And you plan to frighten him cold?"

"Na natural causes actually, donkey! It must appear all natural's all."

"Then a poison might be the medicine for your patient?"

"Na luck. He's too well watched for poison in this case. It would likely na look natural."

"Perhaps your Spirit self-works himself under roses?"

"Do doubt could make Spirit that miserable between now and winter."

Now Cye laughed, "Obviously! Once Spirit has been put down, it could appear he had self-worked."

"Na know if Judge would approve. Do doubt it somehow."

"The world's a white arena, my friend. Perhaps it appears some other, an enemy to Spirit has released him for you?"

"Do imagine that's the same problem as self-worked."

"Then there's nothing left but accidents. All Cian's training and final lead has you rigging bad boards on a flight of stairs!" Cye laughed again a full friendly laugh.

"While you go groping for your Spirit in the dark!"

The pair meandered on in silence for a while and the silence reminded Lane of all the things he couldn't share with Cye. Wouldn't share. And the self-imposed alienation was as painful as his failings. Touching Cye on the shoulder as though in consolation for his challenges, Lane felt a little better, but only a little. Suspiciously hard. If Cian wanted to watch him fail, this task would serve the purpose. Either they knew he did not deserve his place in Cian and had picked Cirrus with that in mind, or they were blind to his flaws. Both were demoralizing. Success was the only solution. Not that success was likely, but further failure was utterly unacceptable.

"So...What'll you do?"

"There are a few who may know history of this boy. I'll be persuasive and hear out their tales. And you?"

"Na see an opening yet, but do know a person, an ancient friend, who might have useful thoughts."

The eyot lay in the frothy torrent, trying to cool off, its four legs splayed out to anchor it to the river's banks and across its back innumerable mite-sized citizens crawled this way and that on their separate missions. Several kestrels rode the wind on lazy wings, suspended on invisible cushions among the wispy white clouds miles above Karabas. Suddenly one of the falcons was plummeting down, a dead weight without wings, rushing toward the earth with outstretched talons as fast as the earth could pull it in, disappearing into the chaotic details of the city.

‡ ‡ ‡

The green veins stood out prominently on the black marble walls, the trace impurities more evident than the dark polished limestone that held them in place. Down four steps into the crater that held the building, the entire front face of Envy's temple, a single ebony sheet of rock, was broken only by a triangular doorway wide enough for four men to enter side by side. Above the first level it stepped up in a rough pyramid to an outdoor shrine at its summit. Lane liked the building and would have been happy to escape the sun for a few minutes, but it had already been a long fruitless day and he wasn't likely to find the person he sought inside.

Continuing his climb through the upstream side of the Upper Bank, Lane passed building after building that did him no good. The private homes were useless, as were the workshop spaces for artisans and craftsmen. Along the clean narrow streets and around the regularly placed open squares, the bustling was beginning to clump around the restaurants and taverns as afternoon approached evening. Lane stopped in front of an outdoor eatery, its bubbling fountain surrounded by customers. But a quick scan of the faces and backs of the heads set Lane into motion again unsatisfied. The old man wouldn't be at a café, or in the sun at all. He would be tucked into a shady corner of some public place where he might be left alone. And so Lane turned into the temple for Charisma because it fit the constraints, but without high expectations.

Two steps up into the temple and it was as noisy as ever. The hexagonal odeon had no walls but was ringed two layers deep in elegant plaster columns that supported a vaulted hexagonal roof of inlaid wood. In the center of this multi-faceted loggia the roof came together in a stained glass dome that cast a patchwork pool of vibrant colors on the empty center stage of the temple. Lane began a tour of the space along the outer colonnade and at the center of each side, just inside the inner row of columns, he passed a stone rostrum where someone was speaking. Lane had no interest in the speeches, serenades, tirades, and poetry that tumbled out of the hall's devotees. Those who did not have a spot at a rostrum stood in the wings or sat in the central kaleidoscopic light shaft practicing their thoughts and contributing to the general cacophony. The only quiet figure at a rostrum, the only quiet figure in the temple other than Lane, was Tory, Charisma's avatar. Roughly carved at her natural size and cast in bronze, she stood close-lipped at her podium with her eyes to the dome and her hands above her head in a "y," waiting like a human lightning rod. It was a magnetic pose further heightened by her commanding pause amid the vain, noisy, ineffective chatter swirling around her.

Lane had given up on the building and was headed down the stairs at the back of the temple when he nearly tripped over the stubby legs of Flood who sat in the shade, leaning against one of the outer columns. Lane froze and took a deep controlled breath, working to reorient himself. Then he flopped down unceremoniously next to Flood and leaned back against the same column.

"Flood! Greetings my ancient! Genius finding you here!"

Flood turned his old head toward Lane and cocking it to the side gave him a puzzled, suspicious look. The clothes covering Flood were a uniform faded brownish gray, but the tiny old man looked cleaner and smelled cleaner than Lane remembered him. The searching eyes reminded Lane that

Flood's eyesight was probably poor, so he picked up one of the wizened hands and tried again.

"It's Lane! We worked together a long time in the high house kitchens."

"Lane?" The question was not to Lane but to himself.

"Remember, Flood. We had bright game together. Like...remember the gourds? When foreign wine came in we'd pour a 'tax' of each bottle into gourds then together drink them outside after the high house fell asleep."

Flood smiled, "That was game indeed." Then a worried look passed over his face like a cloud before the sun, "Did so with you? Sorry son. It's hard ta recall sometimes..."

"Alright, alright good friend." Flood seemed very happy having his hand held so Lane gave it a reassuring squeeze and continued to hold it awkwardly in his. "So...what do you hear from the high house?"

"Na much. Been out of the high house for several years now. The family prepares for the Kamakura two months hence, then another few months and the New Year's celebration with a possible new avatar for Karabas...then of course Cirrus comes of age next spring, of course that'll be the biggest celebration."

"Peach. Cirrus is in good health, hope so? And is looking forward to his accession, sure."

"Cirrus is a good boy...and will be a good man soon. Na think he feels ready for accession but humility makes a better suzerain. He cares very much on family, friends, and the city."

"Peach, peach of course. But he must have vices...all do. Or plays dangerous sport? Or wagers? Or special attention to the dabs?"

"Na. Na. He's a serious boy. He takes exercise but na to excess. He does na overindulge...another sign he'll be a good leader."

Lane could feel the frustration showing a little in his shoulders and dropped them an inch. "He at least must spend time alone."

"Na again. Na proper. He likes people and feels good among them."

"Genius! Give me more good news, history!" Lane had to swallow a snarl. "And you're sure he has na enemies neither..."

"Na. Na of course. He's done nothing to make them hate. There's plenty of family tension sure but Regent has always been very strong for Cirrus since suzerain and his mother died." Flood paused, but on what subject he thought was not clear. "In Karabas are a few who na fancy Cirrus as new suzerain but he's well insulated from those."

"Tell me about Cirrus' siblings. You said there's tension there?"

"Leaf's the next male so always has competition with Cirrus but he knows his place and keeps it sure. Ava dotes on Cirrus dearly and does as he directs. Who knows why Lily so ugly resents her brother. Perhaps just cause she was born first. Anyway she's just a dab..."

"Cirrus must be well happy then if he's so much loved and so in good health."

"He's a serious boy but happy too. Da."

Lane leaned quietly next to Flood for a while, moving through possibilities for some missed opportunity. Flood seemed content with their silence, into which washed the hubbub from inside the temple. With a shock, Lane realized he still held Flood's hand in his and dropped it briskly, standing to go.

"Remind, me, ancient, what was your favorite dish the high house kitchen made while you were there."

A limp look of distant recollection curtained Flood's face. "They used to make candied pheasant as large as life, a crust of hard sugar, stuffed with all kinds of creams, so finely decorated it looked ready ta fly the plate." Then returning slowly from his memories he asked, "Why?"

"Just something for us to talk about next time. Grats, history."

Lane strolled off, leaving the little old man looking both sad and amused. Behind the column on which he leaned, back three strides into the temple, Tory still held court in silence. She stood with her arms raised so that even from behind the bronze statue seemed to be pulling energy into itself, dragging the iridescent beam from the temple's ceiling.

‡ ‡ ‡

A thump, a few muffled words, receding footsteps and the silence was as complete as the darkness. Lane ran his fingertips sightlessly over the inside of the wooden crate and verified that as far down and up as he could reach, it lay thick and solid an inch above his prone position. The cold hard undulations of the wine bottles beneath him seemed to run the length of the box, but now that his ears were idle, a previously unnoticed odor of aged cheese permeated his mind until he could taste it in his mouth. Though he was physically comfortable, this olfactory saturation fed in him an irrational desire to kick and pound his way out of the casket. Lane swallowed down the urge again and again, and a good thing he did for muted sounds of the outside world approached and receded irregularly. Time crept by or sped, there was no way to tell which, until Lane began to worry that he had missed the small hours of the morning and it was day again.

The point came when he could not suffer another moment's interment and he slid one of his spikes out of his pocket and began working as quickly and quietly as possible to drive it between the side wall and the nailed shut lid. The harder he worked the harder it became to breathe the more urgently Lane needed to be free. He found he had to work his lever several times around as much of the perimeter as he could reach before the lid was pried off enough for him to roll out of the box, scraping his back and leg on several nails in his hurry.

Lane moved off without a sound, rubbing his cuts as he padded forward to make sure none were leaving a trail of blood. It took several turns along the corridors of wine that reached all the way to the damp vaulted stone cellar ceilings before he found a rising flight of stone steps. At the top of the stairs Lane looked cautiously into a cavernous kitchen fifty feet on a side, dimly lit by a few candles and the fading embers of two gigantic hearths side by side on the far wall. Windowless as the room was, Lane could only assume from the room's emptiness that it was late enough or early enough for his purposes.

A forest of cooking containers and utensils hung down within arms reach and Lane set several of them swinging as he passed beneath the metal foliage. The kitchen was clean, exceptionally clean for a kitchen, but the thought of all the heat, the din, and the smells packed into that enclosed space each day was uncomfortably reminiscent of working the forges. Lane shuddered involuntarily as he began the climb up the next flight of stone steps, glad to be leaving the place, even in its dormant state.

The banquet hall caught him by surprise. As he took the last stair up into the Palace, his eyes widened and twinkled. As large as the blacksmith's hall above Cian and set with as many fireplaces, the room was, like the kitchen, dimly candlelit. But by that light the walls shimmered in a clinquant network of tiles, chips of mirror, and vast expanses of miniature paintings in gilt so fine they looked like windows into other tiny fabulous worlds. The entire room was edged with molding of semi-precious stones, striped jasper, agate, and onyx delicately arranged in bands and clouds of pinks, reds, and browns, dark blues and greens, all interlocking in a polished exquisite frame for each surface of the hall. Similar to the fortified external surface of the palace, these walls were covered in intricate waterfalls that spilled, split, splashed, and regrouped only to disappear again into the walls or floor. The gurgling from these many fountains gave the room a vibrant life even in its unpeopled darkness.

Continuing through the rooms of the Palace and doubling back several times to avoid the footsteps of its legitimate inhabitants, Lane wound through wondrous rooms until he lost count of them or track of where he was. Nearly all the rooms were curtained with waterfalls, in some making pools that sat along the edge of the walls or running in deep complex grooves through the floors. Where the miniature paintings left off, the walls were carved directly in bas-relief and featured small alcoves with inset statuettes from the Karabas pantheon.

In the open areas between the rooms, indirect sunlight filtered in during the day to the higher floors, feeding the full grown trees planted in soil boxes set into the ground and covered with stone flooring. One atrium in which Lane found himself had several such trees that hid most of the rafters above them. Satisfied that this place was as good as any and better than most, Lane leapt into one of the trees and swung up through it to perch among the birds on a rafter near the corner of the room. From here he could see most of the atrium and was simultaneously hidden from all but the closest scrutiny of the ceiling.

Six trees framed a wide staircase that ran up the center of the space, ascending to a "T" at a balcony with doorways on either end, high above one of which sat Lane. At the top of the staircase hung a large faded tapestry and as he settled in, Lane's eyes ran over the image. A sad serious older man stood by a window, dressed all in black with a gray ribbon tied tightly around the top of his collar. Ornate mullions divided the large window through which the rising full moon could be seen. Spread on the table before the cleric was a snow white swan with the head of a beautiful woman. The woman's ivory hair cascaded across the table and spilled over the edges, parted so her eyes half closed in a swoon could watch the cleric with tearful compassion. The bare white ribs of the swan stuck out grotesquely where her breast had been roughly cut open though there was no sign of blood. Carving knife and fork in hand, the cleric was methodically slicing the meat from the chest and stacking it on an ebony serving platter beside her head.

‡ ‡ ‡

The finch, nestled on hidden feet, was quietly cleaning the top of a wing, digging its beak in and out of its shoulder. Several feet down the timber Lane's boots were still but the thought of kicking the finch was appealing. In the past two days he'd had nothing to eat, one drink from the wall when he jumped down to urinate the previous night, and practically no sleep thanks to the finch's songs, seemingly timed to prevent his getting a moment's rest. Aside from being stiff, sore, hungry, thirsty, and sleepy, he was bored and frustrated. He was beginning to turn over the idea of leaving empty-handed before it was day time again when she appeared below and put her first foot on the stairs.

Lane pushed off from the rafter with fifteen feet of air separating him from the balcony. He realized as he dropped that he was suddenly in a better mood than he'd been in a long time. The floor came up to meet him and as he bent into a crouch he connected the air in his nostrils now with his entrance into the palace. He knew without turning that Lily had a piece of that same cheese he rode in upon, now more pungent with the rind removed.

Landing noiselessly on the balls of his feet and the finger pads of his right hand, his left arm out for balance, Lane froze, listening. Satisfied with the oncoming creak creak creak up the staircase, Lane scuttled forward through the darkened doorway, waited, waited, straightened, and walked back out onto the balcony, nearly colliding with Lily, first scion of the late suzerain of Karabas.

Lily startled back two steps, but then held her ground. Her piercingly blue eyes were wide with surprise and her pale skin flushed momentarily with embarrassment. Very quickly she recovered herself and began watching Lane apprehensively, but there was still a telltale sweat from some recent exertion on her forehead, and her long silver diaphanous gown stuck to her wet skin in several places. This caused her thin figure to be partly visible beneath the loose gown, but from her posture, it didn't seem this was the source of her initial embarrassment. As was the fashion for the Karabas well-to-do, her platinum hair was cropped very short, though in her case so short that on top of her head it stuck nearly straight up. Her cheeks thin, lips pale, her pert breasts small, she cut an altogether elfin figure.

The dense pause stretched on and Lane looked to the silver plate she was holding where a chunk of bread sat next to the cheese he had never seen but knew by smell. Some other smell was mixed in with the old dairy, something sweet and earthy and intoxicating. He ran his tongue over the inside of his teeth trying to taste it with the cheese until he realized it was Lily and a background anointment of nard and sandalwood. Too much time had passed for the moment to be sudden and Lane could see the tension in her eyes and body translating into a wary curiosity. Finally, she removed a hand from the plate, put it to her hip and said "Are you lost?"

"Na precisely." Lane held himself in a comfortable but slightly guilty pose.

"Are you looking for something?"

"You could say so."

"A thief?" Without losing her stateliness, Lily's arrogant tone was slipping into one of intrigued incredulity.

"Na how would've described it, but na wrong neither." Lane smiled at this, warming to the part.

Annoyed by the smile, "Are you not afraid I will scream?"

"Are you nerved you'll need to?" And Lane smiled a little more mischievously at the thought she might also not want attention just now.

"I will take my chances." Lily said with a youthful rebellious tone.

"Hence are na nerved neither. But will go if you ask it."

Lane held his breath while the pause drew out. His heart was louder than usual and he could feel the same quickening in her. Finally, Lily answered by saying, "My name is Lily and you are...?"

"Lane." As he spoke the clatter of a dropped dish echoed into the atrium from some distant room, Lily startled, and Lane rose on the balls of his feet swinging his head to see who was approaching.

"Relax." Lily put a hand on Lane's arm to keep him still. "It is likely just a clumsy valet fetching something." Raising an eyebrow, Lane looked at her hand as she removed it, then back to her face. Tiny hints of color were already fading back off her cheeks. "Here...bread? Cheese?" she said extending the silver plate towards him slightly.

"Grats." Lane took a small crumbly chunk of the cheese and popped it into his mouth. The smell was in the taste but it had a rich astringent flavor as well, overpowering at first but improving as it melted in his mouth. Slowly, Lane broke off another larger piece.

"Have you been doing...this...long?"

Lane bobbled his head indifferently, "A little more than three years."

"I am sure parts of your...lifestyle...are hard," she paused, "But it must be nice living by your own rules."

"Things are na so straight. Wish they were." Now Lane paused, then pointed back at her, "But you. Your freedom – that is peach."

"Freedom," Lily snorted in disgust. "There is no freedom in this house. Especially not for me." Footsteps several rooms away had become audible and seemed to be approaching. "You see." She waved her hand in exasperation towards the doorway from which the sound was coming.

Lane looked once behind him into the dark, then broke past Lily into a jog, taking the stairs two at a time.

"Wait!" Lane paused and turned. "Come back..." Lily paused, caught in mid thought, waiting for the rest to come. "...sometime." Then she looked flustered and added "To see me I mean."

"You and a guard of twenty high house grunts?"

"No! Just me."

Lane held her gaze for a moment and extracted what meaning he could from it. "Will see what can do."

For her benefit, Lane took the second half of the staircase in the air. Nearing the foot he hooked his left hand on the ornate cap at the end of the balustrade, swinging his whole body in a wide arc and soaring out through one of the side archways before his feet even touched the ground.

‡ ‡ ‡

Even from behind and over the ruckus of the room, there was something larger than life about the broad shoulders, well proportioned suntanned neck and head, and the tussletop of light brown hair. Lane had returned to the Rapids looking for Cye, but was nearly as happy to have found Bocc, a long time friend he had not seen in several years. They had shared much of their unruly Lower Bank childhoods until Lane had been sold to the blacksmith's guild and Bocc had become a runner for a small Upper Bank merchant. Since that time Bocc had done well for himself, now a merchant in his own right, importing oil, pitch, bitumen, and wax for sale in the various lighting trades around town.

Bocc was speaking with several friends Lane did not recognize but as Lane clapped him on the back, Bocc turned his head, saw Lane, turned completely and gave Lane a bear hug greeting. Bocc's wide grin of uncomplicated pleasure was untouched by the passing years. Otherwise he had matured into a man's man with an enviable face, broken nose and all. Boisterous, rowdy and passionate, the only way Bocc ever was, could be exhausting in large doses but was exhilarating in short bursts. For Bocc, everything was a competition and around him the stories grew larger with the telling, the jokes funnier, and the accomplishments more grand. Lane and Bocc talked and laughed and drank the evening away, feeling warm and centered at the eye of a storm of disreputability, all shouting and gesturing to enforce the domination of their ideas, their friends, and themselves.

Sona, rumbling into the main room from the balcony, cut off Lane's happy distraction. Sona was wearing an ostentatiously bright orange crossover tunic and the dress of his older friends following him in off the balcony was similarly garish. Given that Sona had never raised the subject with him, Lane assumed his previous unfortunate and disorderly conduct in this tavern had not impacted Sona. As the gaudy group approached, Lane put out his hand to Sona's arm to stop and greet him. Lane could smell the strong spirits Sona had been drinking, and in an attempt to identify the particular drink by smell missed Sona's motion until he had already knocked away Lane's hand in disgust. Sona's refusal to be friendly was no surprise and having made the attempt, Lane was happy to let it go.

Bocc, however, was not. While Lane was chastising himself for having been so distracted and so slow as to let Sona slap his hand, Bocc had stepped forward immediately, grabbing Sona roughly by the arm and swinging him around for an apology he couldn't know would never happen. Sona's companions stood flatfooted, watching with amused interest like a tired audience willing to sit through an encore. Bocc was a large, strong man who had at least in earlier days been handy in a scuffle, but there was no questioning the lethal imbalance of the two. Even so Lane might have hoped, unreasonably with these two, that civility might prevail, had Sona's free hand not headed straight for his long-handled hatchet tucked into a black satin sash tied around his waist. As the weapon rose in Sona's hand, Lane looked from face to face, seeing a blind blood lust in one and a proud fearlessness in the other. With intervention inevitable, Lane reached into his two thigh pockets with a sigh. In the time it took the hatchet to come from beside Sona's ear to a spot two feet forward, six inches off Bocc's shoulder blade, two steel rods had materialized between the combatants, one arresting the further progress of the hatchet and a second one flat against Bocc's chest to keep him out of Sona's reach.

Lane held the pose to let the heat dissipate. The clang of metal on metal was fading and a hushed pause gripped the Rapids. Then all at once, everything started up again. The drinkers kept drinking with cautious eyes on the impending melee. Sona's decorated companions seemed to settle back on their heels to watch the chaos, Bocc heaved himself again at Sona, trying to push Lane aside, and Sona redirected his attack to Lane with evident pleasure. If it had only been Sona, Lane could have carried on without fierce concentration, but Bocc's repeated assaults on Sona took significant effort to disarm without hurting Bocc. Sona rebuffed Bocc's blows distractedly, but it was clear he intended to leave a mark on Lane. At least.

Eyes half closed, diaphragm expanding and contracting as slowly as possible, Lane watched his body from the inside to keep its timing right. Periodically he would check again that Sona's next blow was making its way toward him and in plenty of time he would block the strike, taking care to rap Sona's knuckles each time, but never hard enough to do real damage. This gentle treatment was turning Sona's already dark face black and without a word Lane could feel Sona's intensity increasing and intentions worsening. This sort of sparring was wrong from almost every perspective. Bocc's eagerness to start a fight that was not his, that he did not understand, and that he could not win was tremendously annoying. Not that Lane had a right to complain given his recent behavior in this very tavern, but this was not the place for Sona to start something serious. That Sona could not take his lesson and back out gracefully was also frustrating, but it made Lane feel sorry for Sona. Mostly, Lane just wasn't in the mood.

He reexamined his process and position, making sure he never arrived so early for a block that he missed it altogether. Sona's blows came on steadily and with minimal creativity, and Lane accepted the fact that with the Rapids' crowd not intervening, a blow damaging enough to end the situation would be necessary. As he began picking a spot on Sona that would bring him down with no chance of death, Lane was surprised to find thoughts of Rose running through the back of his mind. They were pleasant memories of her face, her hair, and her scent, but rather than savoring them he let them wash over him and pass away. She was a comfort too connected to a person he must never be again.

The hatchet swung in gradually from the left side and checking the angles and speeds again, Lane switched his attention to Sona's feral expression. As he brought his left stake up to crack on Sona's hatchet hand, he saw a wave of serious evaluation ripple over the jet black eyes in the wake of the surprise, pain, and frustration. The hatchet leaving Sona's hand continued on its current trajectory and Lane leaned to his right to make sure it missed him as it passed. As it brushed his upper arm and went into the watching crowd, Lane noted ruefully that they would probably never let him back in the Rapids again. His right arm extended, inserting the barbed steel tip of his other stake three inches deep into the soft spot just above Sona's left knee. As Sona's body buckled and moved into a kneel, Lane lowered a little with it, looking at the thigh and thinking sadly how much more red there would be when he pulled back.

‡ ‡ ‡

Behind the glass panel the pendulum ticked and tocked back and forth, quiet and persistent. The ornamental clock was on a mantle elegantly carved in teak to mimic in great detail the rough natural growth of the original tree. Under the mantle a fire spit and crackled, discharging its water and sap as it consumed its logs. The room, bright until the eyes adjusted to the firelight, was muted by the long rich swaths of plush vermilion fabric hanging from near the ceiling all the way to the floor. The tall tower room ceiling peaked steeply in a point. Where the heavy textiles had been pinned back near the room's corners, the walls underneath showed glimpses of gold leaf paintings, miniature universes of pastoral scenes and friendly forest animals.

From the window the room had three significant elements: the fireplace to the right, a four poster bed against the opposite wall to the left, and a heavy oak door directly across from the window. The vermilion fabric hung just over the lintel of the window, creating an odd lump by covering some ornamentation centered just above it. Outside the night was hot with a stickiness stoked by a light rain that had been coming down for hours. From the distant lights and indistinct rooftop shapes below, the vertiginous drop outside the window looked particularly severe. Given the muggy weather and the open window, the fire inside the room looked unnecessary.

Lily reclined diagonally across the bed, propped up by so many pillows at her back that she was nearly sitting. The top of her baggy white silk pants were covered by a man's white silk tunic unclasped but crossed over her stomach. She sat staring distractedly into the fire and drawing a golden hairbrush again and again through the few inches of hair on the top of her head. Near her right hip sat a closed leather-bound journal. The brush froze near the base of her neck and Lily stiffened, eyes wide. Two wet hands gripped the windowsill and between them floated the silhouette of a head. A drenched foot appeared, a rush of body parts, and Lane was out of the weather.

Seeing Lily paused in surprise, Lane took the time to bend forward to stretch, then straightened and twisted at the hip, pulling on his arms to try to relieve the tension of the arduous climb. Straightening, Lily had dropped her brush arm, but was otherwise still frozen, and Lane smiled a wide easy smile to hide his sudden realization that he had no specific plan.

"Greetings."

"Hi."

He paused, unsure what she wanted to hear or what he wanted her to think. "Dona be nerved. Didna come to steal."

She sat up in bed, supported from her locked arms buttressed back behind her. "Then why are you here?" The white silk tunic she wore hung open to the middle of her stomach showing skin as smooth and nearly as pale as the fabric.

"You asked me to come, didna you?"

"Yes. I mean what motivated you to do what I asked?"

"Suppose was curious to find out what you wanted."

Lily pushed up into a full upright position crossing her arms over her chest and squirming slightly as she looked at Lane. Then she quickly leaned up against one of the bed posters so that the post blocked the center strip of her now bare chest. She opened her mouth to speak but at first nothing came out and then, "You seemed...interesting...different. I do not get a lot of variety in my social life so...so...I just thought you would be entertaining to see again."

"How different?"

"Unpredictable, maybe. Unfettered."

Lane's hair was slicked to his head with water and he adjusted the locks with a sweep of his hand. Moving to the bed, he sat on the opposite side of its foot, making no effort to hide the drying of his hands on the plush bedspread. Lily had moved off the bed as he sat down, and was now standing by the side of the bed, and leaning into the same post she had kept between them during their rotation.

"And where are your fetters? Are you locked in here? You want for na'thing. You're sister ta the first male scion who soon becomes the suzerain."

His statement brought a cloud over her features, though this dour look actually accentuated Lily's austere beauty. Her icy blue eyes had become suddenly humorless and cold. "Fetters? I have nothing but fetters! My aunt doesn't care, but Cirrus is so twisted up about the appearance of the family. He mistrusts everything I say and everything I do. He decided years ago I was a social liability to be controlled to minimize damage. That door there is not locked, but it might as well be. I'm to be seen at state functions and otherwise kept away from everyone to prevent embarrassment to city."

"But your brother becomes the suzerain soon."

"Exactly. Now at least I am the eldest scion and the regent still rules, but once Cirrus comes of age and becomes the suzerain, he may do as he pleases. What little freedom I have left will be gone. I will be nothing."

"Well that's sad as Cirrus'll certainly become suzerain. He's in perfect health."

"Someone might change that if they dared."

Gasping theatrically, "Na person would dare hurt the soon suzerain!" Lily seemed genuinely emotional and in just the way he had hoped to catch and exploit. But the trend of the conversation was moving a little too directly into an opportunity for Lane. That Lily's needs and his were so aligned was such good fortune, a little suspicion was warranted. Still, Lane's stomach was more settled than it had been in months.

Lily's eyes had lit with a hard bright light. She was quiet for several moments and then said, slowly and softly, with a gentleness at odds with her expression, "They might if they were paid enough." And she held his gaze unflinching as his eyebrows rose. Lily's alabaster skin was pure and unblemished, and though she still leaned in to the post, her pose seemed expectant now and almost suggestive. She couldn't know Lane's task or his occupation unless she had taken a lucky guess. The only person outside Cian who would know the target had even been selected would be the patron who would still have no way of knowing who at Cian would be assigned the work.

"Finding anyone would be extremely stone. Anyone willing ta do the deed. Finding someone willing with also all the skills sounds na possible. Being pickpocket or thief doesna qualify you ta hunt suzerain."

"Well, supposing that someone capable could be found. What do you think it might cost?"

"Honest, do have na clue."

Lily held onto the bed poster and hung out a little from the bed, showing the open tunic hanging just wide enough to expose the central four inches of her nubile chest, smiling, clearly aware of the visual effect. "Well, hypothetically, what would it take to entice you to do it?"

Lane, feeling unbalanced and disadvantaged on the bed, jumped back to his feet. "Soon suzerain?! Bear him na ill will. And you his sister! How could you think so?"

Lily fairly sparkled as she grabbed Lane's arm, "You need not hate him. Compensation could be your motive. Tell me you didn't come here looking for something valuable to carry away."

"It's more complicated than just so." He looked at her hand on his forearm but did not remove it.

"Is it?" A shift of her shoulders and the silk material spread out, draping down over one nipple and just exposing the other. "Will you do this thing for me if I ask it of you?" She waited a moment for him to respond but then continued, "I want to be free of his world. If you did this for me, I would have measured your...worth...and would come away with you."

Her performance was impressive, her direction was suspiciously useful, and the earthy sandalwood vapors directly around her were an overwhelmingly sweet ether. It was no stretch to act flustered and aroused. "Na know that could say 'na' to you." Paused, feeling the tone was off and watching the porcelain figure for a reaction, "But compensation would also be peach." Though whether Lane was allowed to take outside compensation as an apprentice, even for the same task, was unclear.

Her elfin laugh tinkled and danced around him, harrying him with its sharp edges and undertones as the silk top slid off her arms onto the floor. "I will see you get both."

‡ ‡ ‡

Stretched out face down and spread eagle across the rumpled russet covers, Lane's lifeless naked body glistened and shimmered in the firelight. The signs of a struggle ended at the bed's borders, leaving the rest of the room in peace. The rain had also moved on, revealing an eagle's nest view of the nighttime Karabas lamplight constellations below, glowing out of the blackness. Lily perched precariously on the window ledge, her bare legs braced against the far side of the frame. Trailing immodestly down her sides, the wide open silk tunic was all she wore and her lithe body also glistened with sweat.

"You dona really want me to put your brother under roses, do you?" Lane's voice came muffled through the blankets, exhausted and remote.

Lily looked out the window, speaking softly and a little wistfully, "Yes. I do. He has made it clear that I cannot have a real life while his continues." She waited for Lane to speak and when there was no answer, she asked again, "Will you do it?"

"Will you pay me?"

"I'll get for you more than you could possibly have stolen from here."

Lane raised his head slightly and looked at her through the still wet hair that stuck to his forehead and trailed down in chords over his eyes. "That's na a very specific offer."

"Give me a few days to get some things together."

"Your brother's stone ta approach by the likes of me."

"You are right about that. Perhaps you could put something in his food?"

"Na good. You know your family's tiny poison suspicious since your parents met the riff simultaneous at a public banquet. Does na Cirrus have tasters?"

"He does, but not all the time. He is careful, but not paranoid."

Lane had lowered his head to the bed, but raised it again to see if her body language was as coldly humorous as that statement had sounded.

"Still...nuff time to make poison likely cause sudden sleep. Would rather na start a Lane hunt."

"What if he had an accident?"

Lane turned over to his front and slid to sit naked at the foot of the bed. "You have a particular mishap in mind? Does he aught regular and dangerous?"

"It was just a thought." Lily was looking out over the city and she sounded annoyed.

"Na know about this request. Am na sure it's possible." Lane put his head down a bit to accentuate the effect.

"Are you saying you cannot do it?" The soft edged question came padding across the room to rub up against him. Looking up he saw that she'd turned on the lintel to face into the room, her arms out to hold the window sides, and her legs spread slightly.

Lane ignored the proffered tangent, "Will you help? This will na be done by me alone."

"I will help you...as long as the deed cannot be traced back to me. That means I cannot be directly involved...but I can clear a path for you."

"Thought heard you say you were ready to fly away with me."

"Even so."

"Then by both needs, it can na seem Cirrus was worked." Lane's tear ducts filled in an effort to prevent a smile from taking over his face.

Lily slipped over the architrave shelf and stood aside saying matter-of-factly, "You have a long climb ahead of you. I'd ask you to come back but I take it you're now sufficiently...interested." A repressed grin dissolved inside Lane's mouth at the abrupt dismissal. His defined calves rose out of thin ankles and below them well formed well sized feet spread out around the edges to accommodate his weight as he stood. Near his feet and trailing back half way to the window was the debris of his clothing. An odor of freshness came through the square-framed hole in the tower, beyond which was the precarious climb down and the sleeping city far below.

‡ ‡ ‡

The smell of boiling milk was so thick in the stuffy subterranean chamber that Lane could taste it through his nose. Scanning the room, Lane couldn't tell which of the burning sticks could be making the smell or where the devotee had found such powerful incense. The rose and lye smells in the air were thankfully fading away as the odor cacophony must have been dizzying earlier that evening. This late on a summer night the underground temples were generally as empty as this one was now. The few remaining petitioners sat by themselves on the slate benches that hugged the walls of the broad square chamber. Beneath their feet the floors were paved with the same charcoal slate, rising up in the same interlocking plates of deepest grey to form the four walls, and then angling up into a convex geometrical roof of the slate slabs. Diffuse ambient light rose with the smoke from a perimeter of particularly deep braziers whose light came back into the room off matted foreshortened light spots on the ceiling. And hung so artfully from the ceiling by clear threads that the levitation illusion was flawless, a crescent moon of polished silver reflected the light with a pearly glow.

The effort required to see the room itself was substantial as the walls were covered with chalk. The chalk dust haze itself giving a slightly otherworldliness to distance detail, but more than that, it was the chalk still on the walls that absorbed all casual attention. From the bottom to the crest of each wall, thick across the entire floor, and even across the ceiling, drawings, pictorial annotations, text, musical notation, and mathematical equations swirled and danced. Each stream of thoughts involved in its own personal expression but respecting and accommodating the neighboring brainstorms around which they curled. To look on it was to listen inside a thousand active minds simultaneously.

Lane stood behind the life-sized statue of Wima, avatar of Inventiveness, who knelt on one knee at the edge of a pond into which she was staring. The kidney shaped pool at the center of the room was no more than two body lengths across and mirror smooth. Vibrant hyper-real colors painted meticulously onto Wima's porcelain frame gave the still pose a wild, explosive energy in the otherwise hueless surroundings. Lane pulled a strip of newly tanned leather from his pocket and holding both ends, dragged it across the tip of Wima's upright spear on which she leaned. Gouging a series of scars into the leather strap, Lane tossed it over his shoulder noting, even as his mind wandered on, the smell of the leather above the hot milk odor foundation.

Bunched together without respect for individual narratives, Lane's simple drawings crowded in behind Wima's kneeling form - cramped half-formed characters huddled together for meaning. Rose. Don Weaver. Don Maya. Cye. Sona. Lily's allegiance and intentions were far from certain. There was a little aerial view of Karabas and no schematic of another place. Lane had never been to another city but that didn't mean now wasn't a good time to leave. On the other side of the room a man jumped up from the slate bench, spilling a project of clay, pipes, cloth, and wire across the floor, and flew from the room in a disjointed whirring of limbs. Lane's task was both suspiciously hard and now, through Lily, suspiciously well-paved ahead.

Poison can't be made to work. It's a woman's weapon anyway. Lily could walk that road as easily as Lane. And why wouldn't she? Plausible accidents are hard to orchestrate. A fatal illness would be perfect, but even harder to facilitate. Suicide and Cirrus were unfriendly if not irreconcilable. When a scion dies alone or in thin company suspicion is unavoidable. A scion dying in public is worse than suspicious. It's public. Nothing natural about that. A mysterious sickness would be the perfect medicine if such a thing could be created and administered without lasting evidence of its administration.

Scratch after discordant scratch, the incessant grating of chalk chips over slate tablets continued, seemingly as much the natural noise of the place as a result of the solitary figures strewn throughout the hall. Lane stood and stared down at his drawings, waiting for inspiration, going over and over the tactics and directions that couldn't work, waiting for one of them to surrender. Slowly, elongating the moment, he lowered a black boot onto the surface of his roughly gestured sketches and rotated the boot on its heel, back and forth until the images were a semicircle of concentric white texture on the dark gray background.

Lane put a hand to Wima's right shoulder as though she were a friend and, half kneeling, half crouching, brought his head between her head and the upright spear in her left hand. The pond reflected her spear and just below the spear's tip the crescent moon hovered in a bright nacre smile, its two tips parallel with the spear's point. An artifact of man, a shape from the heavens, and a serendipitous perspective diagramming the invention of the traditional weapon of the Karabas guard.

‡ ‡ ‡

The surrounding Upper Bank buildings shrank to a playful toy-like size to accommodate Jofe crawling through their midst. Dark brown bronze so cleverly fitted together that no seam showed along his entire surface, Jofe would have been one hundred feet tall if he'd chosen to stand. Instead he was planted solidly on all fours, head turned to the side with a wide beaming smile of lightheartedness. One with legs around his neck and the other with comparatively tiny arms around his great stomach, two enormous bronze toddlers clung to Jofe, pulling themselves up or him down, possessed by the same naïve exuberance that had hold of their father.

"And his older sister...?" Lane watched Flood for any hints or undertones in the answer.

"Lily."

"Lily..."

The sky was unnaturally blue. Uncomfortably blue. Purest crisp clean blue and through it the midday sun beat down unseasonably hot, making the blue itself feel

181

overwhelming and invasive, seeping through clothing and creeping into the shadows, saturating everything it touched. The rampant blue made Jofe black by comparison and was pushing the crowds attending his temple into the spacious shade of his belly and chest.

"Think she was suzerain's favorite when he was still alive. Perhaps as she was his first scion."

"Did it ever bother him that his first scion was na male?"

"Do na think so. The suzerain always seemed pleased on his eldest daughter."

Several score people sat around the shaded park beneath Jofe's burly torso, fanning themselves and resting while their children played. The ear-piercing shrieks, woops and squeals of pleasure were punctuated occasionally by a howl of pain or a wail of frustration. And through this symphony of signals the parents monitored the children they could not see. The youngsters, immune to the blazing light, played a complex game of tag whose rules had been hallowed by generations of little people before them, climbing up, sliding down and leaping from the calves, angles, and feet of the bronze giant.

"And she? Did she mind she was na son to him?"

"Na know if she minded being a girl but na never acted like a lady in public."

Lane said nothing, waiting, and leaned back against one of the titanic wrists. Though more comfortable now, unless he craned his neck he could no longer see Flood, who leaned directly next to him. So he looked away across the open temple floor and up to the bronze belly that formed the concave ceiling above them. Waiting.

"When Lily was about twelve, Cirrus had recently started learning ta hunt and spent many days that summer hunting game and fowl in the mountains. Natural, the palace staff would na let him go without company for carrying supplies and creating a comfortable base camp from which Cirrus explores. And once the entourage was committed, Lily would beg to come along. Insist she come along, proper. Cirrus and the staff preferred she stay home. Just made our jobs harder. Another scion of the suzerain ta keep out of harm.

"Summer ending and harvest festival only days away Cirrus asked and was granted one final hunting trip that summer and Lily, as usual, inserted herself. She proposed a challenge ta him. A bet. Honor ta the first of them as kill a bird and returns it as proof ta the staff pavilion from where they start.

"She went out on a mountain-worthy pony and carried only a composite bow and a few quarrels. She'd been out a long time when she caught a fantail taking flight and spurred her pony, managing to wing the bird while riding up steep and treacherous slope. So treacherous that even as she hit the bird her pony stepped inta deep crevasse and broke its leg.

She jumped off pony and began ta scour higher ground for that bird. When she finally found it she took off running, several miles, all ways back through the mountains ta the tent we'd pitched."

The morning's rain had been reabsorbed into the world where the sun's blinding directness could reach around the edges of Jofe. At the shaded temple's center the rain had never reached. But near the edge where they sat the ground was still damp, and Lane's nostrils stung with the clean smell of the rain as it disappeared. "Can imagine." Flood looked at Lane, a little surprised at the statement. Lane was still watching the idle and active devotees of Paternalism.

"Game thing is that dona think she loved ponies before, but after then she started ta adore several palace stabled colts."

"And did she win the bet with her brother?"

"Aye. She did. Cirrus never even got a bird. Her run was na necessary."

"And her pony?"

"Never found, so it died do suppose."

Upper Bank residents continued to trickle into Jofe's shadow, filling the park, and from a distance the scene created a litter of tiny animated dolls, waiting for the gigantic metal infants to dismount their father and play with them instead.

"Guess na need say goodbye to you but do need ta leave."

"Do come find again...Lane. Enjoy our visits much."

"Take care, ancient."

The birds around Jofe flitted above his head, perched on his back, flew beneath his abdomen, and harried his limbs like so many mosquitoes. And packed as tightly as he was among the incongruous stone buildings, weighed down with children, pestered by the birds, and bearing the brunt of the sunlight, Jofe had not moved a muscle, not a twitch or tick, in living memory.

‡ ‡ ‡

A waterfall of fiery motes cascaded, glittering and then winking out of existence as they expended themselves. Up the stream at the source of the brilliant orange sparks, a tiny steel splinter dug its head determinedly into the grindstone, throwing off a shower of light with the undesired matter at its tip. The grating sustained screech of the rough stone wheel as it traded matter for matter, like the sound of painful satisfaction, accompanied the fireworks and the burning smell of friction. Temporarily satisfied or exhausted from the effort, the rice grain-sized sliver of metal withdrew, revealing as it did the tiny barbs that ribbed its surface, angled into its sharpened point.

Lane held the tiny metal piece to the light and turned and tipped it. Satisfied, he raised a fine needle the length of his hand into which he fitted the unsharpened end of the slightly finer steel speck. Turning the joined needle upside down he shook the device until the silver splinter dropped into his open hand. Picking up the minute sliver, he pricked the ball of his other hand and when a drop of blood pooled on the skin's surface, Lane carefully gathered the drop into the slight cavity at the end of the long needle. Into this now red receptacle he reinserted the steel splinter so that the blood came up around the edges, making a ruby collar at their intersection.

Again, Lane dangled the needle, tip down, the light of the hot furnace glowing yellow behind it. Swing, twitch, and shake as he might, the barbed head held onto its needle body as its crimson necklace darkened, thickened, and dried. Lane plunged the needle into a yellow sponge on the table and then jerked it back again so quickly its motion seemed only a trick of the light. No sound. No mark upon the sponge. But the thin line of steel he held now ended in a headless red collar.

‡ ‡ ‡

Cye's reclining position was only a foot removed from the rock surface he studied, hammer and chisel in hand. Periodically he raised the chisel briskly, knocked once, paused, knocked twice more in quick succession, and then pulled both implements away again to assess. Despite the irregular supply of rock he dislodged directly above himself, Cye's beige tunic, buttoned smartly at the sleeves and collar, was inexplicably clean.

The blade came up again and clack, clack-clack, another three tiny pieces of stone were flicked off the sculpture emerging from the uneven surface. As far across as Cye was long the egg protruded from the rock, nestled into the curve where the column capital spread out into the ceiling. Along most of its shell the curve ran immaculately smooth except for a few ragged cracks converging near its crest where the casing exploded into a rough blob of stone jamming through from the inside of the egg. This surfacing figure was plausibly and grotesquely premature in its birth so that without Cye's regular attacks of the steel to the stone, it might have been a frighteningly finished piece just as it was.

The hammock supporting Cye was tied around the top of one of Cian's columns, the braided rope securing it snaking over and through several of the column's uppermost sculptures. The hammock brushed the stomach of a large incongruous rabbit character carved from the column so that its ears nearly touched the ceiling, and behind these ears Cye had wedged two thick candles, burning horns atop the already unlikely addition to the local menagerie.

The column dropped down so far from where Cye lay cozied to the ceiling that details along the distant path up the main avenue of Cian's great hall were as indistinct from where Cye lay as his carving would be for those who might pass below. Cye brushed a fleck of stone off a bandage around the middle of his forearm and waited until - click - it struck the floor and sent the echoing news scaling back up the mighty column.

"You've energy for the Kamakura?"

A spider webbing of lines, noosed around the necks and limbs of a dozen older Cian ceiling carvings, converged towards another circular hammock trapping Lane against Cian's roof two body lengths out into the main avenue from Cye's already precarious position. One hundred feet directly above the well worn path to the raised teaching stage, Lane lay with his head turned toward Cye, tools in hand resting at his sides. The light from the two candles on the rabbit's head silhouetted Cye entirely so that Lane could see a crisp shape and no detail. No footsteps stirred the dust below. No voices broke the sepulcher silence. The cavern's many lamps were lit but low, leaving the pair adrift in a half light frozen seething sea of creatures and characters.

"Aye and na."

"How na energized? Thought your bedding was in Humility's quarter. With Bent captain of your Atar team, the contest'll be peach anyway and a win na too rocky."

"Spot. Atar at the Kamakura will shine for sure. It's na that. Deadline for my final lead is coming soon and Kamakura festivities marks summer's end. The luxury of time is stolen away by the gift itself."

"And Spirit? Does he exist even?"

Cye laughed and the sound echoed, rebounding harshly in the tomblike stillness of the manufactured grotto. "Aye. He does exist. Spirit was out of the city for a long time but it seems his migration has come full circle recently."

"Time doesna matter, Cye. Success is sure for you. As always."

"Grats, Lane. Will miss carving Cian with you when our time here is over."

"Samewise, Cye."

Lane released the hammer and chisel and wiped his hands on his loose thin black pants. Pressing his hands together at the first knuckles with his finger pointing inwards at his chest he increased the pressure until several of the joints popped in quick succession, sacrilegiously loud and coarse without background noise to mask it. Though he was too near the ceiling to see it, Lane picked up the hammer and started tossing it absently sideways across his stomach, each departure and arrival heralded only by the thump of the leather wrapped handle on his palm.

"I'll miss Cian too. More Master Weaver and Master Maya than Doyen Horn, but him as well. We're lucky sheep to have such exceptional shepherds."

"Aye. Will miss being with Master Maya and talking with Master Weaver."

"As long as the destination city gets mail, hear tell that Master Weaver sends letters to his Jacks. Masters are na supposed to but..." Cye trailed off for a moment, then, "Have you chosen your migration path after getting Cian card?"

"Na. Though do have a person who wants to come away with me."

"A dab?!" Lane could practically hear the smirk he couldn't see on Cye's face.

"Na sure she's serious. And even if she'd come, hardly know her. And from what do know, would make na sense to leave with her."

"Then why tell me she wants to go away with you?"

"Truthful, na sure why." Lane paused. "Something about her. Complicated." He paused again. "You? Know you where you'll go after Cian?"

"I would rather na pick, proper. The world will point the way."

Neither of them continued and the pause drew into a silence until the staccato triple clacking of metal on rock began again. Lane turned towards the ceiling and his work, the hammer arrested in his hand. Out of the rock above him the shoulder, neck and head of some animal was emerging, pointed down at an angle to stare down Cian's visitors just as they entered the great hall. The beast was far from finished. So far from complete that only its rough outline gave hints to its underlying character. A long, nearly-equine head ended abruptly in a roughly ursine muzzle, both contrasting sharply with the high forehead and deep brows of a man. Lane tried to look into the eyes of the unfinished being, and a momentary shudder of pleasurable horror wracked his body, wondering what this thing might become. In its blind rudeness and undefined mouth its mood was hidden deep, an emotional leviathan waiting to break through the stone surface.

‡ ‡ ‡

Lane's compacted shape perching, dark and feather-patterned, atop the titanic wooden statue rocked gently in the shadows between two rafters. There were no visitors this morning, nor probably would there be today. He floated down the back of the carving, cape spread into a semicircular wingspan, a luxuriously slow, airy descent. There was a soft thud and rustle of fabric as the mantle folded in again. The down-curving beak struck up at a jaunty angle, and beneath it, Lane looked out the door of the temple into a refreshing, warm, autumnal morning.

With the sun still newly minted in Karabas, already crowds of twenty and thirty at a time streamed by Lane's marginalized temple. The drum banging was relentless. Boom. Boom-Boom. Boom Boom, Boom-Boom. Every group, practically every citizen old enough to walk had his own stretched leather and resonating bowl. The incessant pounding was festive at first. Then tiring. Then quickly irritating. Before long, the thumping would become so uniform that it had the decency to fade away entirely from consciousness, leaving some room again for less repetitive sounds.

A dozen drums passed the temple steps, held high by twice as many hands, and Lane fell in behind them, just ahead of the next clump of the beasts. Drafting in a aromatic wake, the thin banner overhead was only a secondary signal to the allegiance of the crowd he trailed. Rich green-on-green fresh cut fujies, the flower of the avatar of Selfishness, were pinned onto hats, up along sleeves, and in garlands festooning the breasts of several of the women. The dying plants smelled intoxicatingly sweet. The Selfishness quarter had little hope in the Kamakura today but the team for Composure from the lower bank, their rival, traditionally did terribly. For the people of a small quarter like Selfishness, having their nemesis humiliated was nearly as good as winning themselves.

Though the street had grown into a road as they swept down towards the river, the alleys feeding onto the main road injected people faster than the infrastructure could accommodate. Individual clusters from each quarter jostled together boisterously. The lightheartedness might last, the revelry would certainly wax as the day wore on, but they would never stay together. Never. Separation from one's friends was a physical certainty today. But just now, however, the press of shoulders was perfect. Physical, impersonally intimate, with a little room left to breathe.

The last stretch before the river belonged to the temple for Strength and it had been visually claimed in Lina's name, draped so thick with clinquant streamers hatched with wide bands of black that the buildings were only occasionally visible. Similarly obscured by these gaudy ribbons, the blacksmith's hall was releasing smoke from its coverless mouth in staccato puffs as though it were trying to blow smoke rings. As he drifted forward slowly with the crowd, Lane came even with the entrance and saw inside bent shadowy shapes continuing to feed the fires as he once had on each Festival day, a lifetime ago.

Arrested by something too good to pass by, the multitudes were backing up on the bridge to watch so that the traffic onto the River Island came to a halt. Animals, avatars, mockeries, the recognizables from Karabas history, no one wore their day clothes today. Face paint, printed fabrics, outlandish hats, and makeshift stilts - most wore their quarter's flower and many of the throng had color coordinated for their quarter as well. But these were overtones riding a sunny tempest of stories, jokes, traditions, and meanings. In the midst of this costume heterogeneity thumping and chattering as loud as they could, the ten men and women standing quietly on the downstream bridge rail stood out. Each was coated with thick pasty gel, each coating roughly colored for the primary color of the quarter they represented. Head to toe it was slathered on their naked bodies, matting down hair and making the rack of taut young bodies both attractively primal and disgustingly dirty. All ten heads faced outwards to the river, down into the furious moiling white water. There might have been at most twice that many insulated bodies poised on the Lower Bank main bridge rail. Many quarters couldn't find a champion to swim for them. Few were dumb enough to do it once and none who survived were ever asked to repeat the performance. Shoulders and stomachs surrounded Lane so tightly that he had to twist and hoist himself up a bit using these same shoulders to see the river's state. A few rocks peeked out through the foam, but struggled just to keep their noses above the rushing froth. The contest might not last a minute.

Directly in front of Lane a young man was dressed as Sarn in his prime, covered in tiny blue violets and carrying a full sized shovel. Why? Lugging that around all day was lunacy. As soon as the lowing of the palace long horns rang out for the first time, this misguided shovel bearer started dancing from foot to foot frantically, trying to see what had not yet happened. The divers were still, tensed. The brassy moan of the horns washed over the crowd again, echoing off the buildings from both sides of the river; and the divers were gone. A comparative hush fell over the crowd. Releasing a long held breath, a cry went up from the front row of the audience and then swept back across the bridge as excitement translated back through the layers of people leaving the exciting event caught at the bridge rail. The idiot's frantic dancing was more than Lane could suffer, and clamping down on a shoulder and handful of violet petals, Lane swung the halfwit behind him, trading places so the man's jerking was someone else's concern.

The tide of humanity was sweeping forcefully on toward the River Island and Lane fought against the press of people to a spot against the bridge rail. In the normal course of events a person who jumped off the bridge would be swept past the tip of the River Island in under a minute. Even a strong swimmer struggling directly against the current might delay when they passed the eyot's tip by at most a few seconds. And indeed, most of the jumpers were long gone and would probably be half a day walking back up through the mountains to the city. Occasionally though, a jumper could grab onto a rock in the rapids, delaying when they passed the island's tip for as long as they could hold their anchor - no mean feat given the unrelenting pressure, capricious turbulence, and icy temperature of the water. Under the current conditions, that three of the ten jumpers had caught themselves on rocks above or just below the surface was remarkable. Contingents from each of these three successful quarters spread along the length of the bridge rail, screaming, chanting, encouraging, taunting members of the quarters whose swimmers were long gone down the river, and generally wasting their breath. From the midst of the foment, the river's thunder would entirely drown out those slight sounds. While the last man past the island's tip was a source of tremendous pride to the winning quarter, it was a secondary victory on the day and truthfully, there was little to watch or comment on. So after a few minutes, as it became clear that the jumpers all had secure holds, the crowd along the rail began to thin. It could take hours before the water cut all but one of them loose, and it was always possible that more jumpers had found purchase on similar jagged river teeth from their leap off the Lower Bank main bridge.

Stepping off the rail and back into the festive crush, Lane was immediately forced down into the shuffling pace of the mob. At least there was still movement. That would last only as long as there was space on the Flat. Once the Flat was full, the futile backup would require considerable energy to work through. Lane looked down and saw he had a temporary, comical honor guard. A brown mouse not much higher than his waist and a black rabbit not much taller than the mouse jostled him from either side, both banging little hand drums with conviction. Their enthusiasm mellowed the tightness in his stomach for a moment. This annual mass hysteria, so central to the rhythm of life in Karabas, its excesses so steeped in city tradition, made it possible for the population to ignore the impending trampling they would give each other as the day wore on. And using that denial they collectively lost themselves each year in the engrossing entertainment of being excited together.

Rounding the edge of the right Alley, the length of the Flat came into view as a rolling sea of heads and hats. For a quarter of a mile down the island and all the way to the walls of both Alleys that framed the rough triangular region, the heads rode so close together that shoulders were scarcely visible. Fifty feet above this undulating surface the simple colored sails used to block the summer sun had been replaced for the day by banners ten feet across, spanning the shrinking chasm between the Alleys, one banner for each quarter. These ribbons with their intricate language of the cities avatars bathed the rippling tide of heads with iridescent illumination, made physical by the dust kicked up by the countless unseen shuffling feet. The banners sagged across the span, rising and filling as the warm autumn breeze ran down the island, then deflating again in a sigh, over and over again in waves down through the queue of the sixty banners.

Quick double step - jump. Lane skipped over an open garbage hole in the ground. With the crowd packed so tight the holes were impossible to see even in the daylight. Several legs would take their last step of the day into that chute. The holes were a convenience across the year whose rough covers during the Kamakura were sometimes washed away by the crowds. His skip enlivened Lane for no good reason. Stride...stride...stride. Sanguine and sturdy. Going with the flow didn't necessitate shuffling with the herd.

To his left, just downstream from the lower basin of the Island Fountain, an enormous cage of wire mesh stood on an eye-level platform. The last event of the day was always a deadly animal with a fortune attached to it, should anyone be brave enough to enter the cage alone and unarmed to try to take it. Lane craned his head to verify the cage was empty, but the press of shoulders, so tight he could not turn around, swept him slowly on toward the heart of the festival. With each step, though, the pace slowed until the shuffling forward of the crowd had become nothing more than a packing in of bodies. And Lane was still only halfway down the Flat. The risers across the base of the Atar board were now visible over the heads around him. Lane would have preferred to drift to the right and head down to the Atar board's tip along the right side, but the eddy he found himself in was pulling strongly to the left, so he shrugged, pointed himself directly toward the left Alley and began forcing himself forward, trusting the current of people to drag him down the Flat as he swam across it.

Exhausting as it was to make progress through the packed throng, Lane got into a rhythm of extending his hands to a pair of unconnected shoulders, forcing them apart like spreading heavy curtains, and stepping quickly into the gap. Stroke, step, release. Stroke, step, release. By the time he passed the risers across the base of the Atar board and had begun pressing himself into the walkway between the left side risers and the board itself, he was dripping with sweat and rather enjoying the tight response of his muscles. Even over the primitive, moist odor of the natives through which he swam, he could smell his own pungent essence, sharper than the millions of decaying flowers around him and yet somehow foreign when he tried to place it.

The atarites spread out across the Flat, tessellating tiles of art upon which no foot tread, the reverence of tradition stronger than any physical barrier could have served. Each painted triangle of clay, three feet along each of its sides, resembled a tiny mountain, often capped with snow and craggy along the rise to its summit with outcroppings and intermediate peaks. Lifting the view from a single tile to the aggregate, one hundred tiles along each side, the entire composition was also a mountain. As Lane pushed along the left side tapering toward the point of the island, the dramatically foreshortened mountain spreading across the ground seemed unscalably tall, covered as it was in a maze of ridges, cliffs, and ravines. The effect was riveting, and Lane wondered what Sylvester would have made if he had had the chance. At this an ugly cloud of bile passed over Lane's face, poisoning his thoughts. Balling and then slowly releasing both fists, Lane plunged his mind back into the present, tempering his attitude with the roar of the bodies around him.

The massive Atar board pointed down toward the island's tip, echoing the rougher triangle formed by the two Alleys. In between the Alleys, temporary stands had been thrown up into a larger, encasing triangle of seats. The rows of seats had been filled for over a day already, though no one actually sat on the benches from the first light of the Kamakura until long after the sun set. Beyond the mounting risers the second and third floors of both Alleys were stuffed with people along every balcony elbowing for a view from every window. A number of bivouacs ran along the Alleys' walls, hung from thick hemp ropes tied to the balconies or slung up over the crest of the long buildings. Atop the Alleys, further risers ran the length of both buildings and from steel poles on the top of these risers, the quarters had anchored their streamers to sail down across the Flat.

The incessant drum banging, the raucous cheering, the occasional shrill whistles, were all joined now by the increasingly frequent coordinated stamping of feet from one section of the stands or another. A clump of people, colored and flowered for their quarter, would take up the stomping, shaking the stands in rough enthusiasm for their team. The teams sat along the first row of the risers, more formally robed in matching pants and a complex torso-wrapping of silks, loose in places but held tight across the chest and stomach. Muted silence, stoic expressions, and matching costumes all marked the Atar teams. The local caravan in which Lane was traveling threw flowers and copper coins to its representatives, mercurially colored for Adaptiveness. Shimmering in layers of glossy silver and gray, the twenty women – interesting - all women – received the shower without response, focusing out across the board or focused inward behind closed eyes.

At the tip of the expansive Atar field, in between the two bleachers that came short of touching on this far end, a wide rostrum nestled into the gap. Dwarfed by the temporary wooden structures on both sides, the rostrum held seating for no more than twenty people in a single row along its front and standing room for another thirty or forty, most of those Cirrus's guards, decked in the traditional emerald and armed with tri-tipped halberds. To either side of the rostrum, bookends to the tip of the Atar board, short fences had been built to save space and room to operate for the drum and horn sections.

The drum, a single instrument so large Lane could have stood upright inside it, nestled into a bowl carved for it into the Flat. A padded hammerhead the size of a human skull rested on the mottled sepia, rubbed smooth leather surface. Back up its shaft the mallet was levered off a short platform that stood next to the drum. Sitting idly on the platform was a shirtless, grotesque, mountain of a man whose features were bulbous and distorted. The growths along his back, shoulders, and neck sprouted such quantities of hair that several seemed as if they might have their own faces as well. Sacks of flab hung off the enormous limbs, hiding the necessarily prodigious muscles beneath. And the monster's posture was freakishly relaxed and contented for such an imperfect mortal shell. As though to offset this embarrassing spectacle, thirteen heralds stood across the Atar board's tip in smart black dress, their long brass horns mounted in front of them.

Split by the rostrum, half the crowd bent back around behind the horns and the other half behind the drum. Lane took a cleansing breath as he broke free of the press and paused at the foot of the rostrum stairs. A cordon of emerald guards enclosed the platform across the front and past the mounting stairs on either side. Soft, slow, untrained, the clown before Lane looked at him and blinked repeatedly without speaking. The guards might as well not be there for all the good they could do. They were symbols of protection mistaken for the protection itself. Lane was tempted to reach out between blinks, remove the dagger from the thick belt binding the guard's green kirtle, slit the unprotected throat with a flourish, and replace the dagger in its unornamented scabbard. He rehearsed the gesture several times in his mind and the guard cleared his throat awkwardly, but said nothing. Torn between wanting to wait the simpleton out and the boredom of the task, Lane finally relented.

"Fetch scion Lily, grunt."

Stretching out blink upon blink, the impasse continued. Perhaps the man was deaf. Or actually simple. Then with no clear next stimulus the man turned and took the stairs heavily, leaving the way before Lane open. The two nearest guards, only arm's length away on either side, made no move to cover the entrance. Comfortably ignorant. Blissfully indifferent, more likely. Lane snorted. And waited. And Lily appeared ten steps above him.

Head to toe she was Dawn. Military dress, authentically dust worn with a smart feminine edge and complete with the Loyalty flower, an orange-blue poinciana, perched on her shoulder like a floral familiar. The artificially thespian moment beat twice, and Lane grinned up at Lily's ethereal face.

"Yes. I was expecting him," she said over her shoulder and then to Lane she held out her hand to beckon him up, "Come up... please."

Lane mounted the stairs with a bounce, passing the lip of the stage by a step's height and then landing definitively next to her.

"Greetings, Lily. You are a dazzle Dawn." His arm slid around her narrow waist and found itself demoted to her elbow by the end of the next stride.

"You are my guest. No more. So behave yourself."

"Da. Bare." Touching the curved beak above him, Lane aped a hat tipping to the guards lining the back wall of the rostrum as they walked. "What dress wears Cirrus today?"

"My brother wears a panther this year. There." And Lily gestured with one hand, slowing Lane to a halt with the other.

The sculpted feline hood and half mask blended the black forehead and muzzle of the animal into Cirrus's lighter tan cheeks, mouth, and smooth jaw. Hinting without menace, a slight stretching extension of claws from the knuckles of the gloves was the only adornment in the otherwise simple, tailless black outfit. The suzerain-in-waiting reclined easily in a tall wicker chair framed in crimson cherry wood, modestly larger than the other similarly styled chairs lining the front of the rostrum.

Over the crest of the chair the regent leaned, whispering into the panther's ear. Her tall, thin body, clad in subdued greens beneath a long charcoal robe, folded at the waist in comfortable respect. Confident brushstrokes of ebony laid out elegant features on a pale skin canvas – and though kindly curved lips moved softly near Cirrus's ear, harder eyes slowly swept the Flat.

The view from the rostrum back up the Flat was magnificent. Fifty thousand people, stacked up to the top of the Alleys and stretching back to the Palace, all funneling into the arrowhead of the Atar board – itself the only uninhabited space – horizontal or vertical – left on the island. The pennants above drowned the crowd in a riot of washing colors and the packed populace, now immobilized by their own density, swayed slowly like underwater vegetation. Loud and constant enough to be silent, the cacophony of the city had become, like the roar of the river, deafening only in its absence.

Gilded to hide their rust, a golden robed crew of sycophantic advisors and city elders ringed Cirrus and the Regent, waiting for an opening to insert themselves. As his aunt straightened up behind Cirrus, Lily stepped quickly forward, dragging Lane with her into the social opening. The ring surged forward a step, saw the opportunity evaporate, and reluctantly shifted back into place just out of earshot.

"Hello, Lily." At the mention of his sister's name, Cirrus turned in his chair.

"Good day, Auntie." The regent's expression did not so much as flicker from its pleasant expression.

"And who is this with you, Lily?" The scrutiny Lane received showed disapproval, but no surprise. He was not the first man Lily had used to needle her aunt and brother.

"He is a friend of mine."

"Yes. I am sure he is."

"Am 'Lane,' regent." And he executed a facetious little bow for her, catching a sweet, tangy odor briefly as his nose advanced and then retreated.

"You don't bow to the regent. You bow to your suzerain, soon to be crowned." Disdain and control. Lane held her eyes for a moment. He liked her and he smiled at her, to no outward effect.

"Oh, let him alone." And Cirrus waved his aunt back into the ring of attendants. Then still sitting, he extended a hand toward Lane. "Bowing is so dull." Lane took the offered hand. Warm, dry, strong, friendly, firm. "Hi, sister." Lily bent down stiffly and Cirrus gave her a formal kiss on her cheek. "Where did you meet this one?"

"I caught him in the Palace, looking for something to steal."

Cirrus gave Lily a dark look, surveyed the immediate audience of Karabas dignitaries, then laughed instead and placed his feet up on the rail of the rostrum. "Well? Did you get anything good, Lane?"

"Aye. Did get some. Grats." Lane grinned. "But proper, am na sure yet how deluxe it will be." No touch of smile creased Lily's face, causing Cirrus to laugh again, more genuinely this time.

The moaning chord of thirteen horns grew to a crescendo and then receded in volume to an echo quickly absorbed by the mass of humanity padding the surfaces of the Flat. Everyone, even Cirrus, leaned forward, watching the still empty Atar board. From beside the seat of the primary scion, the board spread out as though these prime seats were perched at the tip of an unascendable mountain, pockmarked with untraversable ridges and ravines so that even moving laterally across the mountain looked impossible. And onto this surface floated the Atar players, one by one, quickly and matter-of-factly. On they came for several minutes, entering from all three sides of the board, raising and lowering their hands as they stopped on an atarite. Stopping so that no two players were on adjacent tiles. They flew across the surface of the mountain and its look of unscalability heightened the illusion of preternatural motion. The city's roar was relatively quiet, its attention on the strategy as members each placed themselves strewn across the board for reach or clumped together for safety. Onto the mountain they came in a steady stream until there were twenty players for each of the sixty teams, one team for each of the Karabas avatars. The team colors so intermingled that the results of the first phase of the game were apparent only in the gross distributions and balances of the identifying hues.

The players hovered, waiting. The crowd waited with them. The hush became louder and louder waiting for the – thud. Thud. Thud. Thud. Jerseys of magenta shifted on the board, one jersey gliding to one adjacent tile with each beat of the massive drum, until all twenty had taken adjacent positions and – thud. Thud. Thud. Continuing on in time to the incessant pounding, players wrapped in mustard tops began to move. The disfigured giant stood now on his platform, pressing down on the handle to raise the hammerhead, releasing – thud – and catching it on its slight bounce from the drum, pressing down again without a pause. The sweat ran down the piebald back of the beast in sheets, but the routine was invariant. Three seconds between beats was all each player had to choose and move. No talking, no signals, no waiting. And then a long, long wait until their turn to move came around again. Each team moved in order just as did each player on a team.

Sweet warm autumn air filled Lane's lungs. Lily was pulling him toward two empty seats along the rostrum a few steps from Cirrus. "Lane." Lily paused, looking at Cirrus. "Is today the day?"

"Are you of a different mind about your brother?"

Lily continued her fixed stare. "No. But I cannot be involved. I cannot be associated or connected with it in any way. And you are my guest here. This is a very public place. It had better not be here." Lane shrugged a non-committal shrug, which Lily either missed or ignored. "I certainly cannot protect you here."

Lane smiled at this and put a hand on her knee, "Will na expect you to island me. Will na require it. Am exact enough for this work." With a friendly shake of her knee, "It's a bright day. Na be nerved."

A single horn blew a short tone, signaling the first player elimination of the day. Blocked from all three adjacent tiles by other players, a rose-colored player for Beauty knelt on one knee toward the rostrum, and then jogged off the field. The shifting of the other rose-robed players continued without a break. The audience jeered its disapproval at the poor play – there was no good excuse for blocking in another member of your own team due to poor coordination rather than for strategic reasons.

Lane told Lily a joke. He laughed with his head thrown back to help her relax. Even paid her a compliment – one she even deserved. Lily responded to Lane curtly and nervously. Her hard raw beauty floated in the costumed combat dress, framed like an etched silver icon on a rough-worn battle shield. He stopped the dialog, watching her, drinking the vision of her sculpted youth. Lane stood and stepped away, leaving Lily alone with her anxiety.

A brighter chord from several horns saturated the air. The last player remaining on the outside row along the board's right side was stepping in from the edge with a satisfied air. As his second intricately laced boot fell into place on the new atarite, a horde of ununiformed ragamuffins spilled over the first line of spectators along that same side of the board. In a frenzied industrious moment the little hands had seized all hundred and ninety nine tiles, dragging them backward into the risers. Though many of these motley helpers were smaller than the atarites they removed, the board was reduced to ninety nine tiles on each of its three sides in a few heart beats, and both the ragged mob and the banished tiles were gone without a ripple on the surface. The biting tri-tone of horns dissipated in the air, cut short by – thud. Thud. Thud.

"That was a peach step! Da, Master?" Lane leaned in over Cirrus's right side.

Dropping his feet from the front rail and leaving his comfortable recline to peer down over the edge of the rostrum, Cirrus took a moment to study the now tighter board. The black satin material running down the primary scion's strong curved back seemed light, and absorbent – a good choice for today.

"It was an excellent play indeed! Paternity will not last many more rounds now. And Artistry may as well leave the field immediately." Up and down the rostrum rail, the family and sycophants were all now leaning out, watching the contest with increasing intensity. "I will wager though that he pays personally for that move. It certainly helped Humor's cause, but that group he has now pinned in will make sure at least he goes with them off the field."

"It will take three steps at least to get Humor's man off the board. Na less."

"Wrong....'Lane' you said?"

"Lane."

"You're wrong, Lane. I'll give you one hundred pieces if he lasts four rounds."

"But na incentive now for others to go after him..."

"Revenge is always an unofficial part of everyone's strategy." Cirrus and Lane smiled at each other.

"Na the truly great players. Na the players that win."

"You are right, of course. Ideally." But Cirrus was not wearing a tamed face. "Ideally. But really, most players have little discipline. Right? Watch. I stand by my statement. I will give you one hundred pieces if your man makes three moves before he kneels to me."

"Will be sorry ta take your pieces, but will certainly drink with those pieces and toast about your health."

"Do not drink those pieces just yet! Drinks, on the other hand..." and with a finger jab, a gesture, and a pair a fingers he sent a silent demand across the rostrum to a boy in emerald livery at the back of the stage.

On some unnoticed signal, the full herd of horns let loose a blaring announcement. One of the rapids jumpers must have won, though the news of which quarter did not travel as fast. Lane imagined the last swimmer hearing the news himself, numb and senseless from the icy torrent. He imagined the swimmer letting go in an ecstasy of release, shooting downstream past the island tip, perhaps coming to rest in an eddy far downstream, face down, limp in the watery casket. Or perhaps the muscles could not be forced to act and the champion remained in play, clamped to the rock well after the competition had ended. Trapped in place by his own recalcitrant body in a living rigor mortis. Like expanding concentric waves, news of this winner would ripple through the crowd, out from both of the main bridges, crashing through each other near the top of the Atar board, and on to the rostrum with several versions of the same story, all improved on their individual paths through the crowd.

In long colorful snakes of dancers the competitive cotillion played itself out across the daunting mountain range.

Players were ejected from the Atar floor at a regular clip and their environment collapsed at a similar pace, maintaining the close quarters that made the prismatic serpents mesmerizing to watch. The late afternoon sun lit ten of these crisscrossed lines and clumps of players, laying elongated shadows behind each of them. A forked line of older men in periwinkle wraps, recently in position to clear the field, was now being pushed inexorably into the peak of the mountain, forced to consume itself one sacrificed player at a time to maintain the required free space as it was compressed. The city held a collective hush, leaning forward in anticipation, and Cirrus leaned forward with them. From behind Cirrus's chair, Lane scanned the population of the rostrum, all at the rail, leaning out, some precariously, even the serving boys craned their necks to watch Patience run off the board. There it was. Bulging almost imperceptibly under the soft black fabric, the muscles prepared to change the arc of the bone scaffolding that held them in place. Cirrus was reclining.

Lane began a rapid inhale, as he needed to be exhaling in no more than a moment. The back would touch the chair there, there, and there. The moment would have to do. With blinding speed, Lane began to prepare. A jerk of his left arm and he held the long delicate needle between his thumb and forefinger. At the same time his right hand had made it up to his ear, extracted the barbed sliver of metal from the inside of his mask, made it back down to his waist again, and had fitted the splinter on the end of the needle. Exhale, down below Cirrus's left shoulder, a down little more, and...push. Through one of the regular gaps in the wicker of the chair the needle slid. It passed through the black satin draping Cirrus's back without resistance, and immediately returned the resistance of flesh back along its length to Lane's fingers. Deeper. Deeper still? Retract! And out the needle came again, through the pin prick puncture wound, through the cloth that immediately closed into its absence, and threaded peacefully back through the wicker lattice. Without its tip.

There was no way to be certain what effect leaving a barbed metal splinter in someone's heart would have, but whatever the result, it wasn't likely to appear to be poison.

The needle shot back up Lane's right sleeve and he had accomplished nearly an entire step right before Cirrus reacted, jerking forward and clutching both hands to his breast with a gasp. Within moments the primary scion was two circles deep in concern that for a moment went voiced but unheard, drowned out by the shrill tone announcing the removal of another row from the Atar board. Straightening, Cirrus struck off and waved away the hands of support covering him and hovering nearby.

"I am fine. Fine." Cirrus took an experimental breath without a wince. "I just had a chest pain for a moment but it is gone now." With one hand he rubbed his left pectoral and with his other the muscle below his left shoulder blade, then pushed his chest forward to stretch out, then relaxed again and made a show of reclining. "I'm fine." And he thumped his chest for emphasis. The crowd of dignitaries seemed unsatisfied, or disappointed, but they retreated slowly and were reabsorbed by the accelerating competition below them.

Lily crossed and uncrossed and then recrossed her toned arms over the dusty leather jerkin covering her breasts. Without warning after several minutes staring out over the Atar board she clipped out a petulant question. "Well? Is today the day or not? I really cannot be kept waiting like this."

"Your brother will live out the day."

"Then what are you doing here?" Lily's exasperation was understandable but annoying .

"Would you like me to work Cirrus for you now?"

"No! My point is why did you come if you are not here to," she paused uncomfortably but seemingly without concern for who might be listening, "if you are not here to...do your job."

"Job? Have been paid na pieces yet. It is na more than a favor so far."

Lily turned on him at this, "Is money all you are in this for?" and gave Lane a convincing show of actually being hurt.

"Easy rest, little dove. More than pieces brought me here today." Lane drew his hand down Lily's arm from her shoulder to her elbow. His answer seemed to have satisfied both of them, though for different reasons.

Thud. Thud. Thud. The misshapen mountainous coxswain continued to beat out the moments with inhuman consistency. More than three hours into the drumming with no noticeable change in the strength or pacing of the hammer strokes. Perhaps the beast was unaware of the passing of time, and so duration of effort never occurred to him as a limitation.

Chipped away piece by piece, what had started as an expansive mountain range of a board had been whittled down to a precarious peak by the movements of the players. Now three teams of a few members each perched on a board only nine atarites on a side. With six players left, the remaining players for Patience were at an odd disadvantage, being as they were ahead of Dishonesty by a player and at double the three remaining players for Humility. The game would go to Patience unless Humility and Dishonesty implicitly cooperated. Then with Patience off the board, Dishonesty would polish off Humility as well. And as Patience was the traditional rival quarter for Humility, forcing Patience into the third place seat would be a victory of a sort. Still a little sad. So late in the contest Bent was still in play for Humility. He had no control over his teammates so no shame for him, but the city was palpably disappointed as the deal began to play out.

Already, a wedge of Dishonesty's gold and Humility's grey was driving through the pack of Patience's sky blue robes. Loose glittering blouses cinched over golden tights, fans of red roses spreading across their backs, the wedge head looked like nothing so much as a muster of peacocks on a mission. Drafting in their wake came an understated trio dressed in simple light grey tunics tied with darker gray sashes over deep gray shapeless pants. Thud. Thud. Thud. The herd of blue cloaks shifted, splitting to survive, releasing glimpses of their vermillion linings as they retreated from tile to tile.

"Are hale again, Cirrus?"

"I am. I wish people would stop asking me. No. No. It is fine. I just do not need a nursemaid any more. It hurts a little still but I believe it is going away. I am sure it is nothing."

"Hopefully it will na linger too long."

"Yes hopefully..." Cirrus was interrupted by a runner who had been pushing laboriously through the Flat for over an hour to bring the suzerain-to-be firsthand news of the River Race. Flushed and saltwater saturated, the young man's face pressed itself between the rostrum railing bars just below Cirrus's knees.

"Sir. Pessimism held her spot for nearly six hours, sir. Apparently the last of the Lower Bank swimmers had been swept on an hour or more before, but no one could get her attention, sir, and she held on until she let go, sir. They are going to look for her body downstream, sir, but it could take a day or two. Sir, shall we bring her to you when we find her if she is alive still, sir?"

"Thank you. No need to bring her to me. But send her these from me," and Cirrus shook out the dregs and sediment from two silver chalices on the rail in front of him, then handed them through the railing. "If she didn't survive, send them to the temple instead." Jumping aside obediently to release the blocked view of the Atar board, the runner sank back into the churning crowd below, dismissed by the wave of a black velvet paw.

Patience had been washed entirely from the board, leaving Dishonesty with four players and Humility with three. The board was not yet contracted but no reasonable play series left Humility with the board. Second place out of sixty teams was a quality placement. Disappointing but to be expected.

Extending on an elongated wrist past the dark draping forearm cuff, the regent's pale bony hand clamped down in grim concern on the panther's shoulder. Her touch was barely completed before Cirrus was shrugging it off again.

"Please, please do not ask me how I am. The question is so tedious," turning to see the hand attached to his guardian the budding suzerain's tone lightened slightly. "Oh. Hi. The pain is gone. It was just a moment, nothing more."

"You are my ward, sir. The state of your health is my business."

"Then be happy it was nothing serious, Auntie."

Her drawn face remained impassive as she withdrew her hand. Turning toward Lane, her face was framed by a deep jade cloth, itself draped over with a mute grey hood. Wrinkle framed and unpainted eyes regarded Lane casually. Appraising him as though from force of habit.

"The day will be over soon." It was entirely unclear whether this was meant for Lane or for Cirrus. Lane waited, but Cirrus, leaning out with his arms on the rail, was either ignoring the statement, hadn't heard it, or assumed it had not been meant for him. This was probably an invitation for Lane to leave.

"Aye, Regent. It's been a peach day. Will see what night brings."

"And are we likely to see you again, young man?"

"Na likely, Regent. Today was all could ask for. Grats for the opportunity." Lane gave her another bow he did not mean, but this time she accepted it without comment, standing stately and cold as he bent, turning away imperiously as he unbent. He watched her walking slowly down the length of the rostrum, the festival's noises tugging hard at the hem of his attention.

The city was in hysterics. Normally Lane had habituated to the din of the crowd by this point in the Kamakura. But this was different. Waves of coordinated screaming shook the temporary structure, and the swells were increasing. Spreading out like long welcoming arms, the two Alleys of the Flat held up an orange sky marbled with veins of ruby red, slipping in slices through the comb of temple standards high overhead. Tens of thousands of tiny bodies stood thirty rows deep up three flights to the tops of the buildings, jumping about so that they shook the constructions with their energy and were bounced on the shock waves already running through their seats in a reinforcing cycle. As dusk came down over the festival, bitumen torches had been lit and the sharp bitter smoke from the burning pitch flavored the warm air.

Somehow, the Atar board was not as it should have been. Now only four atarites on a side, there were only five players left on the board, itself now seemingly a tiny jagged spike of rock. And only two of those players wore the gaudy dress of Dishonesty. One. Two. Three. Hard to see in the failing twilight, Humility's three remaining members were still there. And the dance of the five players, paced by the consistent pounding of the drum and punctuated by the mob around them, swirled in a tightening spiral. A horn blast and another row was swept away. No room left and Dishonesty backed into a corner. The first with nowhere to go knelt and left the field, freeing the losing spot for his teammate who stepped into the same corner, the only space open for him. Thud, step. Thud, step. Thud, step. And Humility had packed the corner in. Thud. Kneel. Leave. And the silence of the drum was as loud as the pandemonium the city unleashed on itself. The last three members of Humility swooned where they stood, and the tidal wave of Karabas broke its restraints and crashed over them and the tiny remaining island of a board.

Lane watched the audience spill onto the relatively empty Atar stage, leaving nothing but a seething raucous mass of humanity packing the Flat all the way back up stream to the very gates of the Island Palace. At first it was a wonderful catharsis to watch, until the desire to be in the press overcame Lane so that he couldn't wait to swim out into the ocean of anonymous intimacy.

To the stairs in two bounds and ready to soar down to the dirt, skipping the steps just to feel the air. Lily grabbed Lane's arm at the lip of the rostrum. Her radiant face held his eyes for a moment, serious, hopeful, and younger than he had remembered. But proud - and though she gripped his elbow, she waited.

"When Cirrus sleeps evermore, will come find you."

"So you're going to do...it...soon? I will still help you. I will. This was just a bad place..."

"You already have, love. Will come for you." And as he took off from the top step it seemed he might soar away over the torrent of jostling celebrants below rather than plunge down into them. As far as could be seen now up the Flat, it was one directionless parade of waving flags, burning torches, and handheld drum and horns. Through the ribbon ribs curving overhead a heavenly dome of crimson encased the city. And the bodies sucked into the city's heart quivered and shook, feeding off themselves, oblivious to the inevitable squeezing that would shoot them back out to the city's extremities. With a palpable rush of release, feet first, Lane allowed himself to be inserted.

‡ ‡ ‡

Eyelids shuttered up, exposing grey eyes shining out at the uncountable spray of stars who returned the light broken down into individual twinkles. Eyelids shuttered down again. But the darkness was just as bright, magnifying as it did the pounding, raging, febrile enthusiasm in which he swam. Drums, small horns, and increasingly the piercing shrill shriek of whistles raised such a storm that human voices had long since ceased to compete. The violent desperate shoving on all sides, having no outlet, consumed its own energy. In the darkness of his shuttered eyes, Lane felt his stomach muscles react as the pressure and compression ebbed and flowed, transmitted from the hips, elbows, and shoulders encasing him on all sides. With each compression of the crowd, their juices and odors were released, perfuming the night with the rank musty smell of effort.

Lane knew better than to fight the tides, and three hours later his drifting had carried him not quite yet as far even as the lower basin of the Island Fountain. Not that it mattered. He might have killed for a drink of water, but none was to be had this late in the festival, even for that price. But the mob wrapped him in a warm private cocoon, luxuriously hidden and still entirely included in the moment. The collective madness was clearly just that - an intoxicating insanity whose venom was proximity and whose antidote was isolation. The trick was simultaneously staying above it and savoring the pleasure of sinking down into it as well. With a roar, a sheet of scarlet lit his eyelids from the inside and Lane opened them to the slow waving of an enormous flag set ablaze by some foolish soul just forward of him.

If a new avatar was announced on the New Year's Eve, and consecrated the following noon, Humility's quarter would, for the honor it had achieved today, be the quarter divided to carve out a home for the newest temple. Humility's quarter was already small, and the entire crowd would hate to see its team divided, but tradition worked directly against this purpose. So, as often happened, the celebration had an edge of anticipation, a touch of concern for the fate of the victors. New avatars were rarely announced, but then again the previous one had had its New Year's apotheosis only over nine months ago. In any case it was not a serious crisis, as long as Cirrus turned out to be unavailable to preside over the event. Hopefully his heart would not hold out until then.

The crushing press of people broke left and right at the lower basin of the Island Fountain, and Lane's currents dragged him, thankfully, left and biased his eventual discharge from the Flat to be an Upper Bank one. Finding that he could not free either arm, pinned to his sides by sweaty neighbors whose arms in turn he was pinning down, a sudden boyish grin blossomed on Lane's face. He had pulled up his feet so that he held an ankle in each hand and floated along, buoyed up by the pressure of the collective need of those off the island to push their way to its heart and those already at its heart, tired of the noise and the exertion, to force their way back out again through these same arteries. After a minute he released his feet to find that he been lifted sufficiently that, even extended, his feet did not reach the ground. Lane allowed his whole body to relax, born along without effort two or three inches above the surface of the Flat. Flight itself would just then have been a weight compared to this. Less indulgent. Less pure. Less free.

From his slightly elevated vantage point, Lane could see the exhausted who were lucky enough, piling into the lower basin. Standing knee deep in icy water was by that point a lighter chore than fighting the crowd for space to breathe. Along both Alleys, just coming to an end to Lane's left and right, people who still had the strength were clinging to the walls and balconies, perching where they could to wait out the crush. A few limp bodies had been hoisted out of the way, often left draped unceremoniously over balcony rails or roped to sides of the Alley's like battered dolls on display.

Lily floated into the focus of his mind's eye, trying to find a place for herself in his future. He and she might be walking down out of the foothills through a valley of tiny blue flowers, the mountains and their former lives far behind them, holding hands and talking of where they would go. Or maybe instead, her pale elfin face would watch him dumbly through a few inches of water as he removed his hands from her neck and wiped them dry on his pants, kneeling by a bathing pool in the

Island Palace. Or perhaps, covered in the salty balm of sex, he would thrust himself into her again and again, grasping a thin muscular calf in either hand, looking out through a window above the couch into some unfamiliar city, serenaded by their duet of pleasure moans. He could also see himself still warm, jackknifed over the tip of a halberd, held aloft by the guard like a speared fish, Lily breaking off the thin medallion around his neck with a cavalier snap and twirling it in her fingers as she walked away. Then again, Lily might sit alone at the lower basin of the Island Fountain in the blindingly hazy brightness of a winter noontime sun, watching all the colors washing away and waiting for Lane to come for her. The possibilities faded away without conclusion.

The water arc of the Island Fountain captured the glitter of the torches and the pin point starlight so it seemed as though an obedient swarm of fireflies had built a coruscating arch over the stage for one of the festival's evening traditions. Up five steps to a large platform of wooden planks, a cage of links hung without visible support, a sagging cube of chain mail thirty feet across and more than half as high. Access to the cage was through a spineless chain link tube the height of a man, constructed so that opening one end of the tube mechanically closed the other. And despite the desperation with which many in the crowd climbed the walls of the Flat to escape the mob, the stage was empty and the cage had only one occupant.

Piled coil upon shifting coil, the muted brown curving skin of the enormous python would have been nearly invisible too, but for the oil that gave it a colorless glint not unlike the arch above its head. In shifting positions, the interlocking trunk-sized sections of the snake's body slid through each other hypnotically. Watching the complex knot change without changing, moving in place, was like watching the dynamic motionlessness of a standing wave in the river's rapids. The movement of the snake dissolved, eclipsed by the three eyes rising up from the mass of shiny dark scales. The serpent had singled Lane out from forty feet away, swaying back and forth, slowly, left and right, with nothing left in the world except those beautiful eyes.

The relative quiet of those closest to the stage had dropped to a murmur as the python raised its head. Fixed between its wide eyes in the center of its forehead was a dark red gem fashioned as an extraordinary third, unblinking eye. And the nearly black skull of the serpent, larger than a man's even with the jaws shut, hissed to the crowd in the rhythm of its swaying, calling with its eyes "Come to me. Come. Take this bauble from my head. Come dance with me. Come. Make yourself rich. Come show what you are made of. Come. Make your dreams come true. Come to me." The rapt hush gripping the crowd had spread so far around the Flat that the rustle of cotton-on-cotton could be heard, cloth friction as the celebrants shifted helplessly in time to the monster's orchestration.

The marvelous animal's eyes spoke directly into Lane, the mastery of the performance stealing away his very thoughts. The beauty of the thing was too much. Nothing could satisfy the yearning those eyes created. To leap onto the stage. To pass through the barriers. To curl himself around the warm umber body and press and squeeze, harder and harder, until there was nothing left to compress. And nothing to be done about the yearning but to consume the thing, to ingest the beauty. And even this would not be enough. And those captivating eyes reflected the same craving for Lane. An unquenchable rapacious need.

Lane could tell that the crowd still carried his body upstream by the chain links that passed slowly in front of the eyes of the prodigious snake. And though Lane continued to move, the reptilian eyes followed him, locked onto his eyes as if the rest of the crowd were no more than a medium in which his body floated. The pure exigent malice of the gaze transfixed him, but the confidence of the look displeased Lane just enough that he dropped his lids to prove to the beast that he could break their contact. Yet drifting on in that internal darkness, Lane could feel the three colossal eyes tracking him with fell patience. Eyelids up again. The mahogany jewel was right there. And the two wide vertical slits of black. Moving slowly to and fro without ever taking leave of him. Swallowing the night until it was nothing but those black pools. There was a warm tightness in Lane's stomach as he settled back into the blackness inside his head.

‡ ‡ ‡

Though the lecture was over and Don Weaver had knelt in place to complete the apprentice circle, his arms, his torso, and sometimes even his head jumped playfully here and there to catch his own words or tease with the concepts he had just left hanging in the air. Over the raked dirt platform, the crossing conversations knit together the six kneeling figures.

"Leave it be. Many days and more have since gone cold since then. Have you crows na better for gossip and chitter-chat than this topic?"

"You take it very stone, Sona, for one who does na care. If you're na thirsty, why do you keep drinking from the stream?"

"I think it's more than possible," said Don Weaver, clearly enjoying the banter. "I'm oddly confident that Humility's quarter will be divided on the New Year. I have a feeling."

"Do na, Cye! I'm simply bored and easy with talking of Humility's win. Every day and the next makes it a weary subject."

"By this we can at least"

"A feeling?" Lane was skeptical. "Or an inside story from the high house?"

"measure some real loyalty"

"in him."

"You echoes know na and less of my loyalty." Sona's dark stare was fixed on the Wrens, and though Lane waited, Sona would not turn to look his way. Not for lack of opportunities, Sona had not met Lane's eyes in weeks.

"No more than a hunch I can't ascribe. As herald, I'm the last to know the announcement, I assure you."

"Then who will be next named avatar if another is picked, Master?" asked Cye, switching conversations.

"Besides, they split and halved Righteousness last year so Flexibility could have its quarter, space, and room. When ever hardly does that happen twice one year and the next also?"

"If I knew that answer, perhaps I would be the candidate."

"Who shines right? Tast was a sleepy call for Flexibility's avatar year last. This year, na person stands tall. Na yet anywise."

"That I'll give you. Only a swimmer's chance it will matter."

"Then help and please tell me why we still discuss and return again and another. Can na you save Cian for work and work? This stage is na an Atar table for toothless ancients."

Cye jumped in to support their instructor. "The year is not over. Perhaps it could even be the suzerain-to-be himself."

"For what flair? For being a little ill and long horizontal?"

"For succession?"

"The suzerain-to-be"

"is dead"

"this morning."

From Lane's suddenly bloating fingertips back up his arm, an ache spread as the blood slowed to a stop in his veins. Stuck where it was, the air in his lungs began to run stale. Even Lane's thoughts were arrested on the word 'morning.' The simultaneous pressures of the euphoric thought of success and horrifying possibility of failure had clogged his system with a pregnant suspension. Slick and sweet, the lamp oil odor coated his nose with a grimy pleasantness, waiting on an exhale to be released.

"Are you sure, Wren?"

"We came late this morning"

"because we were caught"

"in the commotion"

"on the Flat."

"And how did this feeble end his days and pass on so easy like?"

"They only said his body"

"gave out while he slept"

"last night."

"Gave up? Life is na a contest to quit for sleeping too stone. And they were selling Cirrus as only resting long and easy days from being modest sick." Rising in unison, pausing appropriately, and dropping again, the pairs of identical shoulders seemed entirely content to have no response. Maybe even ever so slightly pleased that that was their answer.

"One of you took Cirrus's life," the joviality had passed off Master Weaver's face, "or one of you just received an unprecedented gift from the fates." Four heads immediately began ratcheting around the circle, checking and gauging, each gaze settling on the one motionless head. Lane was looking across the circle out over Cye's right shoulder with eyes spread just slightly too wide in defocused transfixion. The sweat beaded in individual pearls upon Lane's long black lashes and splashed in little glittering explosions each time the rows of lashes crashed together and retracted.

"That is unexpected and welcome news, Wren. We'll have to see if the patron is satisfied." This second news, that the death was a Cian sanctioned project, twisted the four rotating heads away from Lane for a moment, but the reduced scrutiny did nothing to resuscitate him.

"If the primary scion died in his sleep"

"then does that count as a job delivered?"

"There is na skill in finding luck and unearned fortune. Only hack Jacks need to cross fingers and hope and wish for like extra aid."

"The rules are written by the request, na Sona?"

"There is na like middle place. You do it or you fail. Lucky waits on only the tyros."

The churning dizziness at Lane's center could have been the twilight moments before breath-held unconsciousness. But the feeling grew louder until Lane realized his lungs were pumping again. Some combination of the tickle of breath over his lips and Sona's bitterness slowly drew the corners of his mouth into a smile that he immediately began fighting to repress. To the fuel of the Cirrus news the reactions of his audience were incendiary, stoking a conflagration of invincibility that he mistrusted and craved like a reformed addict. His overheated body drenched his clothes in streams of perspiration which, under the circumstances, he allowed without criticism.

Master Weaver said more but Lane was beyond the triviality of words, exquisitely comfortable in what he could call on his body and mind to perform. Sona was shuffling off to the weapons room with some backward verbal jab and the perceptible sound of a limp. A second shock wave of glee, the imagined response from Master Maya nearly stopped Lane's lungs again, choking him with the hot pleasure of pride and desire. The Wrens were gone as pragmatically as they had been present.

Like an irritant that would not be washed away, the slight shifting back and forth of Cye's figure, one knee up and one knee still down, halfway out of the kneel, finally resolved, swimming into focus in Lane's mind. As Lane's eyes tightened up on Cye, Cye bowed in respect and subservience. Only he wasn't pointed properly at Master Weaver. As he raised his head and then lifted up his body to exit, the warm smile he wore could not have been more clearly pointing Lane's way. Lane's traitorous skin flushed a ruddy brown he could not turn from his teacher to hide.

Then Doyen Horn surfaced in his mind's eye. Ichor surging through Lane with every beat-beat of his heart, pounding in his temples with painful ecstasy, his external calm had become a focusing mechanism to magnify his internal maelstrom. Doyen Horn's hard set weather-beaten face would be proud. Proud of Lane. Proud for Cian. That Doyen Horn might speak these thoughts, might give Lane his due - a primal mirthful howling was building inside his chest, ringing louder and louder throughout the vaulted ceiling chambers of his mind. Such a tempest must burst, releasing its torrent and relieving its pressure. One hundred adversaries would have been no counter balance for this force, but like straw before the cyclone would have been swept aside unnoticed. The ululating silent laughter continued to mount as though it were a clarion call to the seething heavens of Cian to release its monsters, let loose its heroes, that crawling down the myriad columns of the hall they could swarm the kneeling body and between them absorb the full fury of Lane's body reanimated.

Strong hands upon his shoulders, warm arms clasping him from behind, not attacking but congratulating him and claiming him as one of their own. Sight having stepped aside for vision, Lane could not see but still could feel the salty sweet water washing his eye and running down his cheeks to brush the corners of his mouth. Before him floated etched memories of his feats and beyond those, bold ephemeral glorious futures like luminous aurora, waving, shifting, beckoning, promising.

‡ ‡ ‡

Playfully, serpentine tongues of ginger fire licked out from the floor and room's stalagmites at the black heels as they crossed the room in big strides. Doyen Horn was seated near the back of the combat room where the floor sloped up gradually, effectively lowering the ceiling and the free space above the varied height stone spikes. Between two of these mottled cones, Cian's head sat impassively. Dressed in black from head to toe like the character approaching him, his black dress fell softly over crossed legs while Lane's black pants would soon be pulled tight over the top side of his bent thighs. Standing before the inscrutable figure, Lane looked down in annoyance at a flame tipped mole hill moored just where he wanted to kneel. Toeing the protrusion with the front of his boot to vent his irritation, then smiling at the gesture's pointlessness, he stepped to the right and sank down just off center from the angle of Master Weaver's posture.

Lane lowered his head, eyes closed, and the combat room's quiet was intense. Perhaps because he spent slightly longer than usual with his eyes closed, the quiet's completeness seemed to preclude the ongoing presence of Doyen Horn. Lane raised his head faster and less ceremoniously than he had meant to, eager to see if Cian's head instructor had actually vanished. Doyen Horn was still there, as still as death – majestically hardened. Having been summoned, Lane had nothing to say and so contented himself with watching the play of flickering godl and ruby lights on the chest and face in front of him.

When Doyen Horn finally began, the words were right, but the tone was wrong. Dire sternness rather than the thinly veiled warmth he had grown used to from his instructors recently. "Welcome, Lane."

"Na stone, Doyen. You asked for me ta attend?"

"We're pleased with your accomplished task and with your progress. All three of us."

"Much grats, Doyen. Try white ta be bright at what am tasked."

"I have a special task for you, Lane." The specter of the Doyen's displeasure retreated as quickly it had begun to loom. Lane sucked in a breath through quivering nostrils to control his response. The smell of burning sulfur, the perpetual incense of the combat room, filled him with sweet memories of dealing and dodging blows.

"Genius. Am ready for anything. And am honored Cian would think on me for this."

"This task will be harder than your other tasks this year."

"Am looking for this challenge."

"Much harder." The seasoned face contributed nothing beyond the content of the words. Getting nothing from the expression, Lane waited in the spike-strewn shifting twilight. "This person is also trained."

"But is na open fare. Da? It is na a flip for the cold. Work is still a proper lead." Lane paused, waiting for some confirmation. "Da?" Translucent between them hung the rough cold features of Sona's face, intermediating as a promise, a threat, a possibility, as part of the question.

"This person is an active guild member and a guild instructor." Like a sword through cobwebs, Sona's ghost was slashed away and the conclusions reformed themselves into the chaotic sounds, smells, and colors of far off cities where such an instructor target might live. The extravagant richness of the opportunity thickened the shroud between them until the expressionless features opposite Lane were all but obscured by the other worlds of the immediate future.

"Of which city is the Spirit a guild member?"

"This city." Doyen Horn's voice cut through the visions again, scattering them like fleeing remnants of a broken army. Thick, dank, dark air crammed with smoke and anemically lit suddenly packed in the space between Doyen and student. The heartlessly unreadable face floated between the rocks, without clarification or solace. Lane waited for more. Waited for something to change. Waited for a way out. Finally, "Has Karabas guild instructors beyond Cian?"

"No."

In one word his newly exalted blood, so recently contaminated with misgivings, worsened into toxic bile. All three possible targets were unthinkable. The silence drew on so long Lane began to wonder if the audience had ended without the details of his death sentence.

"It is very rare that we hire from within our own ranks, but I believe you could grow into a great teacher here in Cian. This chance to interview is a great honor and high praise."

Through the hazy bounds of the grotto, distorted in columns by the myriad fiery mouths, the scene nearly resolved several times into somewhere else. Anywhere else. And each time the otherwhere faltered, strained, and expired, leaving Lane on his knees in the horrid field of giant stone teeth. "Can decline?" The voice came out no louder than an embarrassment of a hoarse whisper.

"No." The silence that followed went by too fast. Absent any way to prolong it or avoid its termination, the breaths and beats stampeded forward, unchecked and insensible. Hearing Doyen Horn inflating, Lane locked in a breath himself, braced for the hit.

"You have until the end of the year to send Master Weaver. There are no constraints, but your job application will be judged on quality of execution."

Lane hung his head to avoid the pitiless gaze. "Why Master Weaver, Doyen?"

"You know that is not your place to ask." The deadpan voice suddenly had a booming resonance as though someone much larger were speaking through the same body. "I am the patron and that is enough. Your sense of what is fair or appropriate is irrelevant."

If Cian had chosen this as a fitting punishment for Lane's transgressions, it would manifest in some glint in the Doyen's eye. Some hard light of righteous discipline. On the other hand, if Cian were testing Lane's loyalty, his corruptibility, there would be some evidence on the Doyen's face. Some extra lines, some constellation of the features that would signal the Doyen was waiting for a reaction. That he expected, that he desired, a refusal. Raising his head so slowly his neck began to ache with the tension, he saw mute, leathery grey hands lying on black fabric, then dumb, loose black silk floating up the torso, and finally the silent, grizzled elegance of a hoary wolf's face. Nothing. Not a flicker. No sign either way.

"I look forward to your performance, Lane."

Bending at the waist, Lane lowered his head forward again, exposing his arched neck. Darkness gathered around him as he spread his fingers and a whisper of air brushed him just where his head left his body, disturbing the hairs with a sensuous promise of the coming blow. Quick, clean, final.

‡ ‡ ‡

The white blaze streaked back from the flaring nostrils all the way back up the roan's head to a little above its eyes. Set deep into the grey-white flecked hide, the eyes dilated with the nervous exhilaration of outrunning its fear, its captivity, and the continuously startling pounding of its own hooves on the stone paved street. From the broken bit swinging from its tensely outstretched jaw, the foam beading the stallion's shoulders and neck, the animal seemed to be warming into the opportunity it had found to seize. Its elegant, ornately decorated saddle was empty.

Amply warned by the oncoming racket, the street's visitors were pressed up against the stalls and shop windows on both sides, clutching their bags to their chests as though the poor frightened runaway would spook their bags into following his lead. In mid air, with all points pulled in tight, this was not a showy gallop. This action was the wound-tight prolonged sprint of an animal living in its current extravagant stride and the unexpressed elements it was determined to outpace. Its flanks compressed at the end of an exhale, its long white mane streaming behind it, in size a Galloway at least. It cut a magnificently heroic figure as it sailed past the bottom step of the temple to Madness and Addiction. Resting on that first stair of the temple, Lane watched in vicarious exhilaration as the four nailed in equine shoes shot past like bolts from four synchronized bows.

Clop-clop, clop-clop. So fast it was nearly a reverberating single sound, the beast hit the ground and returned again to its airborne rush down the crowded street. As the horse flew out of sight, the traffic reformed, evening out according to the unseen social and psychological forces that space men and women on a thoroughfare. Just as the final effects of the animal's bolt for freedom were fading from the scene, the clattering began again from up the hill. Only this time there was something slower, rougher, and grossly less graceful about the slap slap slap of the several dozen shoes hammering the cobblestones in pursuit of the unruly beast of burden.

‡ ‡ ‡

Thud-Thud. Master Weaver waited with a warm, patient smile as Lane finished his obeisance. Thud-Thud. The incessant pounding of Lane's heart had reached a level where he could scarcely hear above it and the passing days, rather than damping the sound, seemed to be amplifying it. Thud-Thud. With the full expanse of Cian's colonnade behind his mentor, the stage was too small by comparison and they knelt together in unnatural intimacy. Thud-Thud. There was nothing to say and yet here they sat, both waiting for Lane to make a decision. Thud-Thud. To pick a path. Thud-Thud. They should have picked Cye instead. Thud-Thud.

Mercifully, Master Weaver broke the spell. "How can I help you, Lane?"

Lane listened for his answer, hoping it came before the rhythmic pounding overtook him again.

"Am na sure, Master Weaver." At best that bought a few moments more before the mental cacophony returned. "Have conflicting loyalties."

"An unenviable situation. This is a choice between loyalties you owe to two separate friends?"

"Na, Master Weaver. One personal, one work."

"Then shouldn't the professional commitment prevail?"

"Work promises are always stronger?"

"Is your professional commitment explicit?"

"Da, Master Weaver"

"And the promise to your friend. Is that explicit as well?"

"Na, Master Weaver. That promise is implied by how we are together."

"Don't you think your first priority must be to keep your explicit commitments, Lane? Only then, if there is room left over, can you do what you feel is right."

Master Weaver's surface appearance was as imperturbably smooth as a mountain pool, without visible tension or intensity. Inviting and calm with no hint of irony or duplicity. Sensing he was hardly a mirror image of that pool, with a slow breath Lane dropped his shoulders and pushed them back as they fell. Then Lane focused on his hands, relaxing his fingertips out of his palms one at a time.

"Master Weaver...did you ever break a promise to Cian, for example? Cause you thought it was na right? Cause you felt it would break some other promise by so doing?"

"I've never had to make that kind of choice, Lane. I'm careful to only make commitments that aren't likely to conflict, and I keep their relative priority clear in my mind."

Despite himself, Lane's mind slipped back into a comfortable memory, away from the pain of the present interview. Two pairs of tanned legs dangled down over the edge of the bank, the bare feet still another leg's length away from the frothy water. Nestled into his lap, Rose faced out over the river and instead of a view of her face, his was filled with soft brown waves of hair. What they were talking quietly about mattered less than the pebbles they dropped from between her legs down into the waiting rapids. Blinking once slowly, and Rose was gone again.

"That doesn't mean that choices aren't hard. I've dropped out students I really liked. I was sorry to, but I did what ought to have been done."

Flicking to Master Weaver's eyes, they held no touch of hardness. No second layer or inner question. Or at least offered none up. But why didn't his teacher ask him what the work commitment was? Nothing could have been more reasonable. Unless Master Weaver respected Lane's desire for privacy. Or unless he already knew the answer.

"Am na on that list, should hope." Lane manufactured what he hoped looked like a jocular smile.

"So far I'm very pleased with your progress, Lane. I don't speak for Doyen Horn and Master Maya, but I believe they feel similarly." And he gave back to Lane an encouraging smile that drifted into an open-ended silence.

"I heard once about the Doyen for a seaside town called Charios. A very wealthy patron came to the guild with work, but insisted that the Doyen take the task herself. Not long after, the Doyen was lost trying to complete the job, and the patron chose to pay in full for the uncompleted project. Several of the junior guild members were convinced that the patron had set their Doyen up to be undone. In retaliation, this group found and gave a brutal end to the patron. This done, they disbanded and quit the city, never to be heard from again by any guild, in any city, for as long as any of them lived." The silence, unmarred by any Cian murmurs, filled in behind the words as though it had never been broken.

"Still do na know what should do."

"Which would be easier, Lane? To do this thing you are explicitly committed to doing, or not doing it?"

"Na to do it, certain."

"How often is the right thing to do the easy thing to do?"

"Rare, Master." Master Weaver pursed his lips, raised an eyebrow for emphasis, and said no more.

"Master Weaver, would you recommend me to speak with Doyen Horn on this same subject? Would Doyen Horn steer me true?"

"Our Doyen is my mentor, Lane, and he's never yet steered me wrong. I know he may seem hard, but Doyen Horn is extremely thoughtful."

"Am just keen to find a path so you both can be proud of me."

"I know we will, Lane. I'm confident at least that you know what you need to do. Now you just need to decide whether or not you'll do it."

"Grats, Master Weaver. Always, do appreciate all the extra time you give."

"It's what I live for, Lane. To help my students bloom."

Pressing his skull to his knees, Lane held the formal pose well beyond the required time, then arched back, rocked onto his heels, and rose to a stand. The man sitting at his feet was not preparing to die. Either he didn't care or, more likely, he didn't consider death a near term possibility. Passing by Master Weaver to get to the stairs down from the platform, Lane reached out, grabbed the offered wrist and gave a squeeze as his was squeezed in return.

As he stepped down from the raked dirt to the smooth stone floor of Cian, his new black boots caught his eye, intricate gray stitching of spirals swirling out beyond the limitations of the leather. They felt wonderfully comfortable, though they were only a few days old. And watching his boots highlighted the unnaturally long strides he was taking down Cian's central avenue. Concentrating on each step shortened their interval, but then that felt even more forced and artificial than had his longer strides. The more Lane tried to correct his gait, the more awkward it became until it really seemed that the next adjustment might send him pitching forward onto the floor. Hard as it was to ignore this growing palsy, Lane raised his head to the cavern's vaulted heights and watched the pairs of stately columns pass him by until it seemed that it was he who stood quietly and they who marched by in their orderly rows. Each support soldiering on with its opposite, each holding its lit lamps in perfect, reverent formation.

Leaving them behind, he crossed the vestibule and rose up into Cian's twisted gorge. The staircase walls curved down around him, fading as he passed from nondescript to indistinct to black to nothing. And as he rose up Cian's gullet, he allowed himself to glimpse, at the periphery of his awareness, the strong, confident tread of his steps, driven on effortlessly by a swinging of his thighs as though rising were no harder than falling. And then gently, Lane allowed the sensation to pass out of his mind, for fear of disrupting it again. And on up the curling passage he flew.

‡ ‡ ‡

The full, yellow moon, and the bitumen torches of the Upper Bank main bridge produced very nearly the same light. So lit, the colorless pair of figures were shapes against which the relative brightness of his right hand and the pearly whiteness of her left hand shone where they met between the gray folds of their cloaks. She laughed often and easily as they walked, tinkling bells of youthful merriment deceitfully alluring in their guilessness. Though his hood was on his shoulders, hers was unfurled to hide her features and she was careful with each giggle to raise her free hand to her hood to prevent being unveiled.

Master Weaver and his escort stepped off the bridge onto the Flat and their hands swung together. A bright heaven above, the stage was empty except for a few vagrants and pairs of other lovers tastefully resting or passing by the edges of the Flat. As the cloaked pair approached the Palace gates they dropped hands, but even this disengagement was done with a look toward each other, as though instantaneously nostalgic for the sweet purity of the previous moment.

A door just the height of a man was carved into the two story main gates of the Island River Palace, impenetrable cliffs of petrified wood worked with ornate panels of copper, bronze, and brass. The pair stopped before this door and waited a moment, to no effect. Master Weaver rapped twice and in a moment, the top half was opened by someone invisible within. A rough wave of the hand by Master Weaver was stayed by a white hand. His companion raised her hands to pull back her hood enough for the person inside to see her face, and the door was immediately unbarred to them. She stepped into the Palace and, as she did, Master Weaver turned and, rather than looking around, took one long impression of a patch of shadows across the Flat in the corner of the left Alley. Then he turned back and followed her inside.

A clank and the door closed. A rasping thump and it was secured again. Peaceful quiet on the Flat made audible the constant whisper of the Island Fountain as its crafted arch of water, just now a giant handle of captured lunar yellow, dove back into the receiving basin. Lane stepped out of the shadows of the Alley and leaned against one of the ancient stone supports watching the Palace though there was nothing left to see. A minute passed and his solitude had not yet dispelled the lingering presence of Master Weaver. Lane turned his head and stared back down the Alley's colonnade, but nothing resolved out of the dark inanimate shapes stretched out behind him down the covered avenue.

‡ ‡ ‡

Lane squatted, and the brown wool poncho fell all the way down to his boots. Back to his left and back to his right two façades of a high brick building receded. Just in front of him, the Lower Bank of Karabas opened up along the river, dropping down gradually over several miles to dappled plains in the hazy distance. The cool air was perfectly balanced by the midmorning sun, the poncho both insulating from the first and absorbing the second.

Two buildings down along the riverfront boulevard stood the twin to the one upon which Lane was perched. Five stories tall and tall stories at that. Unlike most of the cheaper buildings set back a few streets from the river, the façade of these buildings ran over all five sides. The pentagonal structures were covered in a mosaic of bricks from ochre to maroon, sending waves of colored patterns out from each of its many pentagonal windows until they crashed into each other in perfect tessellation. A plainer three story building sat tucked into the space between the taller buildings, snugly but not interlocked for its having one fewer sides. Lane blinked.

Along the riverfront boulevard a steady stream of people swam, nearly all of them upstream against the current like so many salmon. Master Weaver had just stepped out from the shorter sandwiched building and was immediately caught up in the traffic and carried away, directly beneath Lane's roost. The memorial to mourn the tragic illness and death that had robbed the city of Cirrus, their suzerain-to-be, would start soon, and Master Weaver would be stuck there on the Flat for several hours.

Only once Master Weaver was two minutes out of sight did Lane lean forward into space, leaving the prouder building behind. His head, preceding his feet, continued to curve through the flight so that gradually his feet took the lead again. He gripped the inside of the poncho, and the backside plumed behind him as his head rose above his feet. Progressively, as the flight became a fall, his legs unfolded into a relaxed semi-extension. With a whispered crunch his toes landed first, slowing the fall for his heels, his heels slowing the fall for his knees, which bent and bent until he was still again and the poncho again brushed the rooftop all around him.

Standing, he crossed the roof with brisk strides to the covered hatch in the far back corner. Lane lifted it experimentally with his toe and it came up, unlocked. He lifted it, held on with one hand, and dropped through so that it shut with a thud immediately echoed more softly by his touchdown on the floorboards of a hallway. The building looked as rustically plain on the inside as it did externally. Floorboards, a banister, stairs going down, a covered trap in the ceiling, two doors the same faded white of the walls, and a small clean window at the front was all the hallway had to offer.

Lane placed his fingers on the chest of the rear door by which he stood, but it was locked. He reached for one of his stakes to force it, then returned the steel to its thigh pocket and paced forward to repeat the same gentle gesture of discovery on the forward apartment's door. Why shouldn't Master Weaver take the riverfront view on the top floor? Particularly if he had picked such a plain building in which to lodge. The door swung open at Lane's light pressure and Lane tensed, sensed, waited, then straightened and snorted. The inside was surely Master Weaver's. Unlocked. Why not.

Two rooms with a double width opening between them. The first on entering was a simple kitchen and oversized butcher block that also served as the room's table, set with old wicker chairs still in good condition. Only one decoration: a wall-sized, faded map of a broad area Lane did not recognize, with short hand notes written over much of its surface. No mess. The only obvious personal effects were a collection of wind instruments lying on shelves or standing up in the corners. One thin metal pipe almost four feet long could have been a weapon but turned out to have finger holes down its torso and lip marks at its thin open tip. Only dried food in the cupboards and not much of it. Not enough dishware or flatware to serve a dinner for three.

Through the doorless doorway, the second room was no better. A particularly large straw stuffed leather chair and matching ottoman. No bed? Perhaps this wasn't Master Weaver's only place. A dresser and small doorless closet with enough of Master Weaver's clothes that it was possible that they were all here, nicely folded. Another wall-sized map, this one with at least a dozen differently colored pins pushed into cities across its surface. Below the map was a small bookcase with several hundred letters neatly folded and stacked on end. Sampling them at random, Lane found that they were all personal correspondence to Master Weaver, full of the heartaches and triumphs of everyday life. It took reading several before it became clear that most if not all were from other guild members and several more readings again before Lane formed the hypothesis that many or all of these written conversations were with former students of Master Weaver's. A quick study of another few picked from the top shelf did produce several names of older students who Lane had known or known of in his earlier years at Cian. The letters were almost universally intimate, but none had clearly useful information. Otherwise, the room was clean and bare.

Lane slumped into the chair, threw his arms up on the high sides, and stared around the room again, trying to see what he must have been missing. No locks. No weapons. No traps. No place to hide and wait. This was no place for an ambush. Its simplicity was suspicious. Master Weaver was fond of saying that when something felt right or wrong, that didn't make it a guess. A feeling was just the answer without the explanation as background.

The expansive sepia map, etched with thick black ink marking cities and the roads that connected them, could have been the whole world for all Lane knew. If the map had been more expressive, at the colored pins major road lines of black would have bulged and pulsed as graduated apprentices sent letters of victories, defeats, questions, answers, and musings back toward Karabas. Back toward Master Weaver. And the black ink highways emanating out from Karabas would have surged with his responses, flooding out to these cherished distant colored tacks. Sending them something worth their continued collective deluge of life details. And if Lane fulfilled his task to retire Master Weaver? He watched as the parchment aged and the sepia tightened in on Karabas, choking off the outbound bands of black until they were again just anemic lines of ink. The incoming lines still pulsing with their letters, slowed to a trickle, then a drip, until they dried up entirely, starved for want of a response. And then those lines too were again just faint lines of ink on a map.

‡ ‡ ‡

The downstream tip of the Karabas island, thirty acres falling away from the Flat into a rocky point wedged into the white water, was as unkempt as the Flat was maintained. Weedy trees and clumps of tall grass grew thick where the rocks would let them. Then as the end of the island neared, the vegetation ceded the stage to stone shelves split with boulders rolled down long ago off the Flat. And in the yolk-colored dusk, a few hundred heads grew to the level of the grassy reeds down to the shore where musicians stood or sat on higher rocks, scattered across the final barren reach of the eyot.

Leisurely and undulating, the loosely coordinated music wandered melodically, led sometimes by the winds and sometimes by the percussion, but always weaving in the patterned sound of the rushing river as though it were a key member of the impromptu ensemble. Those playing the hourglass shaped drums crowded in the last few feet of land to be near the pounding surf, though the table-sized drums made the location look uncomfortably crowded. The Atar-shaped metal boards of varying thickness triangles were supported on beds of straw and often legs below them. The boards' players ranged over nearly the entire area where appropriate seating and space for the trays could be found. Brass, silver, wooden, and ceramic flutes and recorders ranged in nimble hands down the final stretch of both coasts, sitting for the most part, or standing when their instruments required it, as it did for one silhouetted figure with a silver recorder that ran from his lips down to his shins.

The direct light of the sun had moved on to some other city, and the silhouetted figure was engrossed in the interplay of the pieces. Back three hundred feet, one of the heads rose up from the patchy reeds. Lane, no more than another silhouette in the spontaneous audience, began to stroll down the slope in the general direction of the silver recorder and its player. Picking his way through the fields of vegetation and the instinctive glances of the strangers by which he passed, Lane was stopped cold by the upturned, wide-eyed face of Cye. The daylight gone, the city was suddenly very cold and a shiver shook Lane.

"Cye! Genius seeing you! What brings you here?"

"Greetings, Lane. Meeting you unplanned is a gift. I came here to," slipping an arm out of the thick blanket in which he was wrapped and sweeping his hand in front of him, "absorb the sounds."

"Samewise. Have na been before and was curious."

"Proper? Without dabs, fixer, or food, I wouldn't have thought such a setting would suit you. Still, I'm glad to have you here now."

"Samewise." Lane paused, hovering in awkward ambivalence over Cye. Cye waited patiently, looking up at Lane from his wrappings. "Do you come here regular?"

"Perhaps once per moon."

"You've never mentioned it to me."

"I find this a good place to be by myself and consider."

"Do you want me to leave? Did na mean to interrupt..."

"No! Don't be simple, Lane. We've spoken fewer thoughts outside Cian than there've been days of late. Stay!"

"Grats. Will."

"Here. The blanket is big enough for three." Cye spread out his arm with a pile of blanket. Lane hesitated, then drew in close to Cye who pulled the rug back over them both. The darker the sky became, the louder and more immersive the rambling, harmonized acoustics became.

"Normal, it's true, such a soft scene is na for me. But have heard that Master Weaver plays here sometimes. So got curious for a look-listen."

"Spot? That's shine. Where? I did na know he played any instrument nor that he played in public."

"Think he's over there, with a long recorder." And Lane pointed, but in mid gesture could not find Master Weaver's form where it had been just minutes ago. It could have been the thickening evening or perhaps the vantage point, and Lane stood up, but the elevation did not recover Master Weaver's shape in the distance. Lane sat down again and Cye rewrapped him. "Maybe na. Thought did see someone his size when it was lighter."

"Could be he just moved a bit."

"Could be."

Cye was quiet for a while, and the first stars began pushing their way through the purple cover over Karabas. With each newly lit solar lantern the late fall took another perceptible step toward winter. Cye and the fleece-lined mantle sharpened the dry chill on Lane's cheeks and gave a crisp ringing quality to the increasingly haunting music that washed over them. When he did begin speaking again, Cye returned to his fantasies of what life would be like after they graduated and quit the city. There was never the explicit mention that they might travel together or end up in the same city, but the invitation was there just the same. Lane joked with Cye and made up questions and comments because the moment felt good, but his eyes were fixed on the empty spot where his mentor had been. Lane did not turn away until the vacancy had entirely merged with the ridge, the air, the sky, and the black distance between them.

‡ ‡ ‡

The tower, a hollowed ivory cone, was a maze of filigree along its inner surface. So delicate, it seemed the first breeze would brush it aside. So densely woven that it entirely hid from the inner view smaller cones that rose up from its outer surface. The external wind and light made its way, rerouted through the lacework marble, into the temple, giving a bite to the atmosphere and a bright glow to the stone. And the temple to Musicality sang for its visitors. In an endless overlapping stream of long moaning chords, the tuned building, its lesser spires and the tiny minarets that grew from each of these, all formed to resonate at their unique pitch, carrying their part of the ever-changing, never-ending harmony of the temple. Sometimes when the winds were high, the shrill notes from the most diminutive turrets carried the tune like warbling banshees. When the wind was lower, as it was today, the baritone of the building itself dominated the song, humming a mighty ohm, both powerfully satisfying and deeply unnerving.

Despite the oncoming winter and the several minute hike up past the last outlying house on the Upper Bank to the rather precarious outcrop on which the temple stood, a surprising number of visitors stood and sat across the unmodulated white marble floor. Many of them held musical instruments which they had hauled up the steep stone steps, but as was the custom, none were played. Near one of the alcoves, as though just entering into the space, the lifesized wood carved figure of Coam was in mid stride, holding a blue ceramic ocarina to his lips. On the floor stretched back from his feet into the alcove, a darker green marble had been inlaid as though it were a rough moon-cast shadow on the temple floor. Out from the column behind him another moon-cast shadow lay along the floor, the shadow of his jealous older brother, who, having crept up to rob and kill his more successful sibling, has been arrested by the beauty of what he hears. The subsequent repentance and begging for forgiveness was such a popular story, it had made Coam's brother, Toam, a sort of also-ran in the greater Karabas pantheon.

A first year female apprentice from Cian had just entered and was looking around like a child in wonder. Master Weaver approached her from across the hall and after a warm hug, they sat side by side where they were on the floor, both leaning back on their arms. She was soft and round, smooth and fresh. She had the sort of rosy nubile aura that make men do stupid things. That kind of attractive innocence would serve her well if it was a mask and would be her death sentence if it wasn't.

Master Weaver listened attentively, nodded in support, laughed out loud when she turned to him with a smile, all with an intimacy both inappropriate and inexplicable given her position in Cian. When his mouth moved, hers was closed, and her eyes riveted on him in a mesmerized trance of complete surrender. Not that Master Weaver treated her with the familiarity he had the cloaked woman on the Flat, but he seemed entirely relaxed. As relaxed and unsuspicious as one could hope to be.

It seemed to stretch credulity to imagine someone so relaxed could be in real danger. To the point where the danger seemed as much in question as the wisdom of being, or at least seeming, so entirely at ease. Such danger as might actually exist for Master Weaver would surely be highest when, like now, he was absorbed with an apprentice he liked. Somewhere more private than such a well lit public space would be advisable. That Cye was the best choice of students to distract their mentor was unfortunate, but unavoidable. Cye's reaction directly afterwards would be terrible. Lane would strike back instantly at anyone who tried to take down Master Weaver – why wouldn't Cye be the same? Hopefully Cye's loyalty to Lane would buy Lane the moment he needed to diffuse the situation.

A melancholic atmosphere took hold of the building as a sharp odor of living pine and decaying leaves permeated the temple's defenses. The effect was amplified by an increasingly rhythmic alto tone, echoing through the temple like a chanted lament of a single word. Insensitive to these new stimuli, Master Weaver and this new favorite continued their quiet, conspiratorial conversation. Beyond them, Coam kissed his instrument in blissful ignorance. Past his algae-colored shadow, in the dimmer light of the temple's margins, the second inlaid shadow was deformed in a spread arm crouch. Whether the brother's arms were spread in menace or revelation was unclear. A black boot came down soundlessly on the shadow's chest, heel, toe, and was gone again.

‡ ‡ ‡

Like an iceberg wedged into a warehouse, ground-to-ceiling vertical sheets of two inch rough glass broke the regularity of stone and wood along the first floor of the Left Alley for fifty feet. This maze of translucent walls was used by day as display space for household crafts, but tonight a layer of snowflakes driven upon the glass had transformed it into austere slabs of unmeltable ice. A radiant full moon had been unsheathed from the clouds, creating a fine edge to the black shadow of a man as it rose up the outer wall of glass. The shadow moved over the wall to the first entrance gap, where the moon's light immediately threw it to the cobblestone floor of the entryway, making a rumpled mess of the pristine shape. Crawling over the irregular stones, the shadow pulled itself up the next glass wall a few steps deeper into the building, regaining much of its former clarity. But as soon as the black shape headed down this second wall, the moon's intensity was intermediated by the outer icy wall, scattering the light and fading the shadow to an insubstantial and tentative thing. As Lane moved another layer into the labyrinth of glass walls, the moon's yellow-white light, magnified and sapphire tinctured by the prisms through which he passed washed his shadow away, leaving him swimming in a silver-blue haze.

Aside from a number of heavy iron hooks screwed high up on the glass walls and a few crates left behind by the day's merchants, the space was entirely bare. With each stratum deeper into the building the light seemed perversely to become brighter and bluer, intensifying the perception of icy encasement. Around the next glass slab was a cul-de-sac in the maze, framed on three sides with mottled glacial blue backlit walls. A bench of glass, reflecting this same preternatural light, running the circumference of the cul-de-sac, protruded at knee height. At the end of the space sat a figure cloaked and hooded in gray wool, and as Lane approached the figure stood and drew back her hood.

Lily's skin and hair had such a luminescent luster to them that it seemed the light passed through her as it did through the walls, as if she had no native colors. She took three steps to reach Lane and she kissed him without preamble. Passionate. But...passionate on principle. The kiss was conveyed like food at a tavern - something already ordered and paid for but not yet delivered. She stopped kissing him as abruptly, but without a trace of awkwardness, and sat down on the immediate shelf of glass. Her youthful elfin features looked magnificent, wrapped in gray in this bath of blue.

"I was beginning to wonder if you were going to contact me again."

"Told you would call."

"I am glad you did. It's been a while since..."

"Told you would care for that too, as did. And would na miss the chance to be rewarded." Lane smiled at her annoyance before it even appeared on her brow.

"How do I know you did anything? Cirrus just fell ill and died."

"Do you believe that is what happened?"

Lily was quiet for a minute, studying Lane's face. The layers of glass smothered any outside sounds, surrounding the pair in sepulchral stillness. "No." Lane just nodded in satisfied agreement, pleased that it was a point that would not require debating. "But...I did not do anything...to help..."

"You did enough." Lane pause and Lily shifted her way back and forth through his pause with a perplexed, troubled look on her face. "What've you brought me as reward?"

"You're serious." Lily seemed to almost chew on the statement under her pursed lips, then apparently abandoned the thought as though she'd spit it out again. "Let us leave together. Tonight. Leave and never turn back. I will bring plenty for both of us."

"Is na about the pieces, Lily. On principle, have delivered for you and should be rewarded."

"And having me does not count?" Head up, chin out. Proud. Probing. Suddenly, she seemed much younger.

"Wouldna think of putting a value on you."

Though she waited, Lane did not continue, and the statement hung in the air, unretortable, unacceptable. Their eyes were locked and her stare was admirably hard for someone who had just delivered an unsolicited kiss. Finally, without taking her eyes off Lane, Lily reached down her neckline and retrieved a large amber-colored square cut topaz set in a thick square silver setting and held around her neck by a braid of silver links. She lifted it carefully over her head and lowered it into the outstretched hand before her. Lane broke from her eyes to take a short look at the beautiful piece. He could see Lily standing in front of a full length mirror in a long low cut white dress and admiring the warm gem where it rested on her chest as an attendant adjusted the hem. Or perhaps a thin pale hand reached over someone else's dresser surface in the dark, slowly, silently lifting a cherry wood lid, and extracting the first item inside it contacted, a large gem on a silver chain that rustled a little as she moved it to a waiting black velvet bag. Though the immersive light was a watery blue, the topaz sparkled a pure golden brown in Lane's broad palm. Lane dropped the necklace roughly into his right thigh pocket, producing a rude clunk against the stake there before it settled into place.

Lily flinched at the sound and then quickly recovered. Both of them were quiet for a while. When Lily reached out and took both of his hands, Lane didn't resist, and having let her, found it more natural to sit beside her than to continue to stand.

"Come away with me, Lane. I do not belong here. I never have." She paused to watch him and Lane was content to let her continue a little. "Now that Cirrus is gone, they won't look for me long. I could leave alone but...you are a bridge for me to something new. And maybe I could be the same for you." Her proud, undeterred delivery in the face of his unresponsiveness only increased his muteness, so he was happy for them both when she said, "There's plenty more reward to look forward to also," with a dazzling smile. A reflexive display of friendly mirth spread over Lane's face. Her smile widened in response.

"Have a thing that still must been done in Karabas. An obligation that can na be dodged."

"And I do not have commitments and responsibilities? Who does not? That is the point of leaving! To erase your commitments. To have a clean slate."

"Will be leaving Karabas on the New Year's first day. Will you wait for me in the morning by the Island Fountain?"

"But why wait?"

"As that is when will leave and na other time."

Lily sat and looked at Lane so long that it seemed she might well leave without him, but when she finally did speak again it was to say "I'll be there." She said it softly, as a concession, but without a trace of resentment or submission. Lane stood up and she stood after him, still holding his hands in hers. "Thank you."

"Couldna have given him early to the sky without you."

Lily started slightly at this and as much to his surprise as hers, Lane pulled her in to return the greeting she had given him. Her sweet, fragrant woodiness ran strong through both his nose and mouth. The transporting strength of the moment was in danger of lengthening indefinitely. Lane closed his mouth to stem the tide. She let go of his hands and he turned out of the dead end. His tall form was well defined in the first phase of his retreat, but as he turned the first corner Lane became a hazy form through the first layer of glass. With each successive turn the silhouette lost definition, melting into the shifting shadows of the moonlit maze.

‡ ‡ ‡

Down the wide stone steps, under the low stone lintel, the grotto opened up on both sides. Across the flagstone floor the furniture congregated in cliques, huddled around the open braziers for warmth. Though it was dark already and the Root nearly deserted, the tables and chairs were not stacked away, but kept each other company in dejected disuse. The canopy of ivy filtered out much of the falling snow, letting isolated flakes drift down to settle on the unneeded surfaces or flash to nothingness when their path brought them into the orbit of the open flames. The ancient living roof to the grotto blocked out any stars that might have been visible, but the establishment had provided its own constellations. In each of the hundreds of water-filled sconces a candle floated, a tiny sun encased to protect it from the winter breezes. Lane imagined that with the braziers put out it might feel that they were floating among the stars. He wished they would.

He and Cye and Master Weaver sat together at a small round wood table directly beside the vine's gigantic trunk where it ruptured and buckled the floor in an ever expanding grip upon the earth beneath. The brazier between Lane and Cye masked the cold but did not remove it and despite the two thick layers he wore, Lane was distracted by the chill. Master Weaver on the other hand, even sitting as he was without the immediate support of the brazier, seemed entirely comfortable. In fact, his sunny conduct this evening made Cye serious by comparison, which created a welcome camaraderie for Lane.

"You've both done a great job these past three years." Master Weaver raised his glass for a toast, not the first of the evening. "Lane. Cye. I'll be sorry to see you go." They raised their glasses and drank with him, finishing yet another glass. "And less than a month to go."

"So you think we'll make it over the finish line, Master Weaver?" Cye grinned the happy, nearly-there smile Master Weaver was looking for.

"As long as you don't find a way to fail us in the next three weeks! Do you think you two can handle it?"

"Think we've got it by the bridle, Master." Master Weaver laughed loudly and leaning forward, clapped them both hearty, conspiratorial claps on their shoulders.

A turquoise liveried server had come up on them quietly and stood politely until the moment was over. He stood behind Master Weaver, in one hand a bowl to catch the juices and his other hand a sword with skewered chunks of blackened goat meat. Given the spot he'd chosen to wait, the tip of the server's sword was a hand's span from the nape of their mentor's neck. The false simplicity of the position, and the illusory advantage it offered whoever could attain that position – Lane exhaled a controlled stabilizing breath through his nose, watching the moisture turn white before him.

The sword went up a little, hesitated, and the server stepped beside Master Weaver, bringing the bowl and the sword over the table. With a quick motion the bowl moved back in the server's hand and a small black-handled knife appeared from under it. Master Weaver began waving his hands to prevent further food from piling up before him, but the small knife managed to get two chunks off the spit before the gesture was finished, the goat meat dropping like little attacks onto the overlapping plates below. The server withdrew, but the resulting crash-crash onto the plates of excess food made it feel like the server had won the encounter.

Giving a mock snarl to the server's back, Master Weaver happily speared one of the chunks, transferred it to a plate closer to him, and took a big bite with gusto. Lane was overfull and wished now he had not eaten so much.

Cye restarted the conversation. "Still do na know where I'll go next year. I should like to get very far way from Karabas do think. I hear there are cities far down beyond the plains where snow never falls."

"True, Cye. There are and some are most wonderful to see. But it sometimes gets so hot you'd give a year's wages for a day's worth of snow. Try them out, but I think you'll find that the heat is harder to escape than the cold."

"Should still like to see those places. Perhaps move from city to city for a while."

"Well, I'm sure you won't have any trouble about work, but just in case, I'd be happy to write you a general letter of introduction and give you a list of cities where that letter might mean something. For you too, Lane, of course!"

"That means a lot to me, Master Weaver. I would cherish such a letter as a memory of you."

"Samewise, grats, Master. Am proud you would speak for me."

"I hope both letters are given the opportunity to help you out." A somber moment was beginning and their teacher jumped in to break it. "Come. Let's not dwell on sad endings. Let's drink again. Passionate times in distant lands!" The strong wine cut the moment, but even as the glasses left their red stained lips, the seconds began to sober again. There might be one more time he could arrange to be alone with these two people. Maybe two. At most. The night was precious. More precious even than the letters that they probably would never receive. Lane's mouth was extraordinarily dry for having just been rinsed with a glass of sweet, rich liquid.

"Master? As long as we send back a quarter of what we're paid, does it matter how much we make?"

"No, Lane. Your gabel is not policed or judged. Tokada requires that you share with the institution that trained you, but no more than share what you receive."

"Is it the same even if we do aught else for a living?"

"You mean a day job? Like the one I have? No. You give one fourth of what you make as a professional."

"What if we're na a professional for a while?"

Master Weaver's brow furrowed. "What would you do instead, Lane? It's what you're good at. It's the only thing you're qualified for."

"Do na proper know. Was just curious."

"Be aware, Lane, that once you leave the guild, it will be very hard to rejoin. Months off is a respite. Years off is an abandonment. The guild doesn't think much of members who quit, even for a while."

Over Master Weaver's shoulder, down the stone steps into the grotto came the recently rebuffed server, returning with reinforcements. Each of the three uniformed meat bearers held a sword aloft and matching white bowls beneath. In a triangular formation they advanced on Lane's position, threading through the pergola's staggered supports, and as they drew near, their loads came into focus.

More to end the topic than because Master Weaver's response settled the matter for him, Lane said, "Will keep that in mind, Master."

Thick slabs of beef. A rotisserie of lamb. Chicken hearts alternated with chicken livers. White gloved hands unified the three long rapiers at their handles above, and below the meat the last few inches of the swords agreed. Down each final reach of metal to their honed tips the same red, oily juices slid, gathering at the ends and dripping in unison into three pools of the gory vital fluid.

‡ ‡ ‡

Narrow wooden steps layered with a fine powder of white grew up into a small three story pyramid. The cloud banks above still discharging the snow hid what moon there might have been, leaving the city with only a few isolated splashes of manmade illumination. A dozen steps from the top sat Master Weaver and beside him Cye. Lane sat up one step, between them, but more nearly behind his teacher than his friend. Behind them all, at the top of Frailty's temple, a forest of extremely thin wooden posts, set a few feet apart, held up a thatched roof patched in many places. Lit by small hurricane lamps hung about the ceiling, Lane could see the top of a huge grizzled sandstone head, wrinkled and veined with age, plastered with sparse long thin hair.

The clink, clink, clink of an amateur trying to beat some metal back into place restarted from out of the darkness and though Lane turned back to look out over the Lower Bank buildings, he could not localize the sound. Gradually, the bloated ball of meats in his stomach had compressed somewhat, but the wine continued to expand in his head softening the night and the chill. The ringing of vibrating metal faded away and the distant, muted mutter of Karabas could be heard, even so late. Then the background sounds were banished again by the screeching somewhere out in the city of metal dragged across a quickly moving stone. The grinding ended and Lane twisted back up the stairs, listening to make sure the man still left at the temple's crown was not walking down the far side, but the resurfaced city murmur was unmixed with any fading footsteps.

"...nineteen years. I was young when I started."

"Do you still enjoy guiding students, Master Weaver?" Cye asked as though there was something in particular he wanted to hear.

"Though I would not have thought it possible when I was your age, guiding students is the thing I enjoy doing most. The classes are fine, but mentoring students like you and Lane is really my reward."

"And do you still practice professionally?"

"I do. Less than I would like, but good opportunities are so scarce for the good students these days that they are often all given out to our best and brightest. Right, Lane?" Master Weaver sent a friendly smile back over his shoulder. "Which doesn't leave much for me or the other Dons."

"Aye, sure and many grats, Master." Lane's hand was in his thigh pocket and when Master Weaver did not turn to respond, he carefully drew out one of his custom stakes and laid it slowly, softly, on his lap. Even done gingerly, the rasping of the frozen metal on his canvas pants sounded like the local whetstone in use again. Looking down to his right hand where it gripped the painfully cold steel, the muscles were clenched so tight his knuckles stood out like white lights beneath his skin.

"Do you ever think of retiring, Master Weaver?" Lane's guts lurched forward and for an instant Lane was worried he had actually pitched forward physically and, knocking into them, would bring them with him in a long tangled series of crashes to a heap at the bottom of the temple. What was Cye thinking asking that? Then came the crunches on the snowy steps he had been waiting for. Neither Cye nor Master Weaver seemed to notice as a young ox of a man stepped briskly down the other side of the same face of the temple on which they sat. He shrugged a heavy overcoat into place on his way down the steps, paused at the bottom to button it up to his chin, then shoved his hands into his pockets and paced off into the blackness. Leaving the three of them alone at the temple. Unlit. Unwatched. Not a soul on the streets or an open window in sight. Lane's teacher and his friend continued their banter. Lane raised his clenched hand a little and navigated the tip of the weapon around and forward.

The sharp tip of the stake drove up into the back of the man's neck and up through the base of the skull and up into the front of the brain, stopped, unable to break through the top shell of bone. Lane's body tensed to actually do it, ready, but somehow he knew now was not the moment. In front of him they continued to chatter like oblivious school children. He wasn't striking. The tip hovered just behind Master Weaver's neck. The moment was passing quickly but maybe not yet gone.

The tension went out of his quadriceps, out of his abdomen, out of his tricep as his hand returned to his lap, and then relief as Lane disengaged his hand from the stake. Why not strike? With his hand released Lane became aware of an odd clopping, as though a lame horse were about to limp into view. When it did turn a corner and took on a vague form, it was not a beast but three elderly women, wide and short, bent with age, but they did not walk gingerly. On hard heeled shoes their six feet made a clip clopping sound as they trudged their way up to the base of the temple. Though it did not seem they needed it, they each clawed handfuls of one another's sleeves so their heavy methodical tread began with a single clump upon the first board at the temple's base. Master Weaver and Cye must have lost the way in their conversation as they were quiet too, watching the trio ascend.

The old women passed near to the men and up close they were more than old. They all had ugly gnarled skin and dark, unreadable faces. Tattered, layered, but apparently thin garments draping their forms. All three, like Master Weaver, seemed impervious to winter's teeth. Tramping the last few steps in unison, the figures made the summit and stepped into the orchard of meager columns. Lane wanted to see them disengage from each other to navigate these poles but their hands were already below his line of sight and they passed into the temple's interior as though they were still connected.

‡ ‡ ‡

Cye, Lane, and the Wrens knelt in the Weapons room, watching the firelight dance upon the thousand polished surfaces and waiting for Sona and Master Maya to arrive. The multilayered surface of devices was an inexhaustible map of new discoveries, but Lane was still shocked to have a ballista longer than he was tall resolve behind a clump of short swords and longer daggers on the wall. It must have been a longer time resident of Cian than he, but how could anyone have missed such a massive launching contraption? A bolt was loaded into it and the bolt must have weighed a hundred times what a hunter would load into a crossbow. Master Maya passed between Lane and the wall. She wore a white top open several buttons down, a black beaded choker, and the traditional long black skirt. The overly serious expression that capped the outfit made her look older, but even that mixed well with her essential desirability. Only once she had knelt opposite them, extra tension around her eyes and a slightly-too-firm placement of her hands upon her thighs, did Master Maya's seriousness expose itself as a tightly controlled presentation to suppress the underlying emotion. She surveyed them, stared pointedly at the spot between Cye and the two Wrens where the unusually late Sona should have been, and began without waiting for him.

"Sona has been finally dropped from the program." Lane bit the inside of his cheeks to repress a guffaw. Sona must have done something historically stupid to have earned an execution from Master Maya, or one of the other instructors, before the final week of the year when Cian traditionally weeded its garden.

"We rarely speak in Cian of those who are not fit to continue with Cian, but I feel that there is in the end a critical lesson for you all in Sona's exit. Sona refused his final assignment." Lane didn't even try to hold back his disbelief, shaking his head in theatrical catharsis.

"You are agents. Those of you who eventually live to become guild members will work as extensions of the will of your patrons and the guild. It is antithetical to tokada to pass judgment on the jobs we do." Doyen Horn had given him until the end of the year to complete his final assignment. Right? There were still two weeks left until the New Year. And he hadn't refused the assignment. Lane shifted on his bent back legs trying to get more comfortable. The Wrens looked unmoved to the point of being bored. Like Lane though, Cye seemed a little agitated.

"Are there any questions?"

Cye frowned, opened his mouth, closed his mouth again and swallowed, then opened his mouth again and let it hang there until the words came out. "What was the job, Master Maya?"

"Did you not hear a word I just said?" Cye's color ran a shade of red Lane had never seen on him - a hot violet hue he had in fact never seen on anyone. Cye closed his mouth with a snap, the color faded from his cheeks and neck, and he seemed himself again in only a moment.

"Are there any good questions?" There were none. The four remaining students sat waiting for instruction and their instructor sat silently watching them with sad and stormy eyes. It could have been that suddenly with a cry of rage and a horribly pitiless mask on her face she sprang forward with a giant scimitar and in one expansive motion removed all four of their heads. But she continued to sit and stare at them. In stark contrast to her stoic expression, tears could have followed each other rapid fire down both of her cheeks, gathering on either side of her chin and dropping in pairs onto the white cotton covering her chest. But there were no tears. It would have been better if there had been.

‡ ‡ ‡

Manic eyes as big as saucers gaped out of the vaguely lupine head. The mouth below leered knowingly. Something about the carved stone had simply but effectively captured the ferocious humanity of the laughing animal. Or perhaps it was the savage inner humor of a man. Dug deep into Cian's gently vaulted ceiling, the creature's neck and shoulders were just visible, thick and burly, but nearly free of fur. Angled down toward the entrance of the main hall, this smug smirking almost snarl was an alluringly inscrutable private joke.

In a spider web of thin hemp lines, a hundred feet over the colonnade's path and inches below the half human muzzle, Lane was pressed against the ceiling close enough to

251

have kissed the beast with only a slight inclination of his head. The piece was done but Lane continued to dabble. Making tiny changes with a chisel that would be entirely invisible from the floor below, he periodically lay the tool on his chest and ran a rag over the cracks and groves to clean out residual sculpting debris. Eventually the sense that further effort was counterproductive overwhelmed his hand and Lane was still, trying to decipher the creature's expression.

"Who do you think the Spirit was?"

Cye, bound into the crook of the nearest column, paused his work, but neither turned toward Lane nor answered him. The woven ropes of his cradle, his thin silky hair, his smooth cheeks, and the figure cresting over his shoulder, were all shaded caramel and honey from the lights below. Just beyond Cye, struggling to break free from its huge stone egg was a wondrously horrible monster of a chick. Its feather matted down with embryonic salve, its tiny eyes shut against the first onslaught of light, in its first feeble cry it splayed an extra set of tiny claws at the tips of its untried wings. And along the upper and lower ridges of its beak, its first shrieking gasp of air exposed rows of infant razor fangs. Lane couldn't place the story attached to the bird though there must have been one, and not having been asked, Cye had never volunteered the details. The bird itself was perfect and so nuanced that from just two body lengths away it could have been alive but for its immobility. Cye was still smoothing out the face of the egg and amplifying the cracks that converged in the avian eruption.

"I can na see the way. It's na like Sona to refuse a task." The hint of a quaver in Cye's voice made Lane turn to watch him more closely. Cye would never say so, and Lane would not press the point, but it was unnerving to be so close to the end and still have victory and defeat still both be so possible. There was something else though.

Cye finally turned toward Lane and there was a sad, serious look where an apprehensive one should have been. "Do you grieve the boar is gone, Cye?"

"To mourn is na to miss, Lane. Perhaps he was given a task he could na win."

"But Sona had na nerve of nought. Nor was he exact in ought he did. That was much of his problem. So why na take the Spirit?"

"Perhaps he could na have that Spirit on his history or that blood on his hatchet."

"Sona! The brut would have killed his parents for practice. Who could have come first before himself?"

Cye shook his head and lay back in his cocoon, lost in thought. When Cye did not turn back, Lane turned himself back to his polishing. Reaching up with his cloth to go around the edges of the thing's open maw, looking through its rough lips and down its gullet, a window of insight flashed open to another time and place. And the vision jerked forward in fits and starts as Lane's mind finished fitting together what might have happened. Sona was kneeling alone with their Doyen in the combat room. Kneeling just where Lane had knelt. Dressed just as Lane had been dressed when Lane had been given his special final assignment. And though Lane could not hear what was said he felt the special assignment for Sona as a collapsing of his chest, as a giant hand crushing the air from his lungs. He did not need to hear Doyen Horn's pronouncement to know the target Sona had been given was also Master Weaver.

An intangible phantom in the scene, Lane whirled around and around the pair, looking for clues. Nothing to suggest whether this meeting was the precursor to or the reprise of Lane's identically staged audience with Doyen Horn. Nothing to suggest whether Lane was Cian's second choice for the task or Sona Cian's chosen insurance should Lane fail. The Doyen's face was etched with lines but clear of content. Sona's face was blanched and his jaw muscles pulsed below his cheekbones. But whether Sona was rejecting the assignment on the spot or would do it later, Lane could not make out. The phantom came back around to Sona's side, watching Doyen Horn over the black clad shoulder, and Lane wondered whether his skin had been as bleached when it had been his turn to kneel in that same spot.

This nightmare made no sense. Cian never gave the same assignment to two people. It wasn't done. But though the hovering spirit tried to shake the vision it would not pass. Doyen Horn was speaking again, and Lane strained to hear if he was relating Lane's non-performance to Sona. A shudder so hard it nearly dissipated the ghost followed hard on the heels of the possible connection for Doyen Horn between Lane's non-performance so far and an effective refusal. Cian never gives the same task to two students because their independent efforts introduce a hidden source of variation, neutering the power of careful planning. As Sona's death, if not his assignment, had done to Lane. Though what Master Weaver may by now have heard from Cian's Doyen could not be read on the grizzled face before them.

That must have happened. But what might have happened next? Still looking deep into the carving's mouth with eyes unfocused, Lane's reconstruction of events shifted scenes. The face before Sona changed, softening and trading its embedded lines for grave creases of attention. Now Sona knelt across from Master Weaver, not in Cian but maybe outside somewhere. As Sona confessed to his mentor, Lane watched in agony as the lines of gravity on Master Weaver's face were overcast by dark thunder clouds of righteous anger. Lane had never seen his teacher in this state and the muted specter behind Sona tried to cry out his support in devoted solidarity. Only realizing after the silent cry passed over the stage without effect that it was himself he was offering to take up arms against. Had Sona really gone to Master Weaver? Really told him he was the target?

The uncertainty broke the imagined scene and Lane saw only the oral cavity again. The window into what might have happened had closed but now Lane wanted to dive back in. To see a future scene in which he knelt before Doyen Horn to ask for guidance. Or one in which he unburdened himself to Master Weaver. He needed some information to change his plan. But the back of the jaws stayed as they were, dark rough unfinished rock. Because there was no other plan. There was precious little time left for the plan he already had.

The confident mirth of the lips had a conspiratorial certainty to them. The twinkling eyes, similarly, had a security to their sparkle that only knowledge of some key fact predestining the outcome could have fueled. Muzzle to muzzle with its creator, the creature's self-assured private amusement was both horribly arrogant and achingly attractive. There was no doubt this thing was laughing at the certainty of its victory. What was not so clearly chiseled into its features was whose side it was on.

‡ ‡ ‡

Some marvel had washed across the dome of the sky from ripe peach to luminescent indigo as the sun receded. Some fantastical rainbow parade. A thin new blanket of snow lay evenly across the Lower Bank's main bridge reflecting the sky's palette from countless crystal mirrors. Even the rapids had sheathed their claws to watch the strange show in relative tranquility – its pounding having settled into noisy purring underfoot. The air was calm and cool enough to preserve the white blanket on the city, but only just, and Lane felt warm as he kicked his feet through the powder on his way across the bridge.

Lane was late, but better that than to hurry, tonight of all nights. With only five days left in the year, no classes left before the New Year, and hard as it had been to arrange, this would certainly be his last chance to see Cye and Master Weaver together. No time for rushed actions. More than that, though, the city's festive fires had been stoked. Perfumes of smoking stoves and cooling honeyed meat pie carried far when, as it was just then, the wind lapsed in its diligent sweeping of the city. Maybe it was the kaleidoscopic sky, but as he stepped off the bridge onto the Lower Bank everyone on the bridge and walking along the riverfront boulevard walked with a touch of a skip, lighthearted in their held hands and friendly nods.

Like an island in this river of civic harmony, on a patch of snow between the riverfront boulevard and a set back building, a gang of youngsters were brawling. The scrum was too dense to total exactly, but there may have been ten or twelve of the urchins and most or all of them had long colored sticks. Bats? But if there had been some game before, they were now engaged in practicing their swings on each other. The fighting was so juvenile as to be essentially harmless, but even so real damage was dealt when luck lent a hand. And the children each yelped when they were struck or poked or gouged, each in their own tone and style. So like some of his fondest memories. Lane slowed to a stop, taking it in.

A light snow had just begun from patches of painted clouds woven into the prismatic sky. Down drifted big wet flakes, sparkling like candies colored mint and melon, berry and orange, coconut and spun confection. Each frozen droplet bringing the whole tinted chaos above down among them in bite-sized miracles. And the ruffians in training had stopped their mutual ministrations. Sticks dragging in the powder from slackened grips, heads upturned in innocent wonder, jaws out, mouths open, they lurched here and there about the battlefield, catching the melting crystals on their little pink tongues. Laughing out loud.

Lane set off downstream while they were still chasing the snow. It was tempting to lick out at the little falling treasures himself, but that frivolity was at odds with the night's grave business. Not pragmatically at odds, but still. Though natural enthusiasm was really a positive prelude to the evening. Lane lunged his head forward and his teeth snapped shut around a soft sweet flake. The tiny melted sip ran down the back of his throat as he simultaneously mourned and savored its transitory nature.

Lane turned left off the water's edge up the wide boulevard blocked a few streets inland by Nagadith's sprawling edifice. The light spreading out over the valley below had lost its brighter flavors and now began with a dark cherry, seeping away quickly to uncolored night. Nagadith had been a convenient meeting place, but it would not do tonight. This week more than most, Nagadith would be crammed with people. That itself might be the excuse to find somewhere quieter for a drink. Somewhere away from slobs like this idiot slumped in the first alley away from the Nagadith square.

The endlessly intricate white marble tiers filled up the square and inhaled those who came within its reach so that the moat of free space around the building was constantly being peopled and depeopled. Lane stopped without entering. Frowned. Turned and walked briskly back up the boulevard to the alley he had just passed. The slumped figure had not sagged down in a heap, but legs bent back in a kneel, head on knees, and hands upon the thighs. The form looked as though it were genuflecting back toward the river. Reflexively, Lane looked to the other side of the dark narrow alley for a person to be receiving the obeisance, but the alley was otherwise vacant. Jogging to the body, Lane dropped to his haunches so as not to block out the only direct illumination, the strip of royal blue firmament between the building crowns.

He did not need to touch Cye to know he was dead, but Lane extended his hand anyway, putting a hand to the shoulder of his friend. No sooner contacted than Lane jerked his hand away, perceiving the shock only afterwards – the shoulder was still warm through the thick outer shirt. The body had been creating its own intensity just minutes before. He returned his hand to Cye's shoulder, feeling the life recede beneath his fingers. Lying neatly before Cye, sunk down into the snow, Cye's long dagger was coated along its length with what was should look red but in this light was black on a waning silver blade. A pool of the same dark stuff approached the simple, elegant weapon, eating up the snow's cleanliness as it expanded out around Cye's folded body. Gently cupping Cye's chin he lifted the limp exquisite head. The eyelids had been shuttered by someone else. Across Cye's neck ran a deep slash, composed and drawn with an artist's touch. No other signs of damage or any extended conflict. A single stroke not unlike the one Lane had intended for Master Weaver.

Lane dropped Cye's head and took a rapid survey of the area. Night had settled in the alley, held back out on the main street where strategically placed torches lit the way and the back of the alley where it ended in the light from an outdoor lantern pooled on the ground, creating a meager oasis of maintained twilight. The walls were sheer up two stories. Three in places. There were a few windows, all closed against the winter evening. Master Weaver must have left already.

As real as if it had happened, Lane and Cye walked together through a city garden, talking as they strolled about their work and their students. Flowering vines spilled down tier after tier, flooding the ground level arboretum with dappled shade and pungent fecundity. Lane would remark on the ironies of the world and Cye would laugh, or send back a return volley of philosophy or give his hand a momentary squeeze in private, intimate agreement. And white, pink, and deep crimson fuchsia petals drifted down from overhead as they went, laying out a royal carpet before them as they passed along.

Doyen Horn was responsible for this waste. Lane's jugular was pulsing so hard he could feel it stretching the skin along his neck with each heated beat. Master Weaver was his task and it will be accomplished. Cye doubled over in an alley, left out like refuse too heavy to dispose of properly. Sona lying in a sleep without end in some dark place he had thought was safe, cut from ear to ear and left to rot in his own bedding. And the Wrens? A jumbled pile of twisted body parts left on some mountain crag or a pair of ever after silent twins with heads on breasts at some outdoor café as though they were no more than napping. Or not. It was his task. Lane clenched his jaw and made a fist with his hand. Rage against Master Horn and painful empathy for Master Weaver swirled inside his gut, incompatible and inextricable. How dare they do this to him. How dare they do this to his mentor.

Cye must have been standing in the alley for a moment to collect himself. Rehearsing how Lane could be used to give him the moment's advantage against Master Weaver that he needed. Aching to tell Lane his secret and unshoulder some of his burden. Knowing he couldn't. Though Cye imagined he was alone, Master Weaver stood directly behind him. As he pulled Cye's dagger out of the sheath that ran down the student's spine, Master Weaver's face aged, wrinkled and creased with remorse, regret, and the losing battle against cynicism. The motion had surely been swift and technical and he would have had time to catch Cye as he sagged, gently folding him into a relevant position. Only once Cye was comfortable did his mentor lay the dagger Cye had made from raw materials out before him in respect for what was gone.

In Lane's imagination, Master Weaver stood again, and Lane could see in his tired mouth and somber eyes that he knew Lane was next. A painful sight to see, but one he could live with. It was the vision of that same face should he duck the task that Lane could not bear to conjure. But ducking was all there was left. Cye could not provide a diversion now. Cian's Doyen had written surprise out of the account almost from the beginning. Master Weaver would be impenetrably on guard outside of Cian. And Cian's role as a safe harbor and neutral zone was equally unassailable. To violate that function was both technical failure and certain death soon afterwards.

Many small herds of chattering revelers had passed the alley with the same inattention Lane had given it. But one mixed boisterous flock had stopped with heads cocked to decipher the scene. Lane stepped toward them one stride, shielding Cye's prostrate form and, folding his arms, coldly received their attention. The group shifted uncomfortably and then pulled each other on into Nagadith's sphere of influence, restarting their rowdiness where they had left it off.

Lane closed his eyes and forced himself to picture the way Cye's hazel eyes had looked as the man who should not have been there unsheathed Cye's dagger. Cye knew how good he was and yet could tell there would be no contest. Cye appreciated in this final moment how good Master Weaver was. Master Weaver stood over the fallen student, looking back toward the rapids and over them to the River Island and over them over the rapids again to the blacksmith's hall on the other side. And in Master Weaver's eyes Lane envisioned sorrow, but something else besides. Sweet tension. Master Weaver was not sure of the next outcome, and Lane fed with pride upon his master's uncertainty. With each chestfull of air his heart beat louder and more demanding in his inner ear. And as he milked the expression before his mind's eye, the concern he could see in that noble face increased, a blooming flower in whose rare winter trumpet Lane could smell alarm.

Standing in front of Cye's reverently bowed form, Lane watched his friend's blood seep forward until it kissed the tips of his boots. He watched the black liquid begin to spread around his feet, but he did not withdraw. Whether the stairs down to Cian were officially part of Cian was not clear. Lane could imagine arguing to Doyen Horn that they weren't.

Kneeling down on one knee, Lane picked up Cye's long dagger and balanced the relic between his hands appreciatively. He moved Cye's hair back a little and the condensed moisture felt like sweat on his hand. He gently replaced the weapon in the well-made scabbard Cye wore on his back.   Then he pulled Cye more upright and lifted him, cradled in his arms. Lane rose, and Cye hung from his arms in a passionate swoon. As they moved out of the alley and back onto the street, the sticky liquid pressed between them made its way through Lane's clothing, soaking in and spreading out to mark the bearer.

Burning brands soaked in naphtha and set in building-mounted sleeves outlined the street, and the traffic funneled along between the lines of light. The blood soaked pair turned against the press of people heading onto the Lower Bank and made their way together toward the pounding white rapids. From several blocks away the water's tumultuous rush through Karabas and down into the valley was audible and grew louder with each step. As the blond man strode the middle of the avenue with his burden, the streaming crowd quieted as he approached, parted to let him pass, reformed in his wake, and their noise returned as he left them behind.   In this way the proud island of two moved through a still river of lowered heads with eyes turned away, studying the dirt and snow upon their shoes.

‡ ‡ ‡

Lane stood with his hands on his hips in the twilight of the apron room at the rear of the forge. The thin line of smoky glow across the bottom of the door gave only ghostly substance to the smithing tools across the walls. Though he could barely make out the top of his black boots, this close atmosphere was lit by a midday sun compared to true darkness. At his feet, cut down into the floor, the rough spiral stone staircase dropped away, opening like a black maw with only its first few teeth visible in the endless procession that wound down its throat. Lane shook his head slowly to clear it, whirling the room around him with a following trail of fading vision chasing his view. The whirling stopped with his head, but the mental thickness persisted. With less than two days left in the year, there was no other way. Forcing himself into motion, Lane tucked the hem of his black tunic into the waist of his black pants, dropped a heavy first step down into the hole, and descended towards Cian.

Lane had never bothered to count the steps connecting the apron room of the forge with Cian's entryway. He considered going on to the bottom of the helix to get that count, but discarded the notion as academic. Lane took each step slowly, examining the surface of the steps, the texture of the walls, and the height of the ceiling formed from the underside of the steps he had already gone down. Stopping to wait two turns of the staircase from the top, Lane's broad hands ran over the inside hub of the staircase, smooth in the middle and increasingly rough above his shoulder and below his knee. Reaching to the outside wall, Lane felt the same pattern, unintentionally rubbed into existence by thousands of hands feeling their way confidently down and up the pitch black passage. When he raised his hand to find the invisible ceiling that finished the definition of the space, he was pleased to verify that he could not reach it even standing on his toes. Another minute passed and Lane's eyes had become accustomed to the gloom so that he could roughly make out his hand as he reached up again to try to brush the carved out underside of the steps some six feet over his head. Slowly he went down another turn of the staircase until the darkness seemed complete, and then stood and waited again, a patient statue waiting out an endless night. One more turn down after this and even after a long stretch of time, Lane could see nothing at all. Though over the years he had taken these stairs at high speed, often two at a time, and thought nothing of it, the current attention to the completeness of the dark was debilitating.

Now here, Lane found the situation much more bleak than it had seemed this morning as he prepared. There was no evidence to suggest whether Master Weaver was below in Cian or above in Karabas and certainly no guarantee his mentor would cross this threshold in the next day and a half. While Lane had never brought a lamp or torch down these stairs and had never seen any of the other guild members or apprentices do so either, it was tradition, not law, that favored Master Weaver coming without a light if indeed he came this way at all. Lane wondered again in an endless mental cycle whether these stairs counted as part of Cian or as part of the forge. Would Master Weaver's footfalls have some identifiable cadence given that he'd never paid attention to this previously uninteresting detail? It seemed wildly unlikely now that he was here that Master Weaver would be the first person up or down this winding passage. And of course, there was no guarantee that Master Weaver would be alone when and if he came. Lane smiled ruefully. It was only the alignment of so many obstacles, unknowns, and uncontrollable elements that made this spot the only location in all Karabas where Master Weaver might just possibly be taken unawares.

Lane patted the long pockets on each of his pant legs. On the left, one of his stakes ran up his thigh alongside a sack of salted chestnuts. In the other the second stake knocked soundlessly against a flask of water wrapped in a piece of cloth. Feeling at his waist, Lane untied a length of string and pulling his hair back, bound it securely. Then putting his wide shoulders to the outside wall and his feet to the center pillar, he experimentally moved up and down from the floor to the ceiling. As he had feared, moving to the ceiling could be done either quickly or silently, but not both. As neither would do without the other, Lane inched his way back up to the crest of the space, shifting his feet and shoulders, wedging himself in place.

Hanging there in the emptiness, Lane worked to keep his breath long, slow, and deep. The fact was that should Master

Weaver descend or ascend these steps, Lane had no plan, no first move, which was all the advantage he would get. Lane let the thought come and then go without fighting or denying it. Following in its wake, it occurred to Lane that perhaps he had picked this situation because the darkness made it possible for him to strike. This perpetual midnight helped to shield him from the sight of Master Weaver and so from the feelings of guilt and disloyalty that had mastered him on the steps of the Temple of Frailty. Feelings now compounded by sadness and sympathy for Master Weaver for the horrible position Cian had created. Lane took a deep breath, exhaling slowly and clearing his thoughts, focusing on the soft, even sound of the air passing through his nostrils.

‡ ‡ ‡

Footsteps on the stairs echoed past Lane. He tensed, reaching his right hand down to the stake in his right leg pocket. The heavy impacts came rhythmically, overwhelming all his other senses until he felt he was choking on the sound. His hand withdrew, crossing back through his other arm to hang down beneath his chest. Master Weaver's feet would never slap the stones like coarse and thoughtless children beating on kitchenware. Lane tried to smell the person as they passed beneath him, but like all the others who had climbed under his watchless eyes since he'd risen to his perch, all he could smell was the furnace smoke drifting down from above. Lane had no idea how long he'd been frozen there or how many people had passed under him already. Had it been a day? Though the traffic was always light, Lane had lost track of the quantity of guild members he'd let pass. He felt certain somehow that Master Weaver had not taken the stairs since he arrived. Lane tried to imagine what Master Weaver would think of this situation, but instead all he conjured up was a profound sadness and a realization that he was cold to his bones.

All feeling had long since left his shoulders and thighs, so after the clomping steps receded into silence, Lane, desperate for a change, decided to risk a few moments standing on the stairs to shake off the terrible stiffness in his muscles. On the first tentative shifting of his weight to his right leg so his left foot could ease a little way down the center pillar, searing pain possessed his body, beginning in his hamstring and shooting up his spine until spots of phantom colored lights danced before eyes closed and rolled back into his skull. Lane groaned through his clenched jaw, creeping his left foot slowly back into place. He had passed the point of no return. Once down, he would never mount the wall again. Drawing another deep, ragged breath to slow his galloping heart and ease the echoes of pain, he hissed the air out through his teeth whispering, "All things are possible."

‡ ‡ ‡

Lane started to gasp, then cut off his breath to suppress the sound. Had he been asleep? Only the lack of pressure on his front or back gave him confidence he was still suspended. The total darkness had gone on so long that Lane no longer saw it, but the approaching footsteps rang through the silence like thunderclaps. Or were they receding? Lane's thoughts had slowed to a wandering crawl in the thick fluid built up in his head, and no answer came to the question. Time was lost to him. The steps seemed to be getting louder, and Lane was gripped by the conviction that this was the approach of his teacher, though he couldn't have said why or even begun to characterize the sound in his current condition.

He withdrew the stake from his right pocket and held it out beneath him. The metal felt like ice against his palm, sucking his heat away, and a wave of sensation shot up his arm into his shoulder, a thousand tiny needles administered simultaneously. The pain exploded into his head and Lane nearly swooned. The thought that brought him back from the edge of unconsciousness shocked him with its obviousness. He had moments to act or lose his last chance. But what if he was wrong? Who might he kill by mistake? Images of Master Maya swept over him in another wave of disorientation but some part of Lane held on to the certainty that this specter now feet from him was his mentor. It felt right. The footsteps advanced but it seemed to Lane, perhaps only a lapse in his mind, that the steps slowed ever so slightly as they drew near. Lane closed his eyes to steady himself, letting the pain, the sadness, and even the uncertainty drain away and dissipate. Then he let go.